Also by Colm Tóibín

FICTION

The South

The Heather Blazing

The Story of the Night

The Blackwater Lightship

The Master

Mothers and Sons

Brooklyn

The Empty Family

The Testament of Mary

Nora Webster

NONFICTION

Bad Blood: A Walk Along the Irish Border

Homage to Barcelona

The Sign of the Cross: Travels in Catholic Europe

Love in a Dark Time: Gay Lives from Wilde to Almodóvar

Lady Gregory's Toothbrush

All a Novelist Needs: Essays on Henry James

New Ways to Kill Your Mother

On Elizabeth Bishop

PLAYS

Beauty in a Broken Place

The Testament of Mary

HOUSE OF
NAMES

- A Novel -

COLM TÓIBÍN

SCRIBNER
New York   London   Toronto   Sydney   New Delhi

Scribner
An Imprint of Simon & Schuster, Inc.
1230 Avenue of the Americas
New York, NY 10020

First Scribner hardcover edition May 2017

SCRIBNER and design are registered trademarks of The Gale Group, Inc., used under license by Simon & Schuster, Inc., the publisher of this work.

For information about special discounts for bulk purchases, please contact Simon & Schuster Special Sales at 1-866-506-1949 or business@simonandschuster.com.

The Simon & Schuster Speakers Bureau can bring authors to your live event. For more information or to book an event, contact the Simon & Schuster Speakers Bureau at 1-866-248-3049 or visit our website at www.simonspeakers.com.

Interior design by Jill Putorti

Manufactured in the United States of America

10 9 8 7 6 5 4 3 2 1

Library of Congress Cataloging-in-Publication Data is available.

ISBN 978-1-5011-4021-1
ISBN 978-1-5011-4023-5 (ebook)

for Hedi El Kholti

HOUSE OF
NAMES

Clytemnestra

I have been acquainted with the smell of death. The sickly, sugary smell that wafted in the wind towards the rooms in this palace. It is easy now for me to feel peaceful and content. I spend my morning looking at the sky and the changing light. The birdsong begins to rise as the world fills with its own pleasures and then, as day wanes, the sound too wanes and fades. I watch as the shadows lengthen. So much has slipped away, but the smell of death lingers. Maybe the smell has entered my body and been welcomed there like an old friend come to visit. The smell of fear and panic. The smell is here like the very air is here; it returns in the same way as light in the morning returns. It is my constant companion; it has put life into my eyes, eyes that grew dull with waiting, but are not dull now, eyes that are alive now with brightness.

I gave orders that the bodies should remain in the open under the sun a day or two until the sweetness gave way to stench. And I liked the flies that came, their little bodies perplexed and brave, buzzing after their feast, upset by the continuing hunger they felt in themselves, a hunger I had come to know too and had come to appreciate.

We are all hungry now. Food merely whets our appetite, it sharpens our teeth; meat makes us ravenous for more meat, as death is ravenous for more death. Murder makes us ravenous, fills the soul with satisfaction that is fierce and then luscious enough to create a taste for further satisfaction.

A knife piercing the soft flesh under the ear, with intimacy and precision, and then moving across the throat as soundlessly as the sun moves across the sky, but with greater speed and zeal, and then his dark blood flowing with the same inevitable hush as dark night falls on familiar things.

*

They cut her hair before they dragged her to the place of sacrifice. My daughter had her hands tied tight behind her back, the skin on the wrists raw with the ropes, and her ankles bound. Her mouth was gagged to stop her cursing her father, her cowardly, two-tongued father. Nonetheless, her muffled screams were heard when she finally realized that her father really did mean to murder her, that he did mean to sacrifice her life for his army. They had cropped her hair with haste and carelessness; one of the women managed to cut into the skin around my daughter's skull with a rusty blade, and when Iphigenia began her curse, that is when a man tied an old cloth around her mouth so that her words could not be heard. I am proud that she never ceased to struggle, that never once, not for one second, despite the ingratiating speech she had made, did she accept her fate. She did not give up trying to loosen the twine around her ankles or the ropes around her wrists so that she could get away from them. Or stop trying to curse her father so that he would feel the weight of her contempt.

No one is willing now to repeat the words she spoke in the moments before they muffled her voice, but I know what those words were. I taught them to her. They were words I made up to shrivel her father and his followers, with their foolish aims, they were words that announced what would happen to him and those around him once the news spread of how they dragged our daughter, the proud and beautiful Iphigenia, to that place, how they pulled her through the dust to sacrifice her so they might prevail in their war. In that last second as she lived, I am told she screamed aloud so that her voice pierced the hearts of those who heard her.

Her screams as they murdered her were replaced by silence and by scheming when Agamemnon, her father, returned and I fooled him into thinking that I would not retaliate. I waited and I watched for signs, and smiled and opened my arms to him, and I had a table here prepared with food. Food for the fool! I was wearing the special scent that excited him. Scent for the fool!

I was ready as he was not, the hero home in glorious victory, the blood of his daughter on his hands, but his hands washed now as though free of all stain, his hands white, his arms out-stretched to embrace his friends, his face all smiles, the great soldier who would soon, he believed, hold up a cup in cele-bration and put rich food into his mouth. His gaping mouth! Relieved that he was home!

I saw his hands clench in sudden pain, clench in the grim, shocked knowledge that at last it had come to him, and in his own palace, and in the slack time when he was sure he would enjoy the old stone bath and the ease to be found there.

That was what inspired him to go on, he said, the thought that this was waiting for him, healing water and spices and soft, clean clothes and familiar air and sounds. He was like a lion as he laid his muzzle down, his roaring all done, his body limp, and all thought of danger far from his mind.

I smiled and said that, yes, I too had thought of the welcome I would make for him. He had filled my waking life and my dreams, I told him. I had dreamed of him rising all cleansed from the perfumed water of the bath. I told him his bath was being prepared as the food was being cooked, as the table was being laid, and as his friends were gathering. And he must go there now, I said, he must go to the bath. He must bathe, bathe in the relief of being home. Yes, home. That is where the lion came. I knew what to do with the lion once he came home.

*

I had spies to tell me when he would come back. Men lit each fire that gave the news to farther hills where other men lit fires to alert me. It was the fire that brought the news, not the gods. Among the gods now there is no one who offers me assistance or oversees my actions or knows my mind. There is no one among the gods to whom I appeal. I live alone in the shivering, solitary knowledge that the time of the gods has passed.

I am praying to no gods. I am alone among those here because I do not pray and will not pray again. Instead, I will speak in ordinary whispers. I will speak in words that come from the world, and those words will be filled with regret for what has been lost. I will make sounds like prayers, but prayers that have no source and no destination, not even a human one, since my daughter is dead and cannot hear.

I know as no one else knows that the gods are distant, they have other concerns. They care about human desires and antics in the same way that I care about the leaves of a tree. I know the leaves are there, they wither and grow again and wither, as people come and live and then are replaced by others like them. There is nothing I can do to help them or prevent their withering. I do not deal with their desires.

I wish now to stand here and laugh. Hear me tittering and then howling with mirth at the idea that the gods allowed my husband to win his war, that they inspired every plan he worked out and every move he made, that they knew his cloudy moods in the morning and the strange and silly exhilaration he could exude at night, that they listened to his implorings and discussed them in their godly homes, that they watched the murder of my daughter with approval.

The bargain was simple, or so he believed, or so his troops believed. Kill the innocent girl in return for a change in the wind. Take her out of the world, use a knife on her flesh to ensure that she would never again walk into a room or wake in the morning. Deprive the world of her grace. And as a reward, the gods would make the wind blow in her father's favor on the day he needed wind for his sails. They would hush the wind on the other days when his enemies needed it. The gods would make his men alert and brave and fill his enemies with fear. The gods would strengthen his swords and make them swift and sharp.

When he was alive, he and the men around him believed that the gods followed their fates and cared about them. Each of them. But I will say now that they did not, they do not. Our appeal to the gods is the same as the appeal a star makes in the sky above us before it falls, it is a sound we cannot hear, a sound to which, even if we did hear it, we would be fully indifferent.

The gods have their own unearthly concerns, unimagined by us. They barely know we are alive. For them, if they were to hear of us, we would be like the mild sound of wind in the trees, a distant, unpersistent, rustling sound.

I know that it was not always thus. There was a time when the gods came in the morning to wake us, when they combed our hair and filled our mouths with the sweetness of speech and listened to our desires and tried to fulfill them for us, when they knew our minds and when they could send us signs. Not

long ago, within our memories, the crying women could be
heard in the night in the time before death came. It was a way
of calling the dying home, hastening their flight, softening
their wavering journey to the place of rest. My husband was
with me in the days before my mother died, and we both heard
it, and my mother heard it too and it comforted her that death
was ready to lure her with its cries.

That noise has stopped. There is no more crying like the wind.
The dead fade in their own time. No one helps them, no one
notices except those who have been close to them during their
short spell in the world. As they fade from the earth, the gods
do not hover over with their haunting, whistling sound. I notice
it here, the silence around death. They have departed, the ones
who oversaw death. They have gone and they will not be back.

My husband was lucky with the wind, that was all, and lucky
his men were brave, and lucky that he prevailed. It could easily
have been otherwise. He did not need to sacrifice our daughter
to the gods.

My nurse was with me from the time I was born. In her last
days, we did not believe that she was dying. I sat with her and
we talked. If there had been the slightest sound of wailing, we
would have heard. There was nothing, no sound to accompany
her towards death. There was silence, or the usual noises from
the kitchen, or the barking of dogs. And then she died, then she
stopped breathing. It was over for her.

I went out and looked at the sky. And all I had then to help
me was the leftover language of prayer. What had once been
powerful and added meaning to everything was now desolate, strange, with its own sad, brittle power, with its memory,
locked in its rhythms, of a vivid past when our words rose up
and found completion. Now our words are trapped in time,

they are filled with limits, they are mere distractions; they are as fleeting and monotonous as breath. They keep us alive, and maybe that is something, at least for the moment, for which we should be grateful. There is nothing else.

*

I have had the bodies removed and buried. It is twilight now. I can open the shutters onto the terrace and look at the last golden traces of the sun and the swifts arching in the air, moving like whips against the dense, raked light. As the air thickens, I can see the blurred edge of what is there. This is not a time for sharpness; I no longer want sharpness. I do not need clarity. I need a time like now when each object ceases to be itself and melts towards what is close to it, just as each action I and others have performed ceases to stand alone waiting for someone to come and judge it or record it.

Nothing is stable, no color under this light is still; the shadows grow darker and the things on the earth merge with each other, just as what all of us did merges into one action, and all our cries and gestures merge into one cry, one gesture. In the morning, when the light has been washed by darkness, we will face clarity and singleness again. In the meantime, the place where my memory lives is a shadowy, ambiguous place, comforted by soft, eroding edges, and that is enough for now. I might even sleep. I know that in the fullness of daylight, my memory will sharpen again, become precise, will cut through the things that happened like a dagger whose blade has been whetted for use.

*

There was a woman in one of the dusty villages beyond the river and towards the blue mountains. She was old and difficult but she had powers that had been lost to all others. She did not use her powers idly, I had been told, and most of the time she was not willing to use them at all. In her village she often paid imposters, women old and wizened like herself, women who sat in doorways with their eyes narrowed against the sun. The old woman paid them to stand in for her, to fool visitors into believing that they were the ones with the powers.

We had been watching this woman. Aegisthus, the man who shares my bed and would share this kingdom with me, had learned, with the help of some men who were under his sway, to distinguish between the other women, the decoys, who had no powers at all, and the real one, who could, when she wanted, weave a poison into any fabric.

If anyone wore that fabric they would be rendered frozen, unable to move, and rendered voiceless also, utterly silent. No matter how sudden the shock or severe the pain, they would not have the ability to cry out.

I planned to attack my husband when he returned. I would be waiting for him, all smiles. The gurgling sound he would make when I cut his throat became my obsession.

The old woman was brought here by the guards. I had her locked in one of the inner storerooms, a dry place where grain is kept. Aegisthus, whose powers of persuasion were as highly developed as the old woman's power to cause death, knew what to say to her.

Both Aegisthus and the old woman were stealthy and wily. But I was clear. I lived in the light. I cast shadows but I did not live in shadow. As I prepared for this, I lived in pure brightness.

What I required was simple. There was a robe made of netting that my husband sometimes used when he came from the bath. I wanted the old woman to stitch threads into it, threads that would have the power to immobilize him once the robe touched his skin. The threads would be as near to invisible as the woman could make them. And Aegisthus warned her that I wanted not only stealth but silence. I wanted no one to hear the cries of Agamemnon as I murdered him. I wanted not a sound to be heard from him.

The woman pretended for some time that she was, in fact, one of the imposters. And even though I allowed no one but Aegisthus to see her and bring her food, she began to divine why she was here, that she had been brought here to help with the murder of Agamemnon, the king, the great, bloodthirsty warrior, victorious in the wars, soon to arrive home. The woman believed that the gods were on his side. She did not wish to interfere with the intentions of the gods.

I had always known that she would be a challenge, but I had come to learn too that it was simpler to work with those who held the old beliefs, who believed that the world was stable.

I arranged therefore to deal with this woman. I had time. Agamemnon was not to return for some days, and I would have warnings when he was approaching. We had spies in his camp by this time, and men on the hills. I left nothing to chance. I planned each step. I had left too much to luck and to the whims and needs of others in the past. I had trusted too many people.

I ordered the poisonous crone we had captured to be brought to one of the windows high in the wall of the corridor outside the room where she was being held. I gave instructions that this malignant creature be hoisted up so that she could peer into the walled garden. I knew what she would see. She would see her own golden granddaughter, the light of her life. We had taken the child from the village. She, too, was our prisoner.

I arranged for Aegisthus to tell the woman that if she wove the poison and if it worked, then she and her granddaughter would immediately be released and allowed home. I ordered him not to finish the next sentence, the one that began, "If you do not . . . ," but just to look at the woman with such clear intent and malice that she would tremble, or, more likely, make an effort not to show any sign of fear.

Thus it was easy. The weaving took, I was told, a matter of minutes. Although Aegisthus sat with the woman as she worked, he could not find the new threads in the robe when she had finished. When it was done, she merely asked him to be kind to her granddaughter while she was here and to make sure, when they were being returned to the village, that no one saw them or knew who had accompanied them or where they had been. She gazed coldly at him, and he knew from her gaze that the task had been successfully completed and that the lovely, fatal magic would work on Agamemnon.

*

His doom was set in stone when he sent us word that before the battles began he wished to assist at the wedding of one of his daughters, that he wanted around him an aura of love and regeneration to strengthen him and fill his followers with joy before they set out to kill and conquer. Among the young soldiers, he said, was Achilles, the son of Peleus, a man destined to be a greater hero than his father. Achilles was handsome, my husband wrote, and the sky itself would brighten when it saw Achilles pledge himself to our daughter Iphigenia, with his followers watching in awe.

"You must come by chariot," his message said. "It will take three days. And do not spare anything in your preparations for her wedding. Bring Orestes with you. He is old enough now to savor the sight of soldiers in the days before a battle and to witness the wedding of his sister to a man as noble as Achilles.

"And you must put power in the hands of Electra when you are away, and tell her to remember her father and use power well. The men I have left, the ones too old to fight, will advise her, they will surround her with their care and wisdom until her mother returns with her sister and her brother. She must listen to the elders in the same way her mother does in my absence.

"Then, when we return from war, power will return to its proper source. After triumph, there will be stability. The gods are on our side. I have been assured that the gods are on our side."

I believed him. I found Iphigenia and told her that she would come with me on a journey to her father's camp and she would be married to a warrior. I told her that we would have the seamstresses work all day and all night to prepare the clothes for her that we would carry with us. I added my words to the words of Agamemnon. I told my daughter that Achilles, her husband-to-be, was soft-spoken. And I added other words too, words that are bitter to me now, words filled now with shame. That he was brave, admired, and that his charm had not grown rough despite his strength.

I was saying more when Electra came into the room and asked us why we were whispering. I told Electra that Iphigenia, older than she by one year, was to be married, and she smiled and clasped her sister's hands when I said that word of Iphigenia's beauty had spread, that it was known about in many places now, and Achilles would be waiting for her, and her father was certain that in times to come there would be stories told of the bride on her wedding day, and of the sky itself bright and the sun high in the sky and the gods smiling and the soldiers in the days before battle made brave and steely by the light of love.

Yes, I said love, I said light, I said the gods, I said bride. I said soldiers steely before battle. I said his name and her name. Iphigenia, Achilles. And then I called in the dressmakers so the work could begin to prepare for my daughter a robe that would match her own radiance, which on the day of her wedding would match the radiance of the sun. And I told Electra that her father trusted her enough to be left here with the elders, that her sharp wit and skill at noticing and remembering made her father proud.

And some weeks later, on a golden morning, with some of our women, we set out.

*

When we arrived, Agamemnon was waiting for us. He came slowly towards us with an expression on his face that I had never seen before. His face, I thought, showed sorrow, but also surprise and relief. Maybe other things too, but they were what I noticed then. Sorrow, I thought, because he had missed us, he had been away a long time, and he was giving away his daughter; and surprise, because he had spent so much time imagining us and now we were here, all flesh, all real, and Orestes, at the age of eight, had grown beyond his father's dreams as Iphigenia, at sixteen, had blossomed. And he exuded relief, I thought, that we were safe and he was safe and we could be with each other. When he came to embrace me, I felt a pained warmth from him, but when he stood back and surveyed the soldiers who had come with him, I saw the power in him, the power of the leader prepared for battle, his mind on strategy, decisions. Agamemnon, with his men, was an image of pure will. I remember when we married first being carried away by that image of will I saw even more intensely that day.

Also I saw how, unlike other men of his kind, he was ready to listen, as I felt he was now, or would be when I was alone with him.

And then he picked Orestes up and laughed and carried him towards Iphigenia.

He was all charm when he turned to Iphigenia. And it was as if a miracle had occurred when I looked at her, as if some woman had come unbidden onto the earth with an aura of tenderness mixed with reserve, with a distance from common things. Her father moved to embrace her, still holding the boy, and if anyone then had wanted to know what love looked like, if anyone going into battle needed an image of love to take with them to protect them or spur them on, it was here for them, like something precious cut in stone—the father, the son, the daughter, the mother watching fondly, the look of longing on the father's face with all the mystery of love, and its warmth, its purity, as he gently let his son down to stand beside him so that Agamemnon could hold his daughter in his arms.

I saw it and I am certain of it. In those seconds it was there. But it was false.

None of us who had traveled, however, guessed the truth for one second, even though some of the others standing around, maybe even most of them, must have known it. But not one of them gave a sign, not a single sign.

The sky remained blue, the sun hot in the sky, and the gods—oh yes, the gods!—seemed to be smiling on our family that day, on the bride-to-be and her young brother, on me, and on her father as he stood in the embrace of love, as he would stand eventually in the victory of battle with his army triumphant. Yes, the gods smiled that day as we came in all innocence to help Agamemnon execute his plan.

*

The day after our arrival, my husband came early to take Orestes with him and have a sword and light body armor made for him so that he would look like a warrior. Women came to see Iphigenia and there was much fuss and wonder as they admired the clothes we had brought with us, and much calling for cool drinks, and much folding and unfolding of garments. After a while, I stood in the space between our quarters and the kitchens listening to the idle chatter there until I heard one of the women mention that some of the soldiers were lingering outside. Among the names she mentioned was Achilles.

How strange, I thought, that he would come so close to our quarters! And then I thought no, it was not strange, he would come to see if he could catch a glimpse of Iphigenia. Of course he would come! How eager he must be to see her!

I walked out into the forecourt and I asked the soldiers which of them was Achilles. He was the tall one, I discovered, who was standing alone. When I approached, he turned and looked at me and I realized something from his gaze, the directness of it, and the tone of his voice as he spoke his name, the honesty in it. This will be the end of our troubles, I thought. Achilles has been sent to us to end what began before I was born, before my husband was born. Some venom in our blood, in all our blood. Old crimes and desires for vengeance. Old murders and memories of murder. Old wars and old treacheries. Old savagery, old attacks, times when men behaved like wolves. It will end now as this man marries my daughter, I thought. I saw the future as a place of plenty. I saw Orestes growing up in the light of this young soldier married to his sister. I saw an end to strife, a time when men would grow old with ease, and battles would become the subject of high talk as night fell and memories faded of the hacked-up bodies and the howling voices rising for miles across some bloodied plain. They could talk of heroes then instead.

When I told Achilles who I was, he smiled and nodded, making clear that he already knew me, and then made to turn away. I called him back and offered him my hand so that he might join his hand with mine as a token of what would soon happen and of the years ahead.

His body appeared to jolt when I spoke, and he looked around, checking if anyone was watching. I understood his reticence and moved some steps away from him before I spoke again.

"Since you are marrying my daughter," I said, "surely you may touch my hand?"

"Marrying?" he asked. "I am impatient for battle. I do not know your daughter. Your husband—"

"I am sure my husband," I interrupted, "asked you to maintain distance in these days before the feast, but from my daughter, not from me. In the days to come, all this will change, but if it worries you to be seen speaking to me before your wedding with my daughter, then I must go back to be with the women and away from you."

I spoke softly. The expression on his face was pained, perplexed.

"You are mistaken," he said. "I am waiting for battle, not for a bride. There will be no weddings as we wait for the wind to change, as we wait for our boats to stop being hurled against rocks. As we wait for . . ."

He frowned, and then seemed to check himself so that he would not finish what he had begun to say.

"Perhaps my husband," I said, "has brought my daughter here so that after the battle—"

"After the battle I will go home," he interrupted. "If I survive the battle, I will go home."

"My daughter has come here to marry you," I said. "She was summoned by her father, my husband."

"You are mistaken," he said, and once more I saw grace, tempered with firmness and resolve. For a second, I had a vision of the future, a future that Achilles would transform for us, a time to come in a place filled with cushioned corners and nourished shadows, and I would grow old there as Achilles ripened and my daughter Iphigenia became a mother and Orestes grew into wisdom. Suddenly, it occurred to me that in this world of the future I could not see any place for Agamemnon and I could not see Electra either, and I started for a moment, I almost gasped at some dark absence looming. I tried to place both of them in the picture and I failed. I could not see either of them and there was something else that I could not see, as Achilles raised his voice as if to get my attention.

"You are mistaken," he said again, and then spoke more softly. "Your husband must have told you why your daughter has been summoned here."

"My husband," I said, "merely welcomed us when we came. He said nothing else."

"Do you not know, then?" he asked. "Is it possible you do not know?"

The expression on his face had darkened, his voice had almost broken on the last question.

I hunched over as I moved from him and made my way back to

where my daughter and the women were gathered. They barely saw me, since they were marveling over some piece of stitching, holding up a piece of cloth. I sat alone, away from them.

*

I do not know who told Iphigenia that she was not to be married but was to be sacrificed. I do not know who informed her that she was not to have Achilles as her husband, but was rather to have her throat bloodied by a sharp, thin knife in the open air as many spectators, including her own father, gaped at her, and figures appointed for this purpose chanted supplications to the gods.

When the women left, I spoke to Iphigenia; she did not know then. But in the next hour or two, as we waited for Orestes to return, as I lay awake and as she went in and out of the room, someone let her know plainly and precisely. I realized I had fooled myself into believing that there would be some easy explanation for Achilles' ignorance of the wedding plans. A few times, I had a piercing intimation of the truth, but it seemed so unlikely that anyone intended to harm Iphigenia, since my husband had greeted us in the way he did with his followers around him, and the women from among his camp had come so eagerly to see the clothes.

I went over my conversation with Achilles, thinking back on each word. When Iphigenia came to me, I was certain that I would, by nightfall, receive some news that would soothe me, and that everything would be resolved. I was convinced of this even as she began to speak, as she began to tell me what she had learned.

"Who told you this?" I asked.

"One of the women was sent to tell me."

"Which of them?"

"I don't know her. I only know that she was sent to tell me."

"Sent by whom?"

"By my father," she replied.

"How can we be sure?" I asked.

"I am sure," she said.

We sat waiting for Orestes to return, waiting so we could implore whoever came with him to take us to Agamemnon, or allow us to send a message to him saying that he must come and speak to us. Sometimes Iphigenia held my hand, tightening her grip and then letting go, sighing, closing her eyes in dread, and then opening her eyes again to stare vacantly into the distance. Even still it seemed to me as we waited that nothing would happen, that all this was maybe nothing, that the idea of sacrificing Iphigenia to the gods was a rumor spread by the women and that such rumors would be easily spread among nervous soldiers and their followers in the days before a battle.

I wavered from feeling unsure and nervous to sensing that the very worst was to come, as my daughter found my hand again and held it harder and more fiercely. A few times, I wondered if we could flee from here, if we could set out together into the night and make towards home, or some sanctuary, or if I could find someone to take Iphigenia away, disguise her, find a hiding place for her. But I did not know in what direction we could go, and I knew that we would be followed and found. Since he had lured us here, I was sure, Agamemnon was having us watched and guarded.

We sat together in silence for hours. No one came near us. Slowly, I began to feel that we were prisoners and had been prisoners since the moment we arrived. We had been fooled into coming. Agamemnon had realized how excited I would be at the thought of a wedding, and that is the strategy he used to entice us here. Nothing else would have worked.

We heard Orestes' voice first, calling out in play, and then, to my shock, his father's. When they both came in, all bright-eyed and boisterous, we stood up to face him. In one second, Agamemnon saw that the woman he had sent had, as he had instructed, told Iphigenia. He bowed his head and then he lifted it and started laughing. He told Orestes to show us the sword that had been forged and polished specially for him, he told him to show us the armor that had been made for him too. He took out his own sword and held it in mock seriousness to challenge Orestes, who, under his father's careful guidance, crossed swords with him and stood in combat position against him.

"He is a great warrior," Agamemnon said.

We watched him coldly, impassively. For a moment, I was going to call for Orestes' nurse and have the boy removed, put to bed, but whatever was going on between Agamemnon and Orestes held me back. It was as if Agamemnon knew that he must play this part of the father with his boy for all it was worth. There was something in the air, or in our expressions, so intense that my husband must have known when he relaxed and faced us that life would change and never be the same again.

Agamemnon did not glance at me now, nor did he look at Iphigenia. The longer his jousting went on, the more I realized that he was afraid of us, or afraid of what he would have to say to us when it stopped. He did not want it to stop. He was, as he continued the game, not a brave man.

I smiled because I knew that this would be the last episode of happiness I would know in my life, and that it was being played out by my husband, in all his weakness, for as long as possible. It was all theatre, all show, the mock sword fight between father and son. I saw how Agamemnon was making it last, keeping Orestes excited without exhausting him, letting him feel that he was showing off his skill and thus making the boy want to do more and more. He was controlling Orestes as we both stood watching.

It struck me for a second that this was what the gods did with us—they distracted us with mock conflicts, with the shout of life, they distracted us also with images of harmony, beauty, love, as they watched distantly, dispassionately, waiting for the moment when it ended, when exhaustion set in. They stood back as we stood back. And when it ended, they shrugged. They no longer cared.

Orestes did not want the mock fight to end, but, within the rules, there was a limit to what they could do. Once, the boy moved too close to his father and left himself fully vulnerable to his father's sword. As Agamemnon gently pushed him back, it was clear to him that it was a game only and that we had seen this and noted it. This realization quickly made Orestes lose interest and move equally fast into tiredness and irritation. But still he did not want it to end. When I shouted for the nurse, Orestes began to cry. He did not want the nurse, he said, as his father lifted him in his arms and carried him like a piece of firewood towards our sleeping quarters.

Iphigenia did not look at me, nor I at her. We both remained standing. I do not know how much time passed.

When Agamemnon appeared, he walked quickly towards the opening in the tent and then turned.

"So you know, you both know?" he asked quietly.

In disbelief, I nodded.

"There is nothing else to say," he whispered. "It must be. Please believe me that it must be."

Before he left us, he gave me a hollow look. He almost shrugged then as he spread out his arms, his palms facing upwards. He was like someone with no power, or he was mimicking for me and for Iphigenia how such a man would seem. Shrunken, easy to fool or persuade.

The great Agamemnon made it plain by his stance that whatever decision had been made, it had been made not by him, but by others. He made it seem that it had been too much for him, all of it, as he darted out into the night to where his guards were waiting.

Then there was silence all around, the silence that can come only when an army sleeps. Iphigenia came to me and I held her. She did not cry or sob. It felt as though she would never move again and we would be discovered like this when morning came.

*

At first light, I walked through the camp in search of Achilles. When I found him, he edged away from me, but as much in pride as in fear, as much for the sake of decorum as nervousness about who was watching us. I drew close to him, but I did not whisper.

"My daughter was tricked into coming here. Your name was used."

"I too am angry with her father."

"I will fall at your knees if I need to. Can you help me in my misfortune? Can you help the girl who came here to be your wife? It was for you that we had the seamstresses working day and night. All the excitement was for you. And now she is told that she will be slaughtered. What will men think of you when they hear of this deceit? I have no one else to implore so I implore you. For the sake of your own name, if nothing else, you must help me. Put your hand over mine, and then I will know that we are saved."

"I will not touch your hand. I will do that only if I have succeeded in changing Agamemnon's mind. Your husband should not have used my name as though it were a trap."

"If you do not marry her, if you fail—"

"My name is nothing then. My life is nothing. All weakness, a name used to trap a girl."

"I can bring my daughter here. Let us both stand in front of you."

"Let her remain apart. I will speak to your husband."

"My husband . . ." I began and then stopped.

Achilles looked around at the group of men who were closest to us.

"He is our leader," he said.

"You will be rewarded if you can prevail," I said.

He looked at me evenly, holding my gaze until I turned and walked back through the camp alone. Men moved out of my way, out of my sight, as though I, in my efforts to prevent the sacrifice, were some vast pestilence that had been sent to their camp, worse than the wind that had smashed their boats against the rocks and then rose up again in further fury.

When I arrived at our tent, I could hear the sound of Iphigenia crying. The tent was full of women, a few women who had traveled with us, the women who had come the day before, and now some stragglers who added their presence to create an air of mayhem around my daughter. When I shouted at them to get out and they did not attend to me, I pulled one of them by the ear to the opening of the tent and, having ejected her,

I moved towards another until all of them, except the women who had traveled with us, began to scatter.

Iphigenia had her hands over her face.

"What has happened?" I asked.

One of the women told us then that three rough-looking men in full armor had come to the tent looking for me. When they were told that I was not there, they believed that I was hiding and ransacked the living quarters, the sleeping quarters and the kitchens. And then they left, taking Orestes with them. Iphigenia began to cry now as the women told me that her brother had been taken. He was kicking and struggling, they said, as they carried him away.

"Who sent these men?" I asked.

There was silence for a moment. No one wished to answer until one of the women eventually spoke.

"Agamemnon," she said.

I asked two of the women to come with me to the sleeping quarters to prepare my body and my attire. They washed me, adding sweet spices and perfume, and then they helped me to choose my clothes and arrange my hair. They asked me if they should accompany me now, but I thought that I would walk alone through the camp in search of my husband, that I would call out his name, that I would threaten and terrorize anyone I saw who did not help me to find him.

When finally I found his tent, my way was blocked by one of his men, who asked me what business I had with him.

I was in the act of pushing him out of my way when Agamemnon appeared.

"Where is Orestes?" I asked.

"Learning how to use a sword properly," he replied. "He will be well looked after. There are other boys his age."

"Why did you send men looking for me?"

"To tell you that it will happen soon. The heifers will be slain first. They are now on their way to the appointed place."

"And then?"

"And then our daughter."

"Say her name!"

I did not know that Iphigenia had followed me, and I do not know still how she changed from the sobbing, frightened and inconsolable girl to the poised young woman, her presence solitary and stern, that now came towards us.

"You do not need to say my name," she interrupted. "I know my name."

"Look at her. Do you intend to kill her?" I asked Agamemnon. He did not reply.

"Answer the question," I said.

"There are many things I must explain," he said.

"Answer the question first," I said. "Answer it. And then you can explain."

"I have learned from your emissary what you intend to do to me," Iphigenia said. "You do not need to answer anything."

"Why will you kill her?" I asked. "What prayers will you utter as she dies? What blessings will you ask for yourself when you cut your child's throat?"

"The gods . . ." he began and stopped.

"Do the gods smile on men who have their daughters killed?" I asked. "And if the wind does not change, will you kill Orestes too? Is that why he is here?"

"Orestes? No!"

"Do you want me to send for Electra?" I asked. "Do you want to find a husband's name for her and fool her too?"

"Stop!" he said.

As Iphigenia moved towards him, he seemed almost afraid of her.

"I am not eloquent, father," she said. "All the power I have is in my tears, but I have no tears now either. I have my voice and I have my body and I can kneel and ask that I not be killed before my time. Like you, I think the light of day is sweet. I was the first to call you father, and I was the first you called your daughter. You must remember how you told me that I would in time be happy in my husband's house, and I asked: Happier than with you, father? And you smiled and shook your head and I curled my head into your chest and held you with my arms. I dreamed that I would receive you into my house when you were old and we would be happy then. I told you that. Do you remember? If you kill me, then that will be a sour dream I had, and surely for you it will bring infinite regret. I have come alone to you, tearless, unready. I have no eloquence. I can only ask you with the simple voice I have to send us home. I ask you to spare me. I ask my father what no daughter should ever have to ask. Father, do not kill me!"

Agamemnon lowered his head as if he were the one who had been condemned. When some of his men approached, he looked at them nervously before he spoke.

"I understand that it calls for pity," he said. "I love my children. I love my daughter even more now that I see her so composed and in the fullest bloom. But see how large this seagoing army is! It is ready and restive, but the wind will not change for us to attack. Think of the men. Their wives are being abducted by barbarians while they linger here, their land is being laid waste. Each one knows that the gods have been consulted, and each one knows what the gods have ordered me to do. It does not depend on me. I have no choice in this. And if we are defeated, no one will survive. We will all be destroyed, every one of us. If the wind does not change, we will all face death."

He bowed to some invisible presence in front of him and then he signaled to the two men closest to him to follow him into his tent; two others went to guard the entrance.

It struck me then that if the gods really cared, if they had been watching over us as they were meant to be, they would take pity and quickly change the wind over the sea. I imagined voices coming from the water, from the harbor, then cheering among the men, the flags blowing with this new wind that would allow their ships to move speedily and stealthily so that they would know victory and see that the gods had merely been testing their resolve.

The noises I imagined soon began to give way to shouting as Achilles ran towards us, followed by men roaring abuse at him.

"Agamemnon told me to talk to the soldiers directly myself, to tell them that it was out of his hands," he said. "I have now spoken to them and they say that she must be killed. They shouted threats at me too."

"At you?"

"To say that I should be stoned to death."

"For trying to save my daughter?"

"I begged them. I told them that victory in battle made possible by the murder of a girl was a coward's victory. My voice was drowned out by their shouting. They will not give in to argument."

I turned towards the crowd of men that had followed Achilles. I thought that if I could find one face and gaze at it, the face of the weakest among them or the strongest, I could shift my gaze to each of them and make them ashamed. But they would not look up. No matter what I did, not one of them would look up.

"I will do what I can to save her," Achilles said, but there was in his tone a sound of defeat. He did not name what he could do, or what he might do. I noticed that he too had his eyes cast down. But as Iphigenia began to speak, he looked at her, as did the men around him, who took her in now as though she had already become an icon whose last words would have to be remembered, a figure whose death was going to change the very way the wind blew, whose blood would send an urgent message to the heavens above us.

"My death," she said, "will rescue all those who are in danger. I will die. It cannot be otherwise. It is not right for me to be in love with life. It is not right for any of us to be in love with life. What is a single life? There are always others. Others like us come and live. Each breath we breathe is followed by another breath, each step by another step, each word by the next one, each presence in the world by another presence. It hardly matters who must die. We will be replaced. I will give myself for the army's sake, for my father's sake, for my country's sake. I will meet my own sacrifice with a smile. Victory in battle will be my victory then. The memory of my name will last longer than the lives of many men."

As she spoke, her father and his men slowly emerged from his tent, and others gathered who had been nearby. I watched her, unsure all the time if this was a ploy, if her soft tone and her voice low with humility and resignation, but loud enough that it could be heard, was something she had planned so that she could somehow save herself.

No one moved. There was no sound from the camp. Her words lay on the stillness of air like a further stillness. I noticed Achilles about to speak and then deciding to remain silent. Agamemnon in those moments attempted to assume the pose of a commander, as he ran his eyes over the far horizon, suggesting that large questions were on his mind. No matter what he did, however, he appeared to me like a diminished, aging man. He would, in the future, I thought, be viewed with contempt for luring his daughter to the camp and having her murdered to appease the gods. He was still feared, I saw, but I could see too that this would not last.

Thus he was at his most dangerous, like a bull with a sword stuck into its side.

With dignity and proud scorn, I walked away from them, with Iphigenia gently following. I was sure then that the weak leader and the angry, uneasy mob would hold sway. I knew that we had been defeated. Iphigenia continued speaking, asking me not to mourn her death, and not to pity her, asking me to tell Electra how she died and to implore Electra not to wear mourning clothes for her, and to use my energy now to save Orestes from the poison that was all around us.

*

In the distance, we could hear the howls of the animals that had been brought to the place of sacrifice. I demanded that all the women who once more had arrived get out of our sight, except the few we trusted who had accompanied us to the camp. I ordered Iphigenia's wedding clothes to be prepared and the clothes that I had planned to wear at the wedding ceremony to be laid out for me. I asked for water so we both could bathe and then special white ointment for our faces and black lines for around our eyes so that we would seem pale and unearthly as we made our way to that place of death.

At first no one spoke. Then the silence was broken at intervals by men shouting, by the sound of prayers rising, by animals bellowing and letting out fierce shrieks.

When word came that there were men outside and they were preparing to enter, I went towards the opening of the tent. The men seemed frightened when they saw me.

"Do you know who I am?" I asked.

They would not look at me or reply.

"Are you too cowardly to speak?" I asked.

"We are not," one of them said.

"Do you know who I am?" I asked this man.

"Yes," he said.

"From my mother I received a set of words that she, in turn, had received from hers," I said. "These words have been sparingly used. They cause the insides of all men within earshot to shrivel, and then the insides of all their children. Only their wives are spared, and they are destined then to search the dust for food to peck."

They were so filled with superstition, I saw, that any set of words that invoked the gods or an ancient curse would instill instant fear in them. Not one of them questioned me even with a glance, not one shadow passed over what I had said, not one hint that there was no such curse, and never had been.

"If one of you lays a finger on my daughter or on me," I continued, "if one of you walks ahead of us, or speaks, I will invoke that curse. Unless you come behind us like a pack of dogs, I will speak the words of the curse."

Each one of them looked chastened. Arguments would not work for them, not even pity, but the slightest invocation of a power beyond their power had them spellbound. Had they looked up again, they would have seen a smile of pure contempt pass across my face.

Inside, Iphigenia was ready, like some deeply molded version of herself, stately, placid, not responding to the sound of an animal howling in pain that rose at the very place where she soon would see light for the last time.

I whispered to her: "They are frightened of our curses. Wait until there is silence and raise your voice. Explain how ancient the curse is, passed from mother to daughter over time, and how seldom it has been used because of its power. Threaten to invoke it unless they relent, threaten it first against your father and then against each one of them, beginning with those closest to you. Warn them that there will be no army left at all, just dogs growling in the deathly stillness that your curse will leave behind."

I told her then what the words of the curse should say. We walked in ceremony from our tent to the killing place, Iphigenia first, with me some distance behind her, and then the women who had come with us, and then the soldiers. The day was hot; the smell of the blood and the innards of animals and the aftermath of fear and butchering came towards us until it took all our will not to cover our noses from the stench. Instead of a place of dignity, they had made the place where the killing was to happen into a ramshackle site, with soldiers wandering around aimlessly, and the leftover parts of dead animals strewn about.

Perhaps it was this scene, coupled with how easy it had been to invoke the gods in the curse that I had invented, that sharpened something already in me. As we walked towards the place of slaughter, I realized for the first time that I was sure, fully sure, that I did not believe at all in the power of the gods. I wondered if I was alone in this. I wondered if Agamemnon and the men around him really cared about the gods, if they really believed that a hidden power beyond their power was holding the troops in a spell that no mortal power could manage to cast.

But of course they did. Of course they were sure of what they believed, enough for them to want to go through with this plan.

As we approached Agamemnon, he whispered to his daughter: "Your name will be remembered forever."

He turned to me and in a voice of gravity and self-importance he whispered: "Her name will be remembered forever."

I saw now that one of the soldiers who had accompanied us went to Agamemnon and whispered something to him. Agamemnon listened closely and then spoke quietly, firmly, to the five or six men around him.

Then the chanting began, the calling out to the gods in phrases filled with repetitions and strange inversions. I closed my eyes and listened. I could smell the blood of the animals as it began to sour, and there were vultures in the sky, so it was all death, and then the single sound of the chant followed by the rippling, rising sound of the chant being repeated by those who followed the gods most closely and then a sudden mass sound directed towards the sky as thousands of men responded with one voice.

I looked at Iphigenia as she stood alone. She exuded an unearthly power, with the beauty of her robes, the whiteness of her face, the blackness of her hair, the black lines around her eyes, her stillness and silence.

At that moment, the knife was produced. Two women walked towards Iphigenia and loosened her hair from its pins, then pushed down her head and hurriedly, roughly cut her hair. When one of them cut into her skin and Iphigenia cried out, however, the cry was that of a girl, not a sacrificial victim, but a young, fearful, vulnerable girl. And the sacred spell was broken for a moment. I knew how fragile this crowd was. Men began to shout. Agamemnon looked around him in dismay. I knew as I watched him how thin his control was.

As Iphigenia pulled herself loose and began to speak, no one could hear her at first and she had to scream to get silence. When it was clear that she was ready to invoke a curse against her father, a man came from behind her with an old white cloth and bound it around her mouth and dragged her, as she kicked and used her elbows, to the place of sacrifice, where he tied her hands and her feet.

I did not hesitate then. I stretched out my arms and raised my voice and I began the curse of which I had warned them. I directed it against all of them. Some of those in front of me started to run in fright, but from behind another man came with a ragged cloth that, despite my efforts, he pulled tight around my mouth too. I was dragged away as well, but in the opposite direction, away from the place of sacrifice.

When I was out of sight, out of earshot, I was kicked and beaten. And then at the edge of the camp, I saw them lifting a stone. It took three or four men to lift it. The men who had dragged me pushed me into a space dug into the earth below the stone.

The space was large enough to sit in but not to stand up or lie down in. Once they had me there, they quickly put the stone back over the opening. My hands were not bound, so I could move them enough to take the cloth from my mouth, but the stone was too heavy for me to push, so I could not release myself. I was trapped; even the urgent sounds I made seemed trapped.

I was half-buried underground as my daughter died alone. I never saw her body and I did not hear her cries or call out to her. But others told me of her cry. And those last high sounds she made, I now believe, in all their helplessness and fear, as they became shrieks, as they pierced the ears of the crowd assembled, will be remembered forever. Nothing else.

*

Soon, for me, the pain began, the pain in my back that came from being cramped under the ground. The numbness in my arms and legs soon became painful too. The base of my spine began to be irritated and then felt as if it were on fire. I would have given anything to stretch my body, let my arms and legs loose, stand up straight and move. That was all I thought about for the first while.

Then the thirst began, and the fear that seemed to make the thirst even more intense. All I thought about now was water, even the smallest amount of water. I remembered times in my life when there had been pitchers of cool drinking water close to me. I imagined springs in the earth, deep wells. I regretted that I had not savored water more. The hunger that came later was nothing to this thirst.

Despite the vileness of the smell, and the ants and spiders that crawled around me, despite the pain in my back and in my arms and legs, despite the hunger that deepened, despite the fear that I would never come out of here alive, it was the thirst that turned me, changed me.

I had, I realized, made one mistake. I should not have threatened with a curse the men who came to accompany us to the place of death. I should have let them do as they willed, walk ahead of us, or alongside as though Iphigenia were their prisoner. That soldier who had spoken to my husband had, I was sure, whispered him a warning. He had prepared him and now, during my time underground, I blamed myself. As a result of my words, spoken too hastily, I was certain that Agamemnon had ordered that if we began a curse, my daughter or I, we were to be silenced instantly by the gagging cloth.

If he had not been prepared, I imagined the men scattering in fear as Iphigenia began to curse them. I imagined her threatening to continue the curse, to finish the string of words that would shrivel them, unless they released her. I imagined that she could have been saved.

I was at fault. In that time under the earth, in order to distract myself from the thirst, I resolved that if I were spared I would weigh each word I spoke and decision I made. In the future, I would weigh the smallest action.

Because of how roughly the stone had been put over me, I could see a sliver of light, so that when it faded and I could see nothing I knew it was night. Through those hours of darkness, I went over everything from the start. We should never have been fooled into coming here. And we should have worked out a way of fleeing once Agamemnon's intentions became clear. Such thoughts made the thirst that I suffered even more intense. That thirst lived in me like something that could never be assuaged.

The following morning, when someone threw a pitcher of water into the hole where they had buried me, I heard laughter. I tried to drink what water I could that had soaked into my clothes, but it was almost nothing. The water had merely wet me and the ground beneath me. It had also let me know, in case I needed to know, that I was not forgotten. At intervals over the next two days, they threw more water in. It mixed with my excrement to make a smell like that of a body as it putrefies. It was a smell that I thought would never leave me.

What stayed with me besides that smell was a thought. It began as nothing, as a piece of bad temper arising from the pure discomfort and the thirst, but then it grew and it came to mean more than any other thought or any other thing. If the gods did not watch over us, I wondered, then how should we know what to do? Who else would tell us what to do? I realized then that no one would tell us, no one at all, no one would tell me what should be done in the future or what should not be done. In the future, I would be the one to decide what to do, not the gods.

And in that time I determined that I would kill Agamemnon in retaliation for what he had done. I would consult no oracle or priest. I would pray to no one. I would plot alone in silence. I would be ready. And this would be something that Agamemnon and those around him, so filled with the view that we all must wait for the oracle, would never guess, never suspect.

*

On the third morning, close to first light, when they lifted the stone, I was too stiff to move. They tried to pull me out by the arms, but I was locked into the narrow space where they had buried me. They had to lever me out slowly; they put their strength under my arms because I could not stand, the power in my legs had gone. I saw no value in speech, and did not smile in satisfaction as they held their noses against the stench that rose in the morning sun from the hole where they had held me.

They took me to where the women were waiting. For hours that morning, having washed me and found me fresh clothes, they fed me and I drank. No one spoke. They were afraid, I saw, that I was going to ask them about the last moments of my daughter's life and the disposal of her body.

I was ready to be left in peace by them so that I could sleep, when we heard the sound of running and voices. One of the men who had accompanied us to the place of death came breathlessly into the tent.

"The wind has changed," he said.

"Where is Orestes?" I asked him.

He shrugged and ran back out into the crowd. A sound rose then, the noise of instructions and commands. Within a short time, two soldiers came into the women's tent and stood guard close to the entrance; they were followed soon by my husband, who had to bend as he pushed through to us, because he was carrying Orestes on his shoulders. Orestes had his small sword in his hand; he was laughing as his father made as though to unseat him.

"He will be a great warrior," he said. "Orestes is the chief of men."

When he let him down, Agamemnon smiled.

"We will sail tonight when the moon sets. You will take Orestes and your women home and wait for me. I will give you four men to guard you on your way."

"I don't want four men," I said.

"You will need them."

As he stepped backwards, Orestes realized that he was being left with us. He began to cry. His father lifted him and handed him to me.

"Wait for me, both of you. I will come when the task is done."

He stalked out of the tent. Soon, four men came, men whom I had threatened with my curse. They told us that they wanted to begin our journey before nightfall. They appeared afraid of me as I told them that it would take us time to prepare. I suggested that they stand outside the tent until I called them.

One of them was softer, younger than the others. He took control of Orestes and distracted him with games and stories as we made our way home. Orestes was filled with life. He would not let his sword out of his hand as he spoke of warriors and battles and how he would follow his enemy until the end of time. It was only in the hour before sleep that he would whimper, moving towards me for warmth and comfort and then pushing me away as he started to cry. His dreams woke us on some of those nights. He wanted his father and then his sister and then the friends he had made among the soldiers. He wanted me too, but when I held him and whispered to him, he recoiled in fright. Thus our journey was filled both day and night with Orestes, so much so that we did not think about what we would say when we arrived home.

All of the others must have wondered, as I did, if word of the fate of Iphigenia had reached Electra, or reached the elders who had been left to advise her. On the last night of our journey, I concentrated on keeping Orestes calm under a high, starry sky as I started to think about what I would do now, how I would live and whom I might trust.

I would trust no one, I thought. I would trust no one. That was the most useful thing to hold in my mind.

*

In the weeks we had been away, Electra had heard rumors, and the rumors had aged her and made her voice shrill, or more shrill than I had remembered it. She ran towards me for news. I know now that not concentrating on her and her alone was my first mistake with her. The isolation and the waiting seemed to have unhinged some part of her so it was hard to make her listen. Maybe I should have stayed up through the night taking her into my confidence, telling her what had happened to us step by step, minute by minute, and asking her to hold me and comfort me. But my legs still hurt and it was hard to walk. I was still ravenous for food and no amount of water quenched my thirst. I wanted to sleep.

I should not have brushed her aside, however. Of that I am sure. I was dreaming of fresh clothes, my old bed, a bath, food, a pitcher of sweet water from the palace well. I was dreaming of peace, at least until Agamemnon returned. I was making plans. I left the others to tell her the story of her sister's death. I moved like a hungry ghost through the rooms of the palace away from her, away from her voice, a voice that would come to follow me more than any other voice.

*

When I woke on the first morning, I realized that I was a prisoner. The four men had been sent to guard me, to watch over Electra and Orestes, to ensure the loyalty of the elders to Agamemnon. They were happy once I was in my chambers, once I asked for nothing more than food and drink and time to sleep and to walk in the garden and restore the power in my legs. If I left my own quarters, two of them followed me. They let no one see me except the women who took care of me and they questioned those women each night about what I said and did.

It occurred to me that I would have to murder all four of them on a single night. Nothing could happen until that was done. When I was not sleeping, I was planning how best this could be carried out.

Even though the women brought me news, I could not be sure of them. I could be sure of no one.

Electra continued to run through the palace, unsettling the very air. She developed a habit of repeating the same lines to me, the same accusations. "You let her be sacrificed. You came back without her." I, in turn, continued to ignore her. I should have made her see that her father was not the brave man she still believed him to be, but rather a weasel among men. I should have made her see that it was his weakness that caused the death of her sister.

I should have had her join me in my rage. Instead, I left her free to have her own rage, much of it now directed against me.

When she came to my room, I often feigned sleep, or turned away from her. She had many things to say to the elders and to the four men her father had sent. They, I saw, grew weary of her too.

But one day, I began to listen to her carefully, as she seemed more agitated than usual.

"Aegisthus," she said, "is walking these corridors in the night. He is appearing in my room. Some nights when I wake, he is standing at the foot of my bed smiling at me and then he retreats into the shadows."

Aegisthus was being held hostage; he had been in the dungeon under our care, as my husband phrased it, for more than five years. It was agreed that he must be well fed and not harmed, since he was a glittering prize, clever and handsome and ruthless, I was told, with many followers in the outreaches, the wild places.

When our armies had first taken Aegisthus' family strong-hold, no one could fathom how two of my husband's guards were found each morning lying in their own blood. Some felt that it was a curse. Guards were detailed to guard the guards. Spies were positioned to watch through the night. But still, each morning, once first light came, two guards were found lying facedown in their blood. It was soon believed that Aegisthus was the killer, and this was confirmed when he was taken hostage, as no more guards were found dead. His followers offered to pay ransom, but my husband saw that, so great was Aegisthus' standing, holding him here, keeping him in chains, was more powerful than sending an army to put down his followers, who had fled into the hills.

When he met with his advisers, my husband often asked, amused, if there was any word of unruliness in the conquered territories and then, on hearing that all was well, he would smile and say: "As long as we keep Aegisthus here, all will be at peace. Make sure that his chains are firmly in place. Have him checked each day."

There was talk of our prisoner as the years passed, of his good manners and his good looks. Some of the women who served me spoke of how he had tamed the birds that flew through the high window of his cell. One of the women whispered too that Aegisthus knew how to attract young women into his cell, and indeed young servant boys. One day when I asked my women why they were trying to suppress their laughter, they finally explained that one of them had heard the sound of the clanking of chains echoing from Aegisthus' cell and had stood outside until one of the serving boys had emerged with a furtive, sheepish look and had fled back into the kitchen to resume his duties there.

There was also something that my mother had told me at the time of my marriage. There was, she said, a story that my father-in-law in the heat of rage had ordered Aegisthus' two half brothers killed and then stuffed and cooked with spices and served to their father at a feast. This stayed in my mind now as I thought about our prisoner. He might have his own reasons to wish to take revenge on my husband were he given the chance.

When Electra mentioned again that she had seen the prisoner standing in her room, I told her that she was dreaming. She insisted that she was not.

"He woke me from my sleep. He whispered words I could not hear. He disappeared before I could call the guards. When the guards came, they swore that no one had passed them, but they were mistaken. Aegisthus moves through the palace at night. Ask your women, if you do not believe me."

I told her that I did not want to hear of this again.

"You will hear of it each time it happens," she said defiantly.

"You sound as though you want him to appear," I said.

"I want my father to return," she said. "Not until then will I feel safe."

I was about to tell her that her father's interest in the safety of his daughters was not something that could be so confidently invoked, but instead I questioned her further about Aegisthus. I asked her to describe him.

"He is not tall. He lifts his face and smiles when I awake, as though he knows me. His face is the face of a boy, and his body too is boyish."

"He has been a prisoner for many years. He is a murderer," I said.

"The figure I saw," she replied, "is the same figure that the women describe who have seen him chained in his cell."

I began to sleep early so that I would wake when it was still dark. I noticed the soundlessness around me. The guards outside my door were sleeping. Some nights I practiced moving from room to room in bare feet, hardly breathing. Not going far. The only sounds I heard were men snoring in one of the rooms in the distance. I liked the sound because it meant that the noise I made was nothing, a noise that could not be easily heard.

I had a plan now, and the plan involved finding Aegisthus and seeking his support.

After a week or more, I risked traveling into the bowels of this building. I would feign sleepwalking, I thought, if anyone found me. I could not work out, however, where exactly Aegisthus was held, in a dungeon floor below the one where the kitchens and storerooms were or in some outer dungeon.

I started to haunt the corridors in the hard hours of night when it was silent. And it was on one of those nights that I came across our hostage face-to-face. He was as young and boyish as Electra had described, with no hint that he had been in a dungeon for many years.

"I have been looking for you," I whispered.

He was not frightened or ready to turn and run. He examined me with equanimity.

"You are the woman whose daughter was sacrificed," he said. "You were buried in a hole. You have been walking in these corridors. I have been watching you."

"If you betray me," I replied, "you will be found dead by the guards."

"What do you want? You must be direct," he said. "If you do not use me, perhaps someone else will."

"I will have guards put at your door all night."

"Guards?" he asked and smiled. "I know the ones who matter. Nothing escapes me. Now what do you want?"

I had one second to decide, but I knew as I spoke that I had decided some time before. I was ready now.

"The four men," I said, "who came with us from the camp, I want them killed. I can guide you to where they sleep. They have guards at their door, but the guards sleep at night."

"All four killed on the same night?" he asked.

"Yes."

"And in return?"

"Everything," I said, and put a finger to my lips and moved back as quietly as I could to my quarters.

Nothing happened then. I realized that perhaps I had risked too much, but I knew that I would have to risk even more were anything to happen. I watched the four guards. I watched the elders who had been left here when my husband went to war. I listened carefully to the murmurings and gossip of the women. I used Orestes as an excuse to wander beyond my own quarters. I followed his sword fights with one of the guards and his young son who often accompanied his father. I knew in this strange time as rumors came of how our army had prevailed that something would move or shift, that somebody would give me a sign, even unwittingly, a sign that would help me, a sign before official news would come to me of Agamemnon's victorious return.

Each night, I made my soundless journeys in the corridors and then I returned and slept, often sleeping beyond the dawn until Orestes came to my side, all energy still, all talk of his father and the soldiers and the swords. On one of those nights, having fallen into the deepest sleep, I was woken by the sound of an owl screaming at my window and then by some other sound. I lay listening, hearing footsteps from outside my door and voices and shouts to the guards that they must protect me with their lives.

When I approached the door, they would not let me leave my room, or allow anyone to enter. Louder sounds then began, men shouting orders, and others running and the high-pitched voice of Electra. Then Orestes was rushed into my room by two men.

"What has happened?" I asked.

"The four men who came with you were found in their own blood, murdered by their guards," one of the men said.

"Their guards?"

"Do not worry. The guards have been dispatched."

I looked out and saw the bodies being carried along the corridor outside and then I returned to the room and spoke softly to Orestes to distract him. When Electra came, I signaled to her not to speak of what had occurred in her brother's presence. Soon she tired of having to be silent and left me and my son in peace. When she returned, she whispered to me that she had spoken to the elders, who had assured her that this had been a feud over cards or dice between the guards and the four men. They had been drinking.

"The guards' faces were all badged with blood," she said, "and so were their daggers. They must have been drunk. They will do no more drinking now, no more killing either."

It was nothing more than a feud between men, Electra added, and would seem nothing to her father when he returned. She had issued an order in my name against any dice or card games. All drinking would be banned too, she said, until Agamemnon returned.

I moved with Orestes into the open air. I spoke to him gently as we went in search of a soldier who would train him further in the art of sword fighting.

It was too dangerous, I thought, to venture far in the corridors at night. In the dark hours, I stayed by my door, watching, listening for the slightest sound.

One night, when Aegisthus appeared as I knew he would, like a fox following a trail, he beckoned me to a chamber where there was no one.

"I have men under my control," he whispered. "We are now ready. We can do anything."

"Go to the house of each of the elders my husband left to govern," I whispered. "Take a child. A son or a grandson. Your men must explain that I gave orders for this and that if they want the child returned they must appeal to me. Take the children some distance away. Do not harm them. Keep them safe."

He smiled.

"Are you sure?" he asked.

"Yes," I said and moved silently away from him and back to my chamber.

Nothing happened for some days. More rumors came of Agamemnon's victories and of the enormous spoils he was conveying back to the palace. The elders came to consult with me when it was clear that Agamemnon would return once some further territories were under his control.

"We must prepare a fitting welcome for him," they said, and I bowed and nodded and asked their permission to call Orestes into the room, and Electra, so that they might hear of their father's glory, so that they too might prepare themselves for his return. Orestes came in solemnly with his sword by his side. He listened as a man might listen, not smiling but mimicking the gestures of a man. Electra asked that she might greet her father before I did, or the elders did, since she had been the one who had remained, who had ensured that her father's rule prevailed while I was away. This was agreed. I bowed.

A few days later, some women came to my quarters in the hours after dawn to say that the elders wished to see me, that they had gathered one by one as the light came up and they seemed agitated. Some, indeed, had wanted to visit me in my room, only to be informed that I was sleeping and could not be disturbed. I sent a woman to find Orestes so that he would not come looking for me and asked her to accompany him to the garden. I dressed carefully and slowly. It would be better, I thought, if the men were left to wait.

They began by asking me where the children who had been taken were, but soon, as I asked them, "What children? What do you mean taken?," they realized that they had spoken too hastily.

"Why are you here?" I asked them.

They explained, interrupting one another, that a group of men, all strangers, had come in the night and taken one male child, their sons or grandsons, and that each group of intruders had said that they were acting on my orders.

"I do not give orders," I said.

"Do you know anything about this?" one of them asked.

"I know that I was sleeping and I was woken to say that you were here. That is what I know."

Some of them now were nervously backing away.

"Have you searched for these children?" I asked. "I am sure this is what my husband would want you to do. The sooner you begin the search, the better."

"We were told that searching would not bear fruit," one of them said.

"And you believed that?" I asked.

They started to talk among themselves until Electra arrived, when they left my presence. I spent the day alone in my room, or with Orestes in the garden. I noticed the guards were more uneasy now, more watchful, and I determined that I would not move from my room tonight, or any night soon. It would not be long before I would walk where I pleased by day, in full light.

Theodotus, one of the elders, the most eminent and sharp among them, came to see me later that day. The grandchild taken, he said, was his only son's only child. Much depended on this boy, whose name was Leander. They hoped that he would be a great leader. As I listened to him, I displayed as much sympathy as I could manage. When he asked me finally if there was nothing I could do, if I really knew nothing, I hesitated. I walked along a corridor with him and, on our parting, I said: "There will be news in good time. For now, can you let the others know that if one of them seeks to contact Agamemnon before his return, or send a message to him about this, or tell him about it when he comes back, then this will not help? It will emphatically not help. If you and they remain silent and obey the law, however, then you would all be wise to hope. Can you convey that from me to the others?"

I suggested that he should come to see me again soon, and perhaps then there would be news. I was certain that by the end of the day he would have told the other men that he believed that I was aware who had taken them, and that it was even possible from how I spoke that I had been fully responsible for their abduction.

By that night I saw a different disposition even in the guards. They seemed more humble, almost afraid. The only one who had not changed was Electra. She told me that the men were searching far and wide for the children and that she agreed with them that bandits were behind what had happened and we must be more vigilant in the short time before her father returned. She spoke like someone who was in control.

Two days later, as further rumors came of our victories in battle and of the large number of slaves captured, I walked alone through the palace and down to the kitchens and the storerooms, asking where Aegisthus was kept. At first, no one would tell me. When I said that I would not leave unless I was shown where he was, I was brought to one of the storerooms, where a trapdoor was lifted.

"His dungeon is down here," I was told.

"Get a torch," I said.

We descended a ladder to the floor below.

"Where is Aegisthus?" I asked as I saw three narrow doors.

They were still unwilling to say, until I made it clear that I was not only determined but impatient. When a door was finally opened, I found my prey sitting happily in the corner playing with a bird. He had furniture in the room, including a bed. The room was lit by a tiny window, which gave a chink of light.

"I cannot come with you unless you release the prisoners in the next cells," he said.

"How many are there?"

"Two," he said.

As I demanded that I be allowed to see the other two cells, the guards were becoming increasingly nervous.

"We have no authority to open these cells," one of them said.

"I am the authority," I replied. "From now on, you will report to me. Open the cells."

The middle one did not have any light. When we opened the door and no one emerged, I believed that it had been empty all along. In the final one, there was a young man who

seemed frightened of us and asked for Aegisthus. I told him
that we would unchain him and that he would be free to walk
out himself to find Aegisthus in his cell, but he shook his head
and said that he did not want to leave his own cell until he had
spoken to Aegisthus. A low, hollow sound then came from the
middle cell, a sound that was like a man's voice, but with no
words. When I took the torch and entered, I found an old man
in the corner. I slowly stepped away from him and returned to
find Aegisthus.

"Who are these two men?"

"The old man has been here for as long as anyone can
remember. No one knows who he is or why he is here. I need
to speak to the other one now."

"Who is he?"

"I cannot say."

Aegisthus moved out of his cell and down to the cell of the
younger man. He closed the door so that no one could hear.
When they both appeared, and Aegisthus began to give orders,
I stood back and watched him, surprised.

"Remove his chains. Give him fresh clothes and food," he
said. "And shelter him until night falls. Then he will depart.
And unchain the old man and leave his cell door open. Feed
him and then let him go too."

And then he hesitated before he smiled.

"And feed the birds," he added. "They are used to being fed."

The guards who had followed us down into this dank cellar
studied Aegisthus with amazement, and then looked at me. A
few minutes earlier, he had been their prisoner.

"Do what he says," I commanded.

We walked together through the palace to my chamber, to
be confronted by Electra.

"This man, this Aegisthus," she said, "is both a prisoner and a hostage. He must be returned to his cell. The guards will return him to his cell."

"He is my bodyguard," I said. "He will be with me at all times until your father returns."

"We have our own guards," she said.

"Who got drunk and murdered four men," I said. "Aegisthus remains here with me as my guard. Anyone who wishes to see me, or speak to me, must know that he is on guard."

"My father will want to know—" she began.

"Your father will want to know," I interrupted, "what happened to the four men he sent here, four men who were his close friends, and he will also want to know what happened to the children who have been taken. This is a most dangerous time. I suggest that you take precautions too."

"No one would dare touch me," she said.

"In that case, don't take any precautions at all," I said.

Soon, many of the elders arrived, wishing to see me. I ordered Aegisthus not to speak as he accompanied me, to walk behind me, to remain silent at all times.

He responded as though this were an amusing game.

I explained to the elders that we must all be careful now in these days before the return of Agamemnon. There must be more vigilance, there must be no more events to make my husband feel that we had not been most careful. For that reason, I had my own bodyguard.

"Aegisthus is being held prisoner," one of them said. "He is a murderer."

"Good," I said. "He will murder anyone who approaches my chamber without permission. And when my husband returns, Agamemnon will decide all matters and we will all be safer, but until then I will protect myself and I suggest that all of you follow suit."

"Does Aegisthus know where our children and grandchildren are?" one of the men asked. "He has followers."

"Followers?" I asked. "This man knows nothing more than what I have told him. I have informed him that there have been grave breaches of the peace here, and his task is to protect me and my son and my daughter until Agamemnon returns. My husband will have much to say to you about how you allowed the children to be taken, and how you allowed his most trusted men to be murdered by their guards."

One of the men made to speak and then stopped. I could see they were afraid.

I asked Theodotus to meet me alone. He seemed eager and wondered if there was news about his grandson.

"When my husband returns, after a day or two, we will raise the matter with him. But you know Agamemnon as I do. He will not be happy to hear news of negligence. When all is calm, and he has slept, then we will speak to him of this. It cannot be dealt with in any other way. We do not want his anger turned on us."

"Yes, that is wise," he said.

Aegisthus, who had been listening, walked behind me to my chamber, where we found Orestes with some of the women. I saw Orestes examining Aegisthus suspiciously. He did not know whether this new man was a guard whose duty would be to play with him, or whether he represented some rank above a guard and thus could not be ordered to take part in a sword fight. Before he could decide, I asked the women to take Orestes and find a guard who could play at sword fighting with him until he was tired.

I ordered Aegisthus then to alert his followers to move from hill to hill and be ready to light fires to signal to us where Agamemnon was and how soon he and his entourage would appear. He disappeared for a short time. When he returned, he said that he already had men on the lookout, but now there would be more, and they would have permission to light fires on hills.

"Where did you go just now?" I asked him.

"I have my people close," he replied.

"In the palace?" I asked.

"Yes, close," he repeated.

I ate alone at my table that evening, my food served as usual by the women. They brought Aegisthus' food to a smaller table near the door.

When Orestes was asleep, I asked that he be moved, as usual, to his own small chamber.

Aegisthus sat in the shadows and did not speak. We were alone. In all the plans I had made, I had not considered what might happen now. I had left any close imaginings out of my mind. I was sure, however, that I did not want him to leave. Even though I supposed that he was armed and alert, with one word, I thought, I could have him returned to his cell.

I needed to be certain of him before Agamemnon returned. But I was still not certain. Did he plan to sit watching over me all night? If I slept, how could I know that he would not leave? Or injure me?

He had a choice, I realized. He could flee and save his life. Or he could wait and see what more he could gain. I had, after all, promised him everything. What did he believe that I had meant? Since I was not sure, I did not see how he could be.

As he studied me, his smile grew more shy, more shadowy.

In the silence between us I knew now what I had stopped myself from thinking in the days before. I realized what I had kept from my mind since the time when I had first heard of this prisoner in chains. I wanted him in my bed. I saw that he understood that. But still he did not move. He gave no indication of what he would do were I to order him to cross the room.

He watched me and then lowered his head. He was like a boy. I knew that he was weighing up what he would do. And I would wait for him to decide.

I do not know how much time went by. I lit a low torch and undressed and prepared for bed, Aegisthus observing me all the time. Once I was ready, I quenched the torch so that we were in darkness. It occurred to me that I might find him at dawn, still watching. And he had, at any time, the chance to go, disappear. If he did, the children who had been taken would not be returned, or he would ransom them. I had risked too much, I thought, but I had had no other choice, or I did not think I had. I wondered if Theodotus might have been a better ally instead. He had seemed to want to take me into his confidence. As I was working out how I might have encouraged him, Aegisthus crossed the room, making enough noise for me to know that he was moving towards my bed. I heard him undress.

His body was thin. His face, when I touched it, was small and smooth, almost like a woman's. I noted some hair on his chest and then the wiry hair between his legs. He was not aroused until he opened his small mouth and edged his tongue towards mine. He gasped when I took his tongue into my mouth.

We did not sleep. In the dawn, when I looked at him he smiled and the smile suggested that he was satisfied or might be soon, the same smile that could, as I later learned, also light up his face after the greatest scheming and cruelty.

But there was no smile when I told him what I was planning. Once he learned that I was preparing to murder my husband on his return from the wars, Aegisthus became serious. When he discovered that I wanted his help in this, he looked at me sharply, then moved from the bed towards the window and stood alone with his back to me. The expression on his face when he turned was almost hostile.

"So this is what you want me for?" he said.

"I will do the killing," I said. "I do not need you for that."

"But you want my help? This is why I am here."

"Yes."

"Who else knows?" he asked.

"No one."

"No one at all?" he asked, looking at me directly, pointing his finger towards the sky as if to ask if I had implored the gods for permission to do what I planned to do. "No one has been consulted?"

"No one."

The look that came on his face then made me shiver.

"I will help you when the time comes," he said. "You can be sure that I will help you."

Soon, he found the old woman, the poisonous weaver, and brought her to the palace, and then her granddaughter. In those days, I began to visit Electra's chambers, with Aegisthus waiting outside like a faithful dog, to discuss with her the ceremony we would create upon her father's arrival. We left nothing to chance. I told her that Orestes would greet his father first. He had become skillful at swordplay and we said we would allow him a short mock fight with Agamemnon while his followers cheered. Then Electra would welcome her father and assure him that his kingdom was as peaceful and law-abiding and loyal to him as when he had left it five years earlier.

When Electra asked if she could mention the name of Iphigenia in her speech, I said no, that her father's mind could easily darken after his long battles, and that nothing should be said by her or by anyone that would undermine his welcome, his happiness.

"Our task is to make him feel at ease," I said, "now that he is once more among the people that he loves. This is what he has been thinking about since he left us, this glorious return."

In the days before Agamemnon's arrival, as fires were lit on the tops of hills to warn us of his approach, I noticed a tension all around me. I made sure to see Electra each day. When she asked me if Aegisthus would be in the line of men to meet her father, I said no, he would not be there. It would be some days, I said, before I would explain to Agamemnon how unsafe I felt in these times and how I had needed a protector for Orestes. She nodded quietly, as if she agreed with this. I embraced her warmly.

I spoke to each of the elders about the tone of the welcome they would offer to Agamemnon. It almost amused me how quickly they had become accustomed to the silent presence of Aegisthus. They must have known, since rumors spread fast in the palace, that he spent each night in my bed; they must have wondered what would happen to him, or indeed to me, on Agamemnon's return.

Aegisthus and I often went through each possibility of disruption or deception. We discussed in detail what would happen on the day of my husband's return. Once Agamemnon was preparing to enter the palace, we agreed, Electra was to be distracted and confined somewhere until it had all ended. And Orestes was to be removed to a safe place so that he too would not witness what was to transpire.

Aegisthus told me that he had five hundred men waiting, each one fully loyal to him. These men would follow orders down to the letter.

I held Aegisthus in my arms then, still worried that something might happen in those first hours when my husband came that would spark his suspicion. It must be open welcome, I thought, it must be all festive. Neither Aegisthus himself nor any of his followers must appear. Thus it would be up to me to make the returning warrior feel that everything was as it should be.

Having charted a great choreography of welcome and good cheer, we made love ferociously, aware of the risks we were taking, but aware too of the gains, the spoils.

*

We could see the chariots in the distance glistening as they came. We sent the guards running out to meet them as we, each of us, rehearsed our roles. First, Orestes with his sword. Then his sister, Electra. Then each elder, each with a different sentence of welcome or praise. I would stand above all this, watching, smiling. Eventually, I would move towards Orestes, who was nervous now, excited, and I would approach my husband and confirm what Electra had said, that his kingdom was as he had left it, peaceful, loyal, waiting for his command. Inside the palace, in the floor below our quarters, Aegisthus and some of his followers would wait, not making a sound, not even a whisper. But in the main corridor, he would leave a number of guards who would be ready to do our bidding.

Agamemnon stood straight in his chariot. He seemed to have grown larger. He was all swagger as he watched us waiting. When I saw that he noticed me, I made sure my look was of pride and then humility. Even when I saw that in his chariot there was a woman standing with him and she was young and beautiful, I gave a grand, distant smile to both of them and then let it soften into warmth. Agamemnon laughed as Orestes approached. He took out his own sword and began to joust with his son, shouting to his followers to come and help him overcome this famous warrior.

We had trained Orestes to move aside and return to the palace and wait in my room, where he believed that he would be joined soon by his father. Electra then stepped forward. She exuded gravity, pomposity, seriousness. She bowed to her father and the woman who was at his side and spoke the words on which we had agreed and then bowed once more while her father greeted each of the elders. Soon he had a group of them gathered around his chariot as he described some battle he had won and detailed the golden strategies that had caused victory to be his.

And then I signaled to my women and they came with tapestries and set them down between where Agamemnon's feet would land and the entrance to the palace. He took the hand of the young, proud woman beside him, who pushed aside her cloak to reveal a red robe of enormous richness. She let her hair hang loose as she stepped with him onto the tapestries. She let her eyes range around, as though this were a country that in her dreams had always belonged to her and had become real merely to satisfy her.

"This is Cassandra," my husband said. "She has been captured. She is one aspect of the gifts and spoils that have come to us."

Cassandra lifted her beautiful head and haughtily caught

my eye, as if I had been placed on earth to serve her; then she looked at Electra, who stared at her in wonder. Many other chariots had come by now, some bearing treasure and others filled with slaves, their hands bound behind them. Cassandra stood apart from this, glancing with disdain at the slaves who were being led away. I moved towards her, and invited her to enter the palace, signaling to Electra that she should follow.

As soon as we were inside, having left Agamemnon to tell more stories and wave his hands in triumph and set about dividing some of the slaves among his men, Cassandra became concerned. When she asked if she could go out to find my husband again, I said no, we the women must stay inside.

This was the moment where all could have been lost, as she spoke in a frightened tone of nets of danger, of snares and dangerous weavings. She lowered her voice as she mentioned murder. She could see murder, she said; she could smell murder. When Electra appeared, she was too excited by her father's arrival to hear what Cassandra was saying. I asked Electra to check the tables for the feast. I knew that Aegisthus' men would be waiting for her. And I knew also that Orestes would be taken from the palace by two of the guards.

As Cassandra continued to speak, her tone more and more strident, demanding that she be allowed to return to my husband's side, I told the guards to remove her to one of the inner chambers. I instructed one of them to tell my husband, if he asked, that Cassandra had sought a place to rest and had been given the most comfortable room for guests and that this seemed to have pleased her.

And then I stood alone at the palace entrance waiting as lines and lines of chariots approached, as the sounds of cheering rose again and again, as my husband repeated a story he had already told to the men hungry for his winning smile, for his familiar touch, for the rich sound of his voice.

Everything I knew I used now. I did not speak or move. I did not frown or smile. I looked at Agamemnon as if he were a god and I was too humble even to be in his presence. It was my task to wait. One word of warning from one of the men would be enough to have changed everything. I watched them, but I saw that they had no chance to speak. Agamemnon was boasting of some danger that he had survived. No one could have punctured the bloated sound he made.

The longer he stayed with them, however, the more comfortable they became and thus the more dangerous. If he does not leave them soon, I thought, one of them will whisper a warning and it will be enough. He had all his guards with him. They were laughing too and showing off their slaves. One word and all that could transform.

I watched calmly, and as Agamemnon moved directly towards me, his face weathered but his bearing open and friendly and sweet, I knew that I had prevailed.

"Cassandra has asked for a bath," I said, "and a bed where she might rest before this evening's feast. Electra has gone with her, and some women too."

"Yes, that is good."

For a few seconds, something clouded his expression, but then he relaxed again.

"I have waited for this day," he said.

"Everything is prepared for you," I said. "In the kitchen they have been working. Come with me to our inner quarters. I have ordered the bath to be filled for you and I have fresh clothes waiting so that when you appear later at the feast the triumph will be complete."

"Cassandra's quarters must be close to mine," he said.

"I will arrange that," I replied.

"It was her warnings that caused me to be fiercer in later battles," he said. "We would not have been victorious without her. That we won those last battles is partly due to her."

He was so involved in the conversation that he barely noticed where we were going. Once again, one warning shout, one strange sound or sight, would have stopped him. But there was nothing except his own voice as he began to describe the details of battles and tell me what spoils were on their way to us.

As we entered the room where the bath had been filled, I knew not to embrace him or touch him. The time for that had passed. I was his servant now as I helped him to remove his robes, as I tested the water for him. What was unusual was the small pang of desire I felt as he stood naked in the room, talking all the while. He had once been beautiful. I felt the old ache of tenderness and it was that very ache, or that change in me, that strengthened my resolve and made me realize even more sharply that if my mood could change, then his could easily shift too. It reminded me how quickly he could become suspicious. Once that happened, he would see how blindly he had been led here, and how vulnerable he was in this room without any guards.

I had planned to wait until his bathing was over and he sought towels to dry himself, but I knew now not to hesitate. I waited for that second when his back was turned. I had the netted robe on a hook on the wall. When he had one foot in the bath, I came behind him and pulled the net around him and tightened it as though I were seeking to protect him. The knife was secreted within my robes.

I saw him trying to struggle and call out. But because of

the robe, he could not move and his voice could not be heard. I caught his hair and pulled his head back. I showed him the knife, pointing it first towards his eyes until he flinched, before I stabbed him in the neck just beneath the ear, moving aside to avoid the jet of spurting blood, and then, pushing the blade farther into his neck, I began to drag it slowly across his throat, slicing deep into him as blood flowed in easy, gurgling waves down his chest and into the water of the bath. And then he fell. It was done.

I went quietly along the corridor to the floor below and found Aegisthus at the place we had agreed.

"I have done it," I whispered. "He is dead."

I retreated to my own quarters then, telling the two guards that I was to be disturbed by no one except Aegisthus.

Some minutes later, Aegisthus came to assure me that both Orestes and Electra had been escorted to safety.

"And Cassandra?" I asked.

"What do you want done with her?"

It was my turn to smile.

"Do you want me to do it?" he asked.

"Yes, I do."

She had come to us in glory and now, in ignominy, she was running through the palace seeking Agamemnon, having divined that something had happened to him. Aegisthus followed her at a slow pace. When I saw her, I calmly ushered her into the bathroom, where she could see my husband bent over naked, his head in the bloody water. As she howled, I handed Aegisthus the knife I had used on Agamemnon and indicated to him that I would leave him to his task.

I returned to my chamber. I found fresh clothes and prepared for the feast that we had planned.

Aegisthus had further work to do. Five hundred of his followers, as promised, had come from the mountains. Once darkness fell, he would lead them directly to the palace. They would surround the houses of the elders and prevent them from meeting until they came to our table. He would have others round up the slaves and protect the spoils.

The soldiers who had returned with my husband would be greeted with fanfare and a great feast in one of the halls on the palace grounds, with rich food and strong wine. As the night wore on, and they grew drunk and distracted enough by the welcome not to notice that the doors of the hall had been locked, Aegisthus' men would lie in wait for them.

At first they would think it was a mistake and they would shout for help. When the doors were opened and they came out in the dark night air to relieve themselves or check their safety, they would be set upon. It would be easy to tie each one up and take them to where the slaves were kept. At first light, slaves and soldiers would be marched away under the guard of Aegisthus' men.

There was rocky land beyond the mountains to be cleared, Aegisthus said, for vines and fruit trees. It would take some years. Most of the slaves and soldiers would remain there under guard, we agreed, but some of the soldiers would be swiftly brought back here as soon as they had been identified as those closest to Agamemnon. We would seek out the ones who knew about the new territories under our control and had the names of the men he had left in charge. These soldiers would know best how to consolidate and keep what had been taken in the wars. They would work for us under our direct protection and watchful eyes.

Some of Aegisthus' other men would stay here to detain troops as they straggled back from the war. They would march them away, to follow the others. They would confiscate what spoils they could and keep the peace, ensuring that nothing untoward occurred by day, ensuring also that there were no secret meetings or small conspiracies by night. They would guard the palace as they would guard their lives. Ten of them, the most loyal and the strongest, who were detailed to be my personal guards, would be instructed to remain always at my side.

*

By the time the feast in the palace began that evening, these ten men had arrived outside my room. Aegisthus' other followers had descended and were making themselves busy. He had trained them years before to be sharp, to make no fuss. There was to be no shouting or triumph; instead there was to be ruthless silence, watchfulness, devotion to the task.

I wore the same dress that I had worn for Iphigenia's sacrifice, the dress that had been made for me to wear at her wedding years earlier. I had my hair done in the same way and the same whiteness put on my face and the same black lines around my eyes.

The food was served as though nothing strange had occurred, although the guests and the servants must have known that two dead bodies lay in the bathing place whose floor was covered in their blood. As the meal came to an end, I spoke to the assembled men.

"The boys, your sons and grandsons, will be released. They will be brought back to your houses in the night when they are least expected. If there is any effort to oppose me, even whispering among yourselves, or meeting in small groups, all will be suspended and the risks to their safety will be great. And also, you must warn the boys when they return never to speak to anyone of where they have been, or mention that they have been away at all."

The men nodded, not even glancing at one another. I asked them to remain at the table for some time as I arranged with Aegisthus' men to have the bodies of my husband and of the woman Cassandra, lit by torches, displayed outside for all to see, and to be left there through the night and the following day and perhaps beyond.

I bade each man good night, standing at the door to watch as they passed the naked body of Agamemnon and the body of Cassandra dressed in red, with their throats cut. The men walked by without stopping, without a word.

*

When I was ready to have the bodies buried, and when all the prisoners had been taken away and the palace was peaceful except for the buzzing of flies, I told Aegisthus that I wished to see Electra and Orestes. I wanted to have them near me now that justice had been done.

The expression on Aegisthus' face darkened when a few hours later I had to give the order for a second time.

"I can release Electra immediately," he said.

"What do you mean release her?" I asked. "Where is she?"

"She is in the dungeon," he said.

"Who told you that you could put her in the dungeon?" I asked.

"I decided to put her there," he said.

"Release her now!" I ordered. "And bring Orestes to me."

"Orestes is not here," he said.

"Aegisthus, where is Orestes?"

"We agreed that he would be taken to safety."

"Where is he?"

"He is safe. He's with the other boys who were captured, or he's on his way towards where they are being held."

"I want him returned now!"

"That is not possible."

"We must send for him now."

"It is too dangerous to travel."

"I am ordering you to have him returned."

As Aegisthus left silence for a few moments, I could see that he was enjoying keeping me in suspense.

"I will decide when it is the right time for him to return," he said. "I will be the one who decides that."

He looked at me with an air of satisfaction.

"Your son is safe," he said.

I had sworn that I would make no more mistakes, but now I saw that I was fully under his power.

"What would I have to do," I asked, "to have you bring him here now?"

"That is something we can perhaps discuss," he said. "But in the meantime, do not worry about him. He's in good hands."

"What do you want from me?" I asked.

"What you promised," he replied.

"I want him returned," I said.

"It will happen," he said. "You must not worry beyond what is necessary."

He bowed and left the room.

*

The palace was quiet in the days that followed. The new guards did not sleep in the night; they were fully alert, prepared to obey Aegisthus' commands. They were afraid of him, I saw, and this meant that they did not swagger, or talk too much. At night, he came to my room, but I knew that he had also been in the kitchens, or some part of the palace where the women gathered, and I knew that he had been with one of them, or two, or one of the servant boys.

He slept with a dagger in his hand.

When Electra came once to see me, she stood in the doorway and stared at me and did not speak before turning away.

The palace remained a house of shadows, a place where someone could still, it seemed, wander in the night without being stopped by anyone. One morning, I woke uneasily at dawn light to find a young girl at the foot of our bed watching me.

"Iphigenia!" I cried out. "Iphigenia!"

"No," she whispered.

"Who are you?"

"My grandmother did the weaving," she said.

I realized then that in all of the care we took in the days since Agamemnon's death, we had forgotten the young girl and her grandmother.

Aegisthus was wide awake. He would, he said briskly, soon arrange their return to the village in the blue mountains from which we had taken them.

I left the bed and approached the young girl. She was not afraid of me.

As I took her hand in mine to walk to the kitchens, to make sure that she and her grandmother had food, the light of early morning was soft and golden. The silence was broken only by birdsong.

Soon, I thought, I would find a way to implore Aegisthus to

have Orestes brought back to me. Since I could not threaten him, I would not oppose him. I would work with him.

And I would, I thought, talk to Orestes gently when he finally came back, as I would speak to his sister in the hope that I could live at ease with both of them now that order had been restored. I saw Orestes growing into a man, learning from me and from Aegisthus how to pull the reins of power, relax them, pull them again, tighten them when the time was right, exerting sweet control. I even imagined Electra subdued and quiet. Forgiving. I would walk in the garden with her.

I saw, as I held this small girl's hand, the possibility of a bloodless future for us. It might be easy if Aegisthus learned to trust me. Perhaps the worst was over. Soon it would all seem right. Soon I would make Aegisthus believe that he could have what he wanted.

Orestes

Inside the palace, Orestes noticed a strange emptiness and silence. The servants, he thought, must have found a way to go out also to welcome his father in victory. He felt small and alone as he went towards his mother's room, where she had told him to go.

He wished that his mother had sent someone to accompany him, someone maybe who was an expert sword fighter or skilled at target practice who could help him prepare for further displays of prowess in front of his father.

Inside his mother's room, he found a place to sit. He put his sword on the ground and waited. He listened carefully. He stood up and went back to the corridor and waited there, looking up and down, but it was deserted. He decided to walk back towards the main door and perhaps find his mother and ask her if he could not stay with her, or with Electra.

As he moved forward, he heard voices. There were men talking in one of the rooms close to where the guards slept. He knew some of the guards there. One enjoyed sword fighting and challenged him now to a game, suggesting they go out in the gardens behind the palace. Orestes wondered if this was the right time, worrying that his mother might come looking for him. But there was something about the man's eagerness and smiling presence that made him feel at ease and ready to acquiesce. The three other guards in the room appeared more stern and remote.

"Will you tell my mother where we have gone?" he asked one of them.

Once the man assented, he felt more relaxed and followed the guard towards the gardens.

When they had fought for a while, two other guards whom Orestes knew appeared. One was friendly and addressed him by name, the other was more distant and preoccupied. Orestes wondered if one or even both of them had the skill to play with him if the other guard grew tired. But instead, the distant one came immediately to break up the sword fight.

"Your mother said that we were to take you along the path that leads towards the road," he said. "That's where the feast will be."

"When did she tell you that?"

"Just now."

"Does my father know?"

"Of course."

"Will he be at the feast?"

"Of course."

"And Electra?"

"Yes."

"And Aegisthus?"

"We were told to take you there."

"Maybe we'll have time for a sword fight before the feast," the friendly one said.

"I think I should wait for my mother," Orestes said.

"Your mother has already gone," the other one said.

"Where?"

"Where we're going."

Orestes considered this for a second. Both guards moved

close to him, each with a hand on his shoulder. They walked Orestes away from the palace.

"We should hurry so we can get there before dark," one of them said.

"But how will the others get there?"

"They're using the chariots."

"Can we not use a chariot?"

"The chariots are for the men who have come home from the battles."

"Give me your sword," the more distant one said. "I'll give it back to you when we get there."

Orestes handed him his sword.

Gradually, as the two men stopped talking and asked him to walk faster, Orestes started to believe that what was happening was not right. He should not have gone with them. A few times, when he turned his head to look back, he was motioned to keep moving by the one he liked less. When he asked how long it would take to find the others, neither guard replied. And when he finally said that he wanted to go back, both guards held him by his shirt and pulled him along.

Then he noticed that night was beginning to fall. He realized that he had been captured, or that someone had given these guards the wrong orders. He thought, however, that once his presence was missed at the palace, they would send out other guards to look for him. Since they had passed houses and been seen by people, these guards would be told in what direction they were moving. He pictured how angry his mother would be when she found that he was missing. He felt that he should convey this to the two guards, but their silence grew more severe and their movement forward more determined. These two guards, he thought, would be in trouble.

When it was dark, they found a place to rest. The guards had some food that they shared with Orestes. But still they did not speak. When he said that he wanted to go home, they both ignored him. And when he added that his mother would have sent out men to search for him, they also remained silent. When he stood up and asked for his sword back, they told him that he should go to sleep and everything would be fine in the morning.

It was only when he remembered the kidnappings that he began to cry. Electra had spoken about the boys who were kidnapped, warning him to stay within the precincts of the palace. He had known some of the boys who had gone missing. Now, it struck him, he was missing too. Maybe this was how the others had been kidnapped; maybe they had been lured away like this.

In the morning, the kinder guard came over to him and asked him if he was all right, sitting down and putting his arm around him.

"It's all going to be fine," he said. "Your mother knows where you are. We're here to look after you."

"You said we were going to a feast," Orestes said. "I want to go back now."

As he started to cry again, the guard did not say anything. When he stood up and tried to run away from them, both guards handled him roughly and made him sit between them.

After a while, there was a sound of voices in the distance. His guards looked at each other warily and forced him to hide with them in the bushes. Orestes determined that he would not call out until those who were approaching were very close, so that they would be able to find him easily. He could see that his two guards were afraid as the voices became louder.

As he was getting ready to shout, his guards stepped out of the bushes and began to embrace a number of men who were leading along lines of prisoners. Orestes saw that the prisoners were fettered to one another in groups of three or four. Some of them had cuts and bruises on their faces. They bowed their heads as they moved slowly by while their guards and the two men accompanying Orestes were urgently whispering and offering darting exchanges of news.

*

A few times, he cried, or sat down and refused to walk any farther, or remonstrated with the guards, but each time, the guard he liked came and put his arm around him and told him that there was no problem, there had been a change of plan, that was all, and he would see his mother and his father soon. When Orestes asked him where exactly they were going and when he would see them, the guard told him not to worry, just to follow, walk as best he could.

They walked all day, letting lines of prisoners moving in the same direction get ahead of them. When Orestes became tired and asked for a rest, his two guards looked at each other hesitantly.

"We have to keep moving," one of them said.

Men they met who were going towards the palace always appeared to know his guards. Each time they encountered them, one guard remained with him while the other moved towards the men to exchange further news in dark whispers before a friendly gesture as they parted.

All along the way, Orestes noticed the vultures hovering on trees or in the thick undergrowth, often bickering fiercely with each other or flapping in the sky above, watching.

On the second day, late in the afternoon, Orestes observed smoke and then he saw that a house and a barn were on fire. As they approached, there were lines of men waiting some distance from the buildings. They were all tied together, standing sullenly, as some of the guards butchered pigs and killed chickens and others gathered together a flock of sheep. A man and two boys stood watching.

Suddenly, a thin woman came running from the barn. She was screaming. First just cries, but then words, including words of abuse hurled at the guards. As she ran towards the man and the two boys with her arms outstretched, one of the guards lifted a pole and, using both hands, swung it at the woman, hitting her full in the face. The blow must have broken bones and teeth, Orestes thought, but before the woman folded and fell to the ground, curling up, there was a second or two of pure silence.

His guards moved him on. He was shivering and crying now, and he was hungry.

Over the days that followed, although he walked between them most of the time, the guards did not threaten him or speak to him roughly. Mostly, they said very little. A few times when he asked about his father and his mother, they simply did not reply. But he heard them talking at night, and he learned that great numbers of the men tied to each other and forced to march were the soldiers who had returned with his father. Others were slaves whom his father had captured.

From stray remarks, he also learned that their orders were to take him somewhere and then join the forces moving back towards the palace. When they talked openly in front of him, they spoke of men and places whose names he did not recognize. The one he liked less was constantly telling the other not to say anything more, adding that they could talk as much as they pleased when their task had been completed.

When he asked his guards one day who gave them orders, they almost laughed at him. When he asked where they were going, they told him he would find out in due time. He studied the guards' faces then and left silence in case one of them would mention his father or his mother. But they told him that the less they spoke, the more progress they would make.

Once, at night, he was close enough to overhear more of what his guards said when they whispered. They used the name Aegisthus but only casually and in passing; there was no mention this time of his father or his mother. Although he was desperately tired from walking, and sleepy now, he tried hard to stay awake and listen, but the talk was about land, hectares of land, land with olive trees and orchards, land that was close to a stream and was sheltered. One of them spoke of building a house and how this was a good time to build because of the slaves and the soldiers who could carry stones.

The people in the villages and houses along the way, he saw, were afraid. Sometimes there were signs that a house had been burned or damaged. If they demanded food from houses, it was quickly provided; if they sought shelter, which they did less often, they were given a place to sleep in a barn or a shed. But as they moved farther along, there were greater distances between the villages and many of the houses they passed had been ransacked. They carried what food they could, but often they were left with nothing.

One evening, when they had walked all day without food, the guard whom he disliked announced that he would go in search of a cottage or a smallholding away from the route that they and the others were following. He would be back before

dark, he said, as he left Orestes and the other guard in a clearing between trees that he said he would be able to identify
easily on his return.

Orestes slept for a while. When he woke, hungry, it was
almost dark but the guard had still not returned. As the moon
rose, he noticed the other guard watching him. He thought to
close his eyes and try to go back to sleep, or pretend that he was
sleeping, but he thought that now might be a good time to sit
up and see if he could encourage the guard to talk, to explain
maybe where they were going and why they had left the palace
in the first place. As the guard remained silent, he wondered
how he should start.

"Will he be able to find us in the dark?" he asked eventually.

"I think so," the guard said. "The moon is full enough."

Neither of them spoke for a while then, but Orestes could
sense that the guard was uncomfortable with the silence. The
man must know everything, he presumed, but he could not
think of a question that would cause him to explain.

"Is it much farther?" he asked quietly.

"What?"

"Where we are going."

"A few days, maybe," the guard said.

They looked away from each other, as though afraid. It was
clear, he thought, what his next question should be. He should
ask where exactly they were going, but it struck him that if he
did this directly, the guard would not tell him. And if the guard
refused to answer one question, then it might be hard to ask
any more. He had to think of a question that the guard might
unthinkingly answer, that might give him even a hint about
their destination.

"I like you better than the other one," he said.

"He's all right. Just do what he says."

"Is he the one in charge?"

"We're both in charge."

"But who gave you orders?"

He had, he knew, asked a question whose answer might matter. Whatever came in reply might let him know how things stood. The guard sighed.

"It's a difficult time," he said.

"For everyone?" he asked.

"I suppose," the guard said.

Orestes could not think what this might mean. He felt that he should abandon all caution and ask a question with the word "father" in it.

"Does my father know I am here?" he asked.

The guard did not respond at first. Orestes was almost afraid to breathe. There was no wind, and no sound even from dogs or other animals in the distance. There was just the silence between them that Orestes knew not to disturb again.

"You'll be looked after," the guard said.

"Other boys were kidnapped," Orestes said. "My mother and Electra will worry that I have been kidnapped. My father too."

"You have not been kidnapped."

"I'd like to get my sword back," he said.

"It will all be fine," the guard replied.

"Are you sure I have not been kidnapped?" he asked.

"No, no, not at all," the guard said. "Just don't worry and come with us, and then you'll be fine."

"Why can't I go back?"

"Because your father wanted you to come with us."

"But where is he?"

"We'll see him soon."

"And my mother?"

"Everybody."

"Why are we walking?"

"Stop asking questions and try to sleep. We'll meet every-one soon."

He slept then and woke to their voices, which sounded hushed and worried. He remained completely still and listened as the guard who had been away said that he could find no food, nothing at all, just deserted houses with no sign of life, the larders empty, no animals in the fields. But there was worse, he said. Someone had poisoned the wells. He had met a sol-dier whose two companions had been poisoned. He had been warned not to drink water from any well. So he had come back not only without food but without water.

"Who poisoned the wells?" the other guard asked.

"They think the farmers did it, the farmers who are hiding now in the uplands, but they haven't found any of them. They don't have time to search."

One of the guards shook Orestes, who pretended that he had been asleep.

"We have to go," he said. "We have no food and no water, but we have to go. We'll find something along the way."

Orestes began to feel thirsty even before they set out. Even one drop of water, he thought, would make a difference. He tried to imagine the day ahead, divided it into steps. How many steps would he have to take in a day? As a way of distracting himself, he pretended that he had only ten steps more to take and then there would be water and a rest. And then after those ten steps, he imagined there were only ten steps more as they walked on.

After about an hour, he noticed the smell of something

rotting. He looked at his two guards, who were holding their noses. As the smell grew more intense, he saw two bodies with flies buzzing around them lying near each other on the road ahead, with vultures feasting on the flesh. From the clothes, he presumed that they were part of the contingent marching towards the palace, the men who would stop and share news with his guards and who seemed at times almost relaxed and confident. As they drew up right beside the dead bodies, the stench was so unbearable that they moved quickly on, but not before Orestes caught a glimpse of the two men's faces, the eyes wide open, the mouths contorted, as though the men had died while screaming or shouting. Once they had passed this scene, none of them looked back.

Orestes could sense that they were more determined than usual to make progress. There was, he saw, nowhere to stop in any case, as habitation became more sparse and the land itself more barren.

He wondered, as a way of keeping at bay the desperate thirst and then a craving for food, and in between spasms of weakness when he thought that he would not be able to go any farther, why he had never fully relished the days when he had been free to wander in the palace. He wished that his mother were here, or somewhere close by, so that he could go to her and lie near her.

When they stopped, exhausted, the guards seemed almost unwilling to resume the journey. They sat on the ground, grimly staring ahead. All around was silence, broken only by the sound of crickets, with lizards darting from under one stone to another hiding place.

Later in the day, when the shadows were longer, they spotted a house in the distance. By this time, Orestes was shivering as though it were cold and holding on to the two guards as they made slow progress. His tongue, he felt, was beginning to swell. He had been obsessively swallowing whatever saliva was left in his mouth, but now there was nothing, his mouth completely dry and his throat sore from the swallowing.

They moved warily in the direction of the house, which was down a long dirt track with olive trees on each side. There were no animal sounds at all and a sense after each step that this holding they were approaching had been abandoned a long time before.

As Orestes sat in the shade, the guards walked around the house, one of them exclaiming when he saw the well, situated at the side. The house, Orestes saw, was in good condition. The guards pushed the door and they went in.

Suddenly, there was a sound from inside, a sound of wood being smashed and then a woman's cry and a man's loud voice, and then the guards shouting instructions to someone to walk out now, to stand in front of the house. Orestes stood up as a couple, disheveled and frightened, emerged, both of them talking at the same time to the guards. As one of the guards told the pair to be silent, the other entered the house again and came back out with a large ceramic jug of water and a cup. He handed the cup to the man and told him to fill it from the jug and drink it.

As the man drank the water, Orestes felt sick and his stomach began to suffer spasms. He tried to stay still but he found himself having to retch into a bush away from the others. When he returned, all he wanted was water. As he went to drink from the jug, one of the guards warned him to wait and told him gruffly that it was possible that the poison, were it in the water, would take time to manifest itself. They would sit and wait, and if, after a time, all was well, they would each drink from the jug. But not until then.

The woman and the man stood, both staring at the ground, as the two guards, who had moved into the shade, watched them. Orestes sat in the doorway. Even though no one spoke, it was clear to Orestes that the couple who had been discovered in the house were terrified, the man as much as the woman. He wondered if the water he had drunk had been, in fact, poisoned, and they were waiting for the signs of this to show.

Eventually, since the water had not poisoned the man, the two guards drank cup after cup so greedily that Orestes wanted to ask them if they had forgotten about him. Now that water was available, he was not sure if he could ever have enough of it. He walked instantly towards the jug when one of the guards indicated to him that he should. They had left enough for two cups for him. When he had drunk the second cup, he tilted the jug to get every drop from it.

Once he had finished, he looked over and saw one of the guards looking down the well. The guard then motioned to the man, ordering him to draw more water from the well. Maybe, Orestes thought, they would be able to carry water with them, or perhaps spend the evening here in this house, or even a day or two. No matter what, he thought, they would need more water. The man stood by the well and tied the jug to a rope and lowered it down as the others looked on. Orestes noticed that the woman was even more nervous now than she had been before. She kept her hands by her sides, but her eyes shifted from one of the guards to the other and then to the house.

When the jug emerged from the well, the guard whom Orestes disliked handed the man the cup and told him to drink some. The man glanced at him proudly, as though he himself were the one in control. He did not speak. He then looked towards his wife. At that moment, as all of them were concentrating on the man and the jug, a number of children ran from the front door of the house as the mother screamed at them, encouraging them to run faster. There were four of them, three boys and a girl. Two of the boys and the girl managed to get away before the guards could properly follow, but the youngest of the boys—Orestes guessed he was four or five—was caught by one of the guards and dragged back and put standing beside his mother. He was crying loudly, words that Orestes could not understand, as the guard returned and stood beside the well.

Orestes started to cry too. He wondered if he should also try to run, follow the children, see where they had gone. He might, he thought, be able to explain to them who he was and where he had come from.

"Drink the water," he heard the guard say to the man.

He watched as the man hesitated and looked at his wife.

"One of you is going to drink the water," the guard said, and walked over and grabbed the boy.

"Let the child drink the water if you are afraid to," he continued.

The mother, crying now, moved to take the boy away from the well.

"Drink!" the guard said. "I want to see you drain that cup. Fill it now and drink."

Still the man would not fill the cup that he held in his hand. He looked to the distance as if help might come, or something might happen. He stood to his full height and the expression on his face became more tense and severe. He and his wife looked at each other as his wife lifted the child and held him higher in her arms.

"If you don't drink," the guard said, "I will bring your boy over here again and I will force a cupful of that water down his throat."

The man appeared deep in thought. Even the child was quiet now. With an expression of dignity on his face, the man filled the cup. He held it in his hand and then he sighed and drank the water down in one gulp. Once he had done that, he walked towards his wife and child, rubbing the small boy's hair and then stroking his wife's head. With his other hand, he held his wife's hand.

Slowly, the man separated himself from the woman and the child and started to cough. The sound at first was gentle, but soon it had a harder edge as the man brought his hands to his throat, as though he were choking. Then, as the pain appeared to get worse, he knelt down. He was gasping and calling out words. His wife, who still held the child in her arms, began to sing. Orestes had never heard anything like her voice before. In the palace when the servants sang, the songs were happy, and even at other times when he had heard singing, it was always a group, never a woman alone.

The voice was rising now and an imploring sound came from it. He understood that it was addressed to the gods.

The man was now shrieking in pain; his whole body shuddered as he lay on the ground, his hands around his neck as if he were trying to push the poison from the base of his throat into his mouth so that he could expel it.

He tried to stand up as some black blood came out of his mouth and dripped into the dust. His eyes were rolling in his head and the pain seemed to have shifted from his throat to his stomach. For a while, as Orestes watched in horror, he held his stomach and roared in pain. But then a gurgling froth came from his mouth. He edged towards his wife, who continued her song, holding the child, who remained placid in her arms. The man became more still; then he turned and lay on his back, reaching so that his hands were firmly around his wife's ankles.

Both guards stared at this scene. The man's eyes remained open, and his mouth too, but there was no sound from him, nor from his wife. The song had ended, and it was clear to Orestes that the man had died. One of the guards then motioned to him to come into the house. In the main room, there was a false wall made of wood, and behind the wall there were beds and a table.

They took what food they could—bread and cheese and some cured meat. They found another jug of water, but the guard shook his head, and even though Orestes felt a thirst more intense than the thirst he had while walking, he did not touch the water. Instead, they left the house, walking along the rough path towards the main route, leaving the woman standing with the child in her arms and the dead man below her lying on the ground.

They walked for some miles before they stopped. They sat down in silence and opened the knotted cloth with the food. Even though he had been ravenous, Orestes felt nausea rather than hunger. Without anything to drink, what they had taken from the house looked stale and dry. He watched each of the guards picking up a piece of bread and trying to eat it. None of them touched the cheese or the cured meat. Eventually, the food was wrapped up and they resumed walking until they chose a place to rest for the night in the shelter of some trees.

On the next day, they came to a deep, fast-flowing stream that they studied hesitantly until one of the guards said that if they did not drink from it they would die of thirst. When they had drunk, the two guards bathed. Although they encouraged Orestes to follow them, he did not want to take off his clothes in front of them. He watched them cavorting in the water, wondering if there were anywhere close by he could escape to and hide, but he was aware that they kept him in their sights at all times and was sure that they would catch him if he tried to get away.

It struck him now more forcefully than ever before that when he made his way back to the palace, he would tell his father about these two men and, if they had run away, he would ask him to find them, hunt them down, to search everywhere if they had to, and then have them brought to the palace in chains and put into the darkest room in the dungeon.

After two days' more walking, still avoiding any wells that they came across, Orestes understood that they were not far from their destination, whatever it was. He was certain by now that he was not here because his mother or father had asked the guards to take him to meet them, that he had, in fact, been kidnapped and that there was nothing he could do to escape as long as the two guards were with him.

Although they seemed friendlier, and he imagined they might even tell him where they were going since they were so close, he decided not to ask. He would find out soon enough, he thought.

For the last stretch, they had to climb, and when the path petered out the guards had to guess which way to go, making wrong decisions a number of times and having to double back. For the first time in many days, they passed some goats clambering among the rocks. In the distance, once they got higher, Orestes could make out a flock of sheep on the plain below.

Then there was a huge cleft in the rock. They walked down

what was like a sloping corridor and turned where there were steps cut leading down farther and winding around the side of a building. No one, he thought, would be able to find any of them in this fastness in the mountains. When they came to a door, they did not have to knock; it was silently opened for them by a man who did not look at them or speak.

Another man who was sitting outside a second door stood up when he saw them, however, and warmly hugged both of the guards. He began to smile and laugh at the very idea of their presence, and their arrival with this boy.

"As though we don't have enough here already," he said cheerfully. "Maybe this one has better manners than some of those I have inside. Do you see this toe? I have had to kick manners into them, and when that doesn't work then they feel this."

The two guards laughed as he lifted a stick he had beside him and whipped the air with it.

"And hungry too. Is this fellow hungry?"

"He eats like a horse," one of the guards said.

"We'll teach him," the man said.

He opened the door, which led into a long room full of beds with several long windows that let in shadow more than light. It took Orestes a moment to see that the room was occupied by ten or more boys, many of them close to his own age. Immediately, when he saw them, he knew that these were the boys who had been kidnapped. What was strange was that although they must, he presumed, have heard the door opening and must even have heard the voices outside before that, and must now be aware that someone new had come among them, none of them looked up at first, and when a few did lift their heads, they did not change the expression on their faces or seem to register anything at all.

No one spoke as he walked between the beds. Slowly, beginning with a boy called Leander, the grandson of Theodotus whom he knew, he started to recognize some of them.

The door was closed. The guards had not come in with him. He was alone with this silent, pale group. When he locked eyes with one of them, he found a blank stare that became sullen and resentful. He moved towards Leander's bed and thought to ask him something, but Leander turned away. Eventually, he sat on the floor at the end of a row of beds and looked around the room, wondering at what point someone would speak, or food would come, or something would happen. The silence was broken only by the sound of one of the boys coughing, a rasping cough that seemed not to be able to give whoever was coughing any relief.

Nothing happened until the smell of cooking rose from the floor below, which caused some of the boys to sit up in their beds. But still no one spoke. When Orestes walked back to the door, all of the boys turned away from him once more. He wondered if they did not actually recognize him, or if they thought that he was allied with the kidnappers.

When the door was finally opened, the boys walked to the floor below in single file, each with his head bowed. The only one who lifted his head as he passed Orestes was Leander. He looked at him for a moment and then shrugged. Once the line had passed him, Orestes joined the end of it, walking down narrow stairs to a cramped dining room with one long table where most of the boys sat, and a smaller table by a window where two of the boys placed themselves. One of them was coughing. It was the same sound that he had heard upstairs; he could see that the boy, whom he did not recognize, was in some distress, and that the coughing was causing him pain and raising the level of tension in the dining room.

Orestes watched the doorway to the kitchen, but no one appeared. Instead, two of the boys came with food that was passed down the table. As he took his place at the end, he saw that nothing was being given to the boy who had been coughing or the other boy at the side table. The rest all ate in silence. He concentrated on each boy on the opposite side in turn, trying to attract a glimmer of recognition from at least one of them, but those who noticed him staring returned only a deadened glance.

When they had finished eating, they stood and walked in single file back to the dormitory, Orestes following.

Since there was no bed for him, he found a place on the floor to lie down. He was woken a few times in the night by the sound of coughing and then finally, in the morning, he was woken again by the boys all around him. When he asked one of them where he should go to relieve himself, the boy did not reply and those close by edged away from him, concerned, it seemed, to stop him approaching them.

When he went to the door, he found it open. The guard whom he had encountered the previous day was sitting outside.

"You," he said. "Two things. You go to the baths this morning. You stink like an old nanny goat. You get fresh clothes with the others. Leave your old clothes there. And you need a slate. You keep the slate beside you at all times."

"What's the slate for?" Orestes asked.

"You'll find out soon enough." The man laughed. "So, you, to the baths now, this second."

"Where are the baths?" Orestes asked.

"Down the stairs here, and then down the next stairs. It will be better for you and everyone when you get rid of that smell."

Having walked down the two flights of stairs, he saw that

four of the boys were already in the baths. As he stood watching in the raked light that came from a slit in the side of the wall, two of them were whispering to each other, while the other two splashed the water vigorously, which muffled the sound. At first they did not notice him as he quietly removed his clothes. When he made to get into the bath with them, the two who had been whispering moved away from each other. All four of them looked straight ahead. He wanted to let them know that he would not tell the guard that they had been whispering, but it struck him that his speaking at all would merely increase their hostility towards him. Soon, all four left the bath, drying themselves in a space in the corner.

Once he was finished in the baths and had dried himself with one of the towels the others had left, he went upstairs to find the guard, who handed him some clothes and a piece of slate and a piece of chalk.

The guard walked with him through the dormitory and found him an empty space and then detailed two of the boys to help him carry from one of the lower floors a bed that he could use. As Orestes stood there in the fresh clothes, the slate in his hand, some of the boys were actually paying attention to him, looking at him closely. But when he nodded at one of them, the boy turned away.

The days went slowly and mostly silently. Three times a day they shuffled down to the refectory. Once a week, they could use the baths. In the baths, two made splashing noises with the water that enabled two others to whisper without being heard. This was, as far as he could make out, the only time the boys ever spoke to one another. Sometimes, in the night, he could hear boys howling and crying in their sleep, and, some of the time, the boy with the cough made a further rasping sound and then struggled loudly for breath, and this noise continued even after the guard, who sat through the night outside the door that led to the dormitory, came in and shook the boy or slapped him.

And then there was the slate. Slates had to be left at all times beside each bed so that they could be clearly seen. For any infringement of the rules, each boy had a mark on his slate, and this mark could be placed there only by a fellow captive, who would also place a symbol to identify himself. It took Orestes some weeks to work out the full details of this, as he never once saw a boy marking another's slate. It must have been done in the night, he realized, but even on nights when he was awake he did not witness it.

At intervals there was an inspection, led by the guard whom Orestes had first met, but it could include one or two other guards. They would check the slates and then select the boys who had marks on their slates for punishment. These boys were taken outside or down into the dining room or the baths but sometimes also right outside the door. The severity of the beatings did not concur with the number of marks on the slate, but depended on the mood of the guards. Nonetheless, having a number of marks on your slate meant that you were more likely to be taken out and punished than if you had a clean slate, or very few marks.

But, Orestes noted, no matter how few marks the boy with the cough, whose name he discovered was Mitros, had, he would always be taken out. When he returned, he lay on his bed crying and then coughing until the two sounds merged.

As the marks on Orestes' slate began to accumulate, he could not work out to whom the symbol beside the mark belonged. The mark was always made by the same person, put there during the night. Finally, one morning, as he studied the symbol, he noticed Leander looking at him. As Orestes knit his brow and then glanced up as if to ask if the symbol belonged to Leander, Leander nodded. A few times subsequently, Orestes tried to catch Leander's eye, but Leander paid him no further attention.

The guards seemed to enjoy looking at Orestes' slate, showing the marks to each other and commenting on them, but over the first few weeks, they passed on. He was not told to stand out until the fourth week.

He stood beside a shivering Mitros, having presumed up to now that he would not be touched, having believed that his status in this place was different from that of the others. He had not even planned how he would respond if he were selected for punishment. As he was roughly pushed through the doorway of the dining room, he saw that the guard had a stick in his hand.

"If you touch me," he said, "just touch me, my father will learn about it."

"Your father?" the guard asked.

"My father will find out about this."

"Is that your father with his throat cut?" the guard asked.

Orestes stood back for a second and took in the mocking expression on the guard's face. He then looked around the room. Had there been a knife close by, he would have used it on the guard, but the only thing he could see was a chair at the smaller table that was falling apart, and it was easy to pull off a leg and lunge with it towards the guard.

"Touch me now!" he said, wielding the leg of the chair.

The guard looked at him and laughed.

In that second, one of the guards who had been moving stealthily behind Orestes managed to overpower him. He pinned his arms behind his back while the other guard began to hit him on the face full force with the back of his hand. When his arms were released and he fell on the ground, both guards kicked him before the one who had taken him down to the dining room whispered into his ear: "Your father isn't any use to you now, is he? We won't be hearing that again, will we?"

They left him there. Later, he hobbled back to the dormitory, noticing the intensity of the silent watching as he limped past the others towards his bed. For the next two days, he did not go to the refectory except to get water, but stayed in bed, unable to sleep, trying to piece together what might have happened to his father.

An image came to him then of his mother and Aegisthus. He was not sure when it was, but it must have been the morning, a morning when he had come to the room earlier than usual, and his nurse at the doorway had pulled him back but not before he had caught a glimpse of his mother and Aegisthus, and saw them naked and making sounds like animals. The image stayed with him now, became as solid in his mind as the image of his father's face as it brightened when he returned, and the memory of his father's voice and the cheering all around, and the smell of horses and men's sweat and the sense of happiness he felt that his father was home.

The following week, as he found himself in the baths with Leander, he edged away from him and began to splash water with one of the other boys so that Leander and the fourth bather could whisper without being heard. But Leander pulled him towards the shadowy end of the baths and let the other two cover for them.

"I want to escape," he whispered. "I need to help Mitros escape too before they kill him. I can't escape with him on my own. I want you to be the one to help me."

"Why are you putting marks on my slate?" Orestes asked.

"Some of the boys hate you because of your family. They asked me to do that."

"Why do they hate me?"

"I don't know. I'm not sure. And I wanted to see what you would do when they came to punish you. You were brave. I thought I could trust you not to be afraid."

"How can we escape?"

"Some night I'll wake you. You be ready. It will start with Mitros coughing. Tell no one, and stop looking at me all the time."

"I don't look at you."

"You do, and stop it. Ignore me. You look around too much. Begin to behave like all the rest. Fit in."

"When will we escape?"

"We must stop talking. Move away now."

During the days that followed, Leander continued to put marks on his slate, but not too many. He tried to follow Leander's advice and stop looking at him. But it was hard and made him feel alone and frightened. He began to worry about escaping, about where they would go, about what plans Leander had, and about what would happen if they were caught. When he woke during the night or in the morning, he thought it might be best just to stay here and hope that he would be rescued somehow. He wondered if there was a safe way to let Leander know that he did not want to go with him and Mitros, but no one ever spoke except in the baths, and when he went to the baths the next time, Leander was not there.

One night, as Mitros' cough worsened, Leander came and tapped Orestes on the shoulder. When he opened his eyes, he could just make out Leander's shape. As the rasping sound from

Mitros began, Leander whispered to him: "Get dressed and follow me to the door." When he tried to reply, Leander put his hand firmly over his mouth to stop him speaking. Orestes desperately wanted to go back to sleep then, knowing that, if they did not escape, the day ahead would be hard, but at least the fears he felt would be familiar and predictable. He waited, nervous and uneasy, until Leander pulled him out of bed and stood with him while he dressed.

They went towards the door of the dormitory and waited there, as Mitros' coughing grew louder, even more piercing and alarming than usual. When they heard the door opening, Leander and Orestes slipped to the side. The guard came into the dormitory. Then Leander led Orestes out into the corridor, where they searched among the objects near the guard's day bed. When Leander found a knife, he handed it to Orestes. He himself picked up a flat piece of wood. And then they waited as the guard in the dormitory put his hand over Mitros' mouth and appeared to hurt him in some way so that Mitros let out a muffled howl that caused others in the dormitory to wake and cry out.

Orestes heard the guard make some threatening noises; he noted his footsteps as he approached the door. He tried to hold his breath. He had no idea what the exact plan was, but presumed that he should try to attack the guard and stab him before he could shout for help.

They let the guard shut the door. As he lay down and yawned and made as though to settle back into sleep, Orestes inched forward, and, holding the knife hard, stabbed him with as much force as he could in the neck while Leander brought the wood hard down on his head. As the guard let out a roar, Orestes held him by the hair and ran the knife hard into his neck again, pulling it out and stabbing him in the chest with all his strength until he could not dislodge the knife from the bone. Leander clubbed the guard in the face. And then they both stopped. Orestes listened as Leander held him by the shoulder. There was no sound, except some coughing from within the dormitory. Leander, using his two hands, made Orestes stand still against the wall as he went back into the dormitory.

In his absence, Orestes could, from the shadowy light that came from the stairwell, make out some shapes of things in this small space. He looked at the door to the outside, wondering where the key might be.

He was going through the guard's possessions in search of the key when Leander and Mitros appeared. Leander located it on a ledge and went swiftly to open the door and whispered to Orestes to come quickly.

Once they were outside, Leander locked the door and led them both away in the moonlight that illuminated the passage between rocks and then the steps and then the broad vista when they emerged into the open. They stood and listened, but there was no sound of anyone coming behind them.

"We walk in the same direction as the wind," Leander said.

As Mitros' cough began again, Leander held him, putting one hand on his chest and the other on his back. Mitros started to vomit, doubling over.

"You'll be better when we are away from here," Leander said.

"No, I won't," Mitros whispered. "You should leave me. I won't be able to walk as fast as you."

"We'll carry you," Leander said. "The only reason we escaped is you, so we can't leave you."

They descended towards the plain, Orestes looking back

all the time, aware that in the brightness anyone could make them out from the hills above and follow them. Since Mitros would not be able to run, he wondered if they would be wiser to find a place to hide for a few days, but Leander was pressing ahead with such cold certainty and determination that Orestes knew he would not entertain any changes to his plan. Thus Orestes and Mitros followed him, Mitros with his head down, like someone who had been already defeated.

When the sun came up, Orestes saw that they were moving towards where it would eventually set. He had presumed that both Leander and Mitros would want to return to their families immediately, but they were not following the route that he judged would lead back home.

He waited until night, when Mitros was asleep, to ask Leander what his plan was.

"We can't go back," Leander said. "None of us can. We would be kidnapped again, at least I would be, and Mitros too."

"Is my mother still alive?" Orestes asked.

Leander hesitated for a second and then reached out and touched his shoulder.

"Yes."

"How do you know?"

"I heard the guards talking."

"And Electra?"

"Yes. She is alive too."

"But my father is dead?"

"Yes."

"How did he die?"

Leander made as though to speak a number of times. Finally, he fell silent and did not look up.

"Do you know how he died?" Orestes asked.

Leander once more hesitated and shifted his position.

"No," he whispered, but still he did not look at Orestes.

"But you are sure my mother is alive?"

"Yes."

"Why did she not send men to search for me?"

"I don't know. Perhaps she did."

"Is Aegisthus alive?"

"Aegisthus?" Leander appeared suddenly alert. He looked at Orestes directly, as though puzzled by the idea that he had asked such a question.

"Yes, he is alive," Leander said eventually in a low voice. "He is alive."

Once more, as with the guard, Orestes felt that if only he could think of one single right question to ask, then he would find out what he needed to know. But, he sensed, no direct question would work. He could not think what to ask instead.

"Did Aegisthus kill my father?" he abruptly asked, regretting the question almost immediately.

"I don't know," Leander replied quickly.

Orestes sighed.

In the morning, Leander spoke to them about what they should do.

"The only thing I know is that we must not kill anybody else. No matter what. That is the first rule. If we kill someone, then people will come after us. What we want is to find a place where we can stay. Even if we are attacked, we must not kill."

Looking at Mitros, who nodded in agreement, Orestes wanted to say that Mitros would not have the energy to kill, and that, in any case, they had no weapons, since he had left the knife lodged in the guard's chest.

"We need to carry small rocks that we can throw at people,

injure them maybe, encourage them to leave us alone. And we need to get food and water by sending Mitros to a house to ask for it. Unarmed. Just asking. No one will feel threatened by him. We need to look at each house carefully. If we think it is hostile, we must pass on."

"The wells could be poisoned," Orestes said.

Leander nodded distractedly.

"We can offer to work for people," he said, "in exchange for food and shelter, but we don't want to stay anywhere near here. If we do, we will be found. We have to move faster than they can. Maybe Mitros will get stronger. If he doesn't, then the two of us will have to get stronger so that we can carry him, or at least support him part of the way. We will walk every day from as soon as we wake until it is too dark. If we don't do that, they will catch us."

The tone of voice reminded Orestes of his father in the camp with the other men, when he wanted his father to play or carry him on his shoulders, but when his father was too busy. He shivered as it occurred to him that he would be safer back in the dormitory with the others, and almost more content. He would have more time to think about things, conjure up images of having sword fights with his father, or coming to his mother in the morning and finding her waiting for him, or sitting between Electra and Iphigenia as they talked, or moving easily among the servants and the guards.

When they came to a well, Orestes wondered if he should be the one to test the water for poison. If it were poisoned, he did not want to have to stand and watch as Mitros began to vomit and choke and slowly die, and Leander seemed so powerful and strong as he led them forward that his being stricken by poisoned water was unthinkable. Maybe they should all three drink at the same time, he thought, but then he felt that if he were to volunteer it would impress Leander, be a sign of his bravery.

When, having left Mitros by the side of the road, they approached the well, Leander took the spring water in the cup of his hand and smelled it. He stood up and looked around.

"Let me drink it," Orestes said.

"One of us will have to," Leander said.

Leander dipped his hands again into the water, and, cupping as much of it as he could, he drank, and then he indicated to Orestes to follow his example. Orestes had a vision then of all three of them writhing from the poison. As soon as he drank, however, he felt that the water was good. They waited for a while, cupping the water in their hands again and again and drinking, before Orestes went to let Mitros know that he thought the water was pure.

Later that day, they came across a man with a herd of goats.

"Make sure he can see our hands," Leander whispered.

On noticing that the man had moved away from them nervously, Leander told Orestes and Mitros to stay back. He would approach the man, he said. They watched him walking slowly, swinging his arms, towards the man, patting the goats on the head gently as he passed them.

"Everybody trusts him," Mitros said. "When they kidnapped us first and were going to leave me on the side of the road because I was sick, he stopped them. The guards paid attention to him."

"Did you know him before you were kidnapped?"

"Yes, his grandfather used to come to my father's house. His grandfather brought him everywhere. They let him listen when the men talked among themselves, the older men. They treated him like one of themselves."

"I remember him," Orestes said. "We played together when I was small, but I don't remember you."

"I was too sick to play. I always had to stay at home. But I heard your name. I knew your name."

They watched as Leander and the man with the goats remained deep in conversation. Orestes wanted to sit down, but thought it better if they both stood so that they could be clearly seen.

"Do you think we are being followed?" he asked Mitros.

"My family will pay money for me, but the family of Leander will give everything they own. The kidnappers must know that. They must feel that someone stole a fortune from them when we escaped. They can't sell us back now."

"How do you know they were planning to sell you back?" Orestes asked.

"Otherwise they would have killed us," Mitros said.

"So why didn't we stay and wait?"

"Leander didn't think I could survive much longer, and he was worried too that all of us could be killed if the guards thought that our families had sent men to rescue us and they were getting too close."

"Why didn't they send men to rescue us?"

"Because Aegisthus is in charge now. Or so Leander says. He heard it from one of the guards."

"In charge of what?"

"Everything."

"Did he order the kidnappings?"

Mitros hesitated for a moment and looked over at Leander and the man. He seemed to be pretending that he had not heard the question. Orestes decided to whisper it to see what would happen.

"Did he order the kidnappings?"

"I don't know," Mitros whispered in reply. "Maybe. Ask Leander."

"Leander said that some of the boys hate me because of my family."

Mitros nodded, but did not offer any comment.

They watched as Leander remained with the goats while the man approached them.

"Are you ready to work, the two of you?" the man asked.

They both nodded, Orestes trying to look eager.

"I have barns to clear out," the man said. He studied Orestes carefully and then Mitros.

"In return you get food and shelter, and when it's done you go."

Orestes nodded.

"Is there someone following you?" the man asked.

Orestes realized that he had only one second to decide how to reply. He did not want what he said to contradict what Leander might have said.

"Mitros is not well," he said softly. "So maybe Leander and myself will do most of the work."

The man narrowed his eyes and glanced over at Leander.

"We'll keep you well hidden if anyone comes," he said.

They followed the man and his herd until sunset, when they reached a small house and barns close to some trees. Leander never left the man's side, talking to him all the time, while Orestes and Mitros walked behind. Orestes wondered how long it would be before some food—even some bread—would be produced and they could eat it, or if they would have to do some work first, or wait until the man was ready to eat and then share the food with him.

The man's wife, at the door as they approached, gave the impression that she was deeply worried about their presence. She walked into the house, away from them, with her husband following. When the man came back out, he ordered three large dogs and a number of smaller ones to circle them. The man led the goats into a barn and seemed in no rush to return. Mitros began to pat one of the dogs and play with it, but the other dogs were less friendly, snapping at their ankles. It would be easy, Orestes realized, to hold Leander and him and Mitros here, using the dogs as guards, until the men following them arrived. He tried to work out if the man might have been able to guess that they were worth money.

"What did you tell him about us?" Orestes asked Leander.

"I told him the truth," Leander said. "Nothing else would have made sense. He saw the blood on my clothes. I told him we were in a fight. But I didn't tell him that we killed a guard and I didn't tell him how much money our families would pay for us. He doesn't know who we are."

"He can sell us all the same," Mitros said. "Even if he thinks he won't get much, it might be worth his while to sell us rather than protect us."

"If we don't get food, we'll starve," Leander said. "And there is no other house for miles. He said that the next house is more than a day's walk. After that, it's the sea. There's nothing here. We might have walked the wrong way."

He was preoccupied.

"His wife doesn't like us," Mitros said.

When the man came into view again, he shouted to the dogs, which circled the boys more keenly, one of them snarling as it did so. When Mitros tried to pat the dog with which he had been friendly earlier, the dog moved away and sat near the front of the house, wagging its tail. The man went into the house and closed the front door.

They waited then, afraid to move, as the day waned. In the last half hour of light, they watched the swallows and martins frantic in the air, almost too loud for any other sound to be heard.

The dogs seemed to grow more alert as time passed. Although Orestes wanted to relieve himself, he knew that the dogs would respond to even the smallest change. Once it was dark, he saw the stars appearing in the sky, but there was no moon as yet.

"Do nothing that I don't tell you to do," Leander whispered. "Watch me. Is that agreed?"

Orestes pressed Leander's hand with his own to indicate his assent. Soon, as silence reigned around them, Mitros started to cough, which caused the dogs' barking to grow louder. Orestes and Leander held him to prevent him doubling over with the pain.

"Just don't move," Leander said. "The dogs will get used to the noise."

As the moon came up, the man appeared from the house. He shouted some words to calm the dogs.

"You can walk on now," he said. "All three of you. We have decided we don't want you here. It is too dangerous."

"We have no food," Leander said.

"The dogs will attack you if you don't walk," the man said. "And if you ever come near here again, they'll go for your throats."

"Even some bread?" Leander asked.

"We have nothing."

"Which is the best way to go?"

"There is no good way, except back to the mountains from where you came. All the rest is sea."

"Who owns the next house?"

"It's guarded by dogs as well. They won't even bark. They will tear you to pieces when they smell the blood."

"Are there islands?"

"There are no boats. They took our boats to fight their war."

"Is there water to drink?"

"No."

"No spring or well? No stream?"

"Nothing."

"Who lives in the next house?"

"It doesn't matter. She's an old woman but you will never see her. Her dogs are like wolves. You'll only see her dogs."

"Can you give us water before we set out?"

"Nothing."

The man whispered something under his breath to the dogs.

"Walk slowly in single file," he said in a louder voice to the three. "Don't turn."

Orestes noticed that the man's wife had appeared at the door, standing in the shadows with the dog that Mitros had petted close to her. The dog was still wagging its tail.

"My friend's cough—" Leander began.

"The dogs will follow you for a mile," the man interrupted. "If you try to turn back or even speak to each other, they will attack. If your friend starts to cough again, they won't know what that is and they'll attack him."

"I can't . . ." Mitros said.

"Concentrate hard," Leander whispered to him.

"Leave now," the man said and then shouted some orders to the dogs, which followed slowly behind them. They walked on until the dogs turned back and then they continued and did not look behind again. Soon they came to a place that was sheltered by some bushes. They sat down. Mitros was the first to fall asleep. Leander said that he would stay awake while Orestes slept. He would wake him later so that he could then keep a lookout.

At dawn, Orestes noticed the seabirds and felt that their cry grew louder and more alarming as they flew directly over him and his sleeping companions. Anyone pursuing them would know where they were, he thought, just as anyone ahead of them would know that they were approaching. The crying of the seagulls, in particular, was shrill. When he looked up into the sky, Orestes saw hawks hovering high above them in the pale morning light. Anyone for miles around would now be sure that there were intruders in the landscape.

As they walked on, they could smell the salt from the sea, and a few times as they climbed small hills, Orestes caught glimpses of its blueness. He was aware that they were walking away from food, and from water that they could drink. The house that the man had mentioned, the house guarded by dogs, was the last chance they would get. He presumed that Leander was working out a plan, but Leander was even more downcast than Mitros, and Orestes was afraid to ask him what he had in mind.

As they stopped for a rest, panting with thirst, in a rock-strewn field, Mitros lay back with his eyes closed. Leander searched for stones or pieces of rock that he could hold in his hand.

Slowly, Leander gathered them into a pile. He removed his vest and tried to make a sling that would carry as many rocks as possible, testing the weight, throwing out some when they seemed too heavy. Without asking any questions, Orestes followed suit, noticing a new brightness in Leander, an expression on his face that exuded determination and something almost close to confidence.

When they alerted Mitros, he opened his eyes and stood up and walked behind them. They made their way forward more slowly now, listening for the slightest sound, as Leander fashioned a stick for himself from a stunted tree, later stopping to do the same for both Orestes and Mitros.

Once he began to dream of food and water, Orestes did not think he could move another step. As he tried to imagine their destination, it became the palace with his mother at the door waiting for him, and Electra and Iphigenia inside.

With a shudder, he wondered where Electra was and if she had been kidnapped too, or if she had been taken to be killed as Iphigenia was killed, with screaming and the bellowing of animals. For a moment, he wanted to cower so that no one could see him, but he was beckoned forward by Leander.

They walked for some hours towards the setting sun. Orestes was tired carrying the stones. Mitros was having more and more trouble walking. Since they were burdened by the weight of the stones, they could not support him. All Leander could do was talk to him in a soft, cajoling voice, even though he too was out of breath as they climbed a hill.

For some of the day, there had been no birds above them in the high sky, but now, as their shadows lengthened, the seabirds returned, flying lower and lower, seeming almost angry as they swooped down close.

Leander stood behind Orestes as they studied what lay ahead. Orestes checked every inch of the landscape, but saw no sign of any habitation. Orestes wondered if the man had been fooling them when he told them that there was a house here. He could see that Leander was worried, but he knew that it was best not to ask what he thought as they sat beside Mitros, who was lying flat on the ground with his eyes closed.

Leander spoke to Mitros gently and said that it would not be long before he had a bed to sleep in and some food and water. He must come with them for this last stretch. Orestes could see the sea on two sides now; they were heading towards the end of the land. If there was no house here, or no well or spring, he knew that they were finished and would have to turn back.

Ahead of them, the vegetation became more dense, which made him think that there was a water supply. And there could easily be a house hidden by the bushes and the pine trees. As they moved, the seabirds that had been following them seemed to withdraw, and there was only the sound of sparrows and other small birds. This sound was soon broken, however, by the barking of dogs. Leander signaled to the other two to run into the shelter of a bush on one side of the path as he went behind a thin pine tree on the other side. When they were settled, he began to whistle.

As the first dog rushed ferociously along the path, Leander hurled stones at it, causing it to stop in its tracks and snarl. Orestes tried to aim precisely at the dog's head, managing with one jagged rock to make the dog fall on its side. Leander stepped out and began to beat the dog on the head with a stick, returning to his supply of rocks for one hard enough to smash its head. As he did so, a second dog came down the path. Within a few seconds, it had Leander by the arm with its teeth, making him scream and writhe in pain. Orestes shouted to Mitros to get a heavy rock from his pile, as he took the stick and began to beat the dog.

While Mitros threw rocks at the dog, Orestes hit it harder and harder. Finally, the dog fell over, with blood coming out of its mouth, leaving Leander gasping, his hand moving quickly to his arm to stop the bleeding. All three of them looked ahead, Orestes aware that if more dogs came in groups, they would not be able to withstand them. As Mitros held Leander, checking the wound in his arm, Orestes heard the sound of barking. He had time to fetch a number of rocks before a large black dog came bounding towards them, showing its teeth. He concentrated fiercely as he took aim and directed a rock towards the dog's open mouth, instantly choking it. The dog fell on its back with a howl of pain.

Now there was just the sound of whining. The first dog, still alive, was trying to get to its feet, even though half its head was open. Orestes stepped quickly towards it, and slammed a rock down on the animal's body. He went across and knelt beside Leander, noting the huge raw tear in his arm.

"Make him sit up," Orestes said.

Slowly and with difficulty, crying out in pain, Leander moved into a sitting position. As he opened his eyes wide, Orestes saw him checking the scene with something close to his old vigilance. He stood up, holding his right arm with his left hand.

"There could be more dogs," he said, as if nothing much had happened.

They sat in the shadows as the light began to wane and the birdsong grew louder. Orestes felt so tired that he thought he could lie on the soft grass between the trees and fall asleep. He imagined that both Leander and Mitros felt the same.

He was half-dozing when he heard the voice of a woman. He looked in between the branches to see her bending over one of the dogs, crying out its name. She was old and very frail. When the woman saw the other dogs, she let out a shriek, moving from one to the other, calling each by name, eventually cradling the head of one of them, using lamenting words. Orestes watched her stand and look around her; he was aware for a second that if she looked closely she would see him. From the way she squinted, however, he could tell that her sight was not good. She moved away, back to where she had emerged from, still crying out words and the names of the dogs, raising her voice as if trying to wake the dogs up from death.

They waited as darkness fell. Orestes believed that if the woman had more dogs, then she would not have lamented the dead ones with such intensity. Nonetheless, he was listening for the smallest barking sound. He heard other animal noises, the bleating of goats, and sheep and chickens, but no sound that suggested a dog. As Mitros began to vomit, Orestes felt the urge also. Leander warned them to be quiet. Afterwards, Orestes lay exhausted, close to Mitros, who reached out and held his hand for a moment. He did not know whether the grip was to let him understand how exhausted Mitros was, or how hungry and thirsty, or how afraid. Leander sat apart from them as though he was angry. When the moon appeared, he stood up.

"I want both of you to remain here and be quiet," he said. "I'm going to talk to her."

As they waited for Leander to return, Orestes heard many sounds that suggested footsteps, someone approaching. In all the undergrowth around them, he realized, there was movement, small animals scratching about. There was also a sound that he did not recognize at first. It was like a human sound, someone breathing in and out. He listened and indicated to Mitros that he should listen too as this sound, like someone larger than they were who was sleeping peacefully, breathing with ease, came and went. It made him certain for a short time that there was someone nearby, someone who would wake soon and who would have to be dealt with. And then Mitros whispered to him: "It's the sea." Suddenly, that made sense. It was the waves swelling and coming in towards the land and breaking and then, in a quick, hushed breath, going out again. He did not know that this sound could be so loud. In the camp when he was with his father he had seen the sea, and he must have slept near it, but he had never heard it like this before. He was sure also that this breathing sound had not been there earlier. Maybe, he thought, the wind had changed or the sound belonged to the night.

As they waited, it was almost as if they were being rocked in a boat, so regular was the rhythm of the water. Orestes felt that if he concentrated on the sound of the sea and forgot everything else, then at least he would not have to think, but as time wore on and Leander did not return, he worried that he would be left in charge of Mitros with no idea whether he should make an attempt to approach the woman's house as Leander had done, or lead Mitros back along the road, where they would have no protection from the other dogs, or from the guards who might be in pursuit.

When Leander approached, he had to call their names as he could not immediately locate them. The fact that he was almost shouting suggested to Orestes that he was confident that it was safe. They stood up when they heard his voice.

"She says we can stay," he said. "I've promised her that we will stay until she wants us to go. She has food, and there's a well. She's afraid of us, and she's crying because of what we did to her dogs."

Bats began to swoop down on them as they walked towards the house, causing Mitros to cover his head in fear. Leander told them to follow slowly and watch every step, as the house was close to steep cliffs. Mitros became so afraid of the bats that he had to snuggle in between the two others, seeking protection.

The woman at the door seemed enormous, almost ominous, in the shadows cast by an oil lamp. She stood aside as they entered and then followed them inside. Orestes looked around the room, feasting his eyes on a ceramic jug of water and a cup beside it from which he imagined Leander had been drinking before he came to find them. Since both he and Leander were bare-chested, having used their vests to make slings for the rocks, he felt oddly uncomfortable in the small space of the room. The woman ignored him and Mitros as she set about examining the wound on Leander's arm, on which she had earlier put a white poultice.

Orestes eyed the cup, wondering what would happen were he simply to ask if he could drink and if he could share his drink with Mitros.

"Drink," Leander said. "You don't have to ask. There is a well just outside. She has promised me that it is not poisoned."

As Mitros almost ran across the room towards the water, the old woman moved swiftly out of the way and stood against the wall watching them.

"I thought for a second there of calling the dogs to protect myself. But I can't call the dogs," she whispered. "I don't have any dogs to call. I have no one to protect me."

"We'll protect you," Leander said.

"You'll go when you are fed, and you'll tell others that I am here unprotected."

"We will not go," Leander said. "You must not be afraid of us. We will be better than the dogs."

When Mitros had drained a cupful of water, he handed the cup to Orestes, who filled it and drank it down. Leander began to cry out in pain as the woman removed the poultice on his arm and replaced it with a thick white liquid that she spread over the wound.

"Someone has to be on the lookout all the time," Leander said. "If they are still following us, they'll come here. The farmer will direct them here."

"And they'll burn the house," the old woman said. "That is what they'll do."

"We won't let them near the house," Leander said, as he stood up, his shadow growing against the wall.

"I'll stand guard tonight," Orestes said.

"When the food is prepared, we'll bring it to you," Leander said.

"How long will it take for the food?" he asked.

"There's bread here you can carry with you," Leander said.

As Orestes left the house, the old woman shouted something that he could not make out. Then she spoke to Leander, as though he were the only one who might understand her.

"He must not stray too far. There are cliffs. Only the animals know where it is safe. He should take one of the goats with him and follow the goat."

"Are the goats yours?" Orestes asked.

"Yes, who else could own them?"

The old woman left the room for a moment and then returned with a thick tunic that she handed to Orestes.

Leander led Orestes out into the dark and stood with him for a while until they could make out shapes by starlight. He patted one of the goats that the old woman had called.

"Can you keep awake?" he asked.

"Yes," Orestes said. "And I can see and I will be careful."

"If you hear the smallest unusual sound, come and wake me. She has other goats and there are sheep in fields away from here. You might hear them in the distance. And the hens will make noise at first light. And there might be other sounds, bird sounds. But if you think you hear the sound of a dog barking too near, or a human sound, then wake me. We can try to defend ourselves. In the morning, we can make this house secure, or more secure."

"How long are we going to stay here?"

Leander sighed.

"We're not leaving."

"What?"

"Not until . . ." he began. "Not until she dies or until she wants us to go. That's what I promised her."

"But maybe we could find more dogs for her."

"This is where we're staying," Leander said. "We must not think of leaving."

Orestes slowly followed one of the goats once Leander had left him, gauging where the cliffs were by the sound that came from the waves. Since there was a light wind rustling the leaves of the trees that grew in some abundance around the house, he tried to work out what a new sound, the sound of an intruder, might be like. He hoped that Leander would soon bring him food, something more than the bread he had now.

When the food finally came, he ate it ravenously, wanting more, regretting that he was not at the table with the others so that he could see if there was more. And then he was alone, with the sound of the sea and the rustling leaves and the intermittent hooting of an owl, and nothing else, no other sound.

He dozed off in the hour before dawn and woke with a start

at the light. The dawn must have been stealthy, he thought, because it had not woken him until everything around was bright and there were new sounds, birdsong and a cock crowing. He sat up and listened in case there was anything else, but he did not think so. He would not tell Leander that he had fallen asleep.

Over the next two days, as Mitros stayed in bed, or remained close to the old woman, Orestes and Leander gathered rocks and small stones. They tried to break the rocks up so that each one could be thrown a distance. At intervals, they practiced throwing the stones and small rocks to hit a particular target, before building mounds among the bushes on each side of the narrow path that led to the house.

They also began to explore the land around the house, Leander noting the fruit trees that had been recently pruned and the stone walls between fields and the animals that all seemed well cared for. He also looked carefully at the house itself and the outbuildings and stores with cured meat and grain and wood for the fire.

"She could not have done this on her own," Leander said.

When night fell, Mitros offered to go outside and guard while the others ate. Later, Leander would take his turn to sit through the night at the highest point, to which they had made a path marked with rocks and stones. As the old woman served them the food, he asked her if she had always been alone.

"This house is filled not by me," she said, "but by the others who have gone. It is their voices I hear and I talk back to them when I can. But I don't need to cook for them anymore, so the store is full."

"But where are they?" Leander asked.

"Scattered," she said.

"Who?" Orestes asked. "Who lived here?"

"My two sons were taken to be in the army, taken for the war, and their boats taken too."

"When were they taken?" Orestes asked.

"Some moons ago. They're all gone and won't be back. They left me the dogs and now the dogs are gone too."

"How many were here before?" Leander asked.

"Their wives fled with the children, including the boy with the limp, the one I loved best," she said, ignoring his question. "You are wearing his clothes."

"And why didn't you go too?" Orestes asked.

"No one asked me to go," she said. "At a word from one of them, I would have gone. When you are fleeing in the night, no one wants an old woman."

She sighed.

"We thought they just wanted the sheep and the goats and the chickens, the men who came," she said. "But all they wanted were young men and boats. If we had known that, we could have hidden the men. In one second, they took them and we knew they would not be back."

"Where are they now?" Orestes asked.

"They are in the war."

"What war?"

"The war," she said. "The war."

"And the others?" Leander asked.

"The others were afraid to stay. Only one of them, the boy with the limp, looked behind as they set out."

She went silent and they ate without saying anything. When they had finished, Mitros came back in. The old woman smiled at him and tossed his hair playfully, affectionately, as she put his food on the table. He seemed to Orestes to have drifted into a realm of his own, avoiding Leander and Orestes as much as he could, and spending his time shadowing the old woman.

The following morning, as Orestes and Leander were sitting together beside a mound of rocks, not speaking, just looking into the distance, they saw a dog slowly approaching, wagging its tail. As the dog passed, they crept into the bushes, each with a rock in his hand, Orestes sure that someone was coming and tensing himself for attack. They watched and waited, but there was no sign of anyone. The dog appeared to have come alone. Eventually, Orestes left Leander to look out and went to the house, where he found the dog with its paws on the table being petted by both Mitros and the old woman.

"It's the dog from the house. He became my friend outside the house," Mitros said.

"What house?"

"The house where the other dogs surrounded us. This fellow didn't join them. He just wagged his tail. He's friendly."

The old woman put out a bowl of water for the dog, which slurped it down quickly and then moved back again to be close to Mitros.

When Orestes went out to tell Leander what had happened, he smiled.

"Everyone likes Mitros. Except the guards. They didn't like him. And those other dogs didn't like him either. But the old woman likes him."

Before he went to rest, Leander warned Orestes to remain sharp in case the farmer came looking for his dog.

"What will I do if he comes?"

"Tell him that there's a trap ahead and if he moves closer to the house it will snap shut on his leg."

"What will I do if he doesn't believe me?"

"Shout loudly and throw stones. Hit him hard on the legs with stones. Frighten him."

*

Slowly, they grew used to the old woman's house. She trained them to look after the animals and instructed them about harvesting crops and growing vegetables and managing the fruit trees. Mitros stayed with her in the kitchen when he could, going out only to collect eggs or milk the goats, accompanied always by the dog. Orestes and Leander took turns at watching through the night, three nights each in a row. Orestes became familiar with the night sounds and taught himself not to fall asleep in the hour before dawn, when he was most tired.

He imagined sometimes that Leander and Mitros were his sisters, Electra and Iphigenia. In his dreams, he would go in search of one of them. He imagined also that the old woman was his mother. He wondered if Leander and Mitros were thinking the same thoughts as he was, and if they dreamed that this house was like their real houses and that the people they shared the house with were like the people at home.

One morning when he was sitting at the table in the kitchen with Mitros, with Leander standing guard in the bushes and the old woman looking after the hens, the dog began to paw the ground and look around the room expectantly. Mitros laughed and started to pat the dog on the head until its pawing became more frantic. Orestes stopped eating to watch the scene. When the old woman came in, the two boys did not even look up at her, they were so wrapped up in the dog. When she saw what was happening, she let out a scream, and then ran to the door.

Orestes and Mitros followed her to find out what the problem was.

"The dog!" she said. "It means someone is coming. Get Leander!"

Orestes had never heard her use Leander's name before. The only name she had seemed to know before then was Mitros' name. He ran down to where Leander was and found him sitting in the shade close to a heap of rocks. When he told him what had occurred, Leander told him to move to the other side of the path, stay close to the mound of stones and do nothing. He was to wait for a sign from Leander before he threw a stone.

They waited but no one came. Orestes was sorry that he had not asked Leander at what point he could go back to the house. He had been up all night and he was tired. When he peered across the path to the bushes, he could see no sign of Leander. He guessed that he must be waiting there, hidden, still alert. As more time passed, he was tempted to call to him, but he realized that if Leander thought that he could go then he would have shouted across to him.

He did not see the two men approaching. Instead, he was surprised by the sound of one of them shouting as he was hit in the head by a rock that Leander had thrown. Since Orestes had kept a rock in each hand all the time, it was easy for him to move quickly. The two men, he saw, had stopped. One of them held his hands over his head. The other was looking around him, puzzled about where the rock had come from. Orestes recognized them as the guards who had taken him away from the palace.

Orestes stood back and aimed carefully and coldly, deciding to go for the man already injured, hitting him with one rock on the head and hitting him a second later directly in the face. The other man ran in the direction of the house, avoiding the two rocks that Leander threw. Orestes took up one more rock and threw it after him, hitting him hard on the shoulder, but it did not stop him.

Leander sprang from where he was, having removed his shirt and filled it with rocks, to follow the man. As he did, Orestes noticed that the man who had been hit was still standing. He took aim once more with two rocks, one of them smaller and sharper than the other, and hit him twice. The man fell over. Then Orestes also removed his shirt and gathered some rocks and ran onto the lane to follow Leander.

When he caught sight of him, Leander was standing alone, having dropped the rocks. He was looking around in panic, desperately trying to see where the man he had pursued had gone. Suddenly, from the bushes where he had been hiding, the man jumped at him, one hand going for his throat. Orestes, still some distance away, reached for one of the rocks, but before he could throw it the man had managed to trip Leander over. He had something in his hand, which Orestes guessed was a knife, as the two rolled on the ground in combat.

As he came close, he saw that the man was forcing his way on top of Leander, straddling his body, pinning one of his arms down. Leander was holding the man by the wrist as the man attempted to bring the knife down and stab him in the neck.

Orestes dropped the rocks, aware that if he put one thought into what he should do, he would miss the chance to surprise the intruder. He tried not to make a sound as he approached, then put his hands around the man's head, pushing his thumbs as fiercely as he could into the man's eyes. For those seconds, it was as though he had no body of his own, no mind, nothing except the force of the thumbs. He did not breathe until he felt something give way within the eye sockets as the man let out a scream, dropping the knife and freeing Leander's other hand.

In one move, Leander got to his knees and, taking up the knife, began to stab the man in the chest and neck. When there was no sound from him, they laid him on his back flat out on the ground.

"We have to go for the other one," Leander said. Orestes almost wanted to stop to explain to Leander who this dead figure was, and who his companion was—the gentler one, the one who had treated him less harshly. But Leander had already gone ahead and he had to follow.

The man was not on the lane. They made their way forward carefully in case he was hiding in the bushes. When they reached the clearing, they saw him below them in the distance, swaying slowly from side to side, holding his head. When he looked behind and saw them, he tried to run.

"Wait for me," Leander said as he went back to get some rocks.

"We can catch up with him," he said when he returned. "Tell me when you think you can hit him."

Having gathered some rocks, they both went forward with as much speed as they could muster. It was clear to Orestes that their prey would not be able to outrun them, but he was worried that the man would have a knife, as his companion had. In that case, the man's only chance was to get close enough to one of them to use it.

Orestes decided to run faster, hoping that if he could make progress without losing any rocks, then he could stop and take aim before Leander, who was ahead of him, reached the man. He felt that he could do anything if he did not worry for a second or even calculate. His aim would be right and he would be able to judge the moment to start throwing the rocks. The man was desperate, it appeared, to get away from them, but it was still clear to Orestes that he could suddenly turn and threaten them.

Instead of following Leander and the man, Orestes ran diagonally across the clearing where the raised ground continued. He made sure that he did not lose any rocks from the shirt that he held cradled against his chest. He ran with even greater speed when he noticed the man looking behind him again. He was calculating, Orestes thought, working out at what point he should stop and be ready to attack Leander with a knife if Leander were foolish enough to approach.

Orestes was ready now. Having selected a rock, he took aim and threw but the man was not running in a straight line so the rock missed him and alerted him to where Orestes was. Orestes had no choice now but to pick up the shirt filled with rocks and run as quickly as he could manage towards the moving figure. He would no longer have the advantage of the slope, but if he put all his energy into his speed he might, he thought, get close enough to throw another rock from the side, even if the angle would not be as good.

He stopped and took up another rock. He breathed in and summoned up the same strength as when he had attacked the other man. And then he threw. The rock hit the man's shoulder. Quickly, he chose another rock. This second one hit the man's head, causing him to fall backwards.

When Orestes caught up with Leander, he said nothing. They both had their eyes fixed on the figure lying on the ground. When they got closer, they could hear him moaning and gasping. Orestes put down the rocks and knelt to take one from the five or six that were left. He ran towards his victim and hit him hard in the head.

The man was lying on his back but his eyes were wide open. When Orestes caught his desperate gaze, the prone figure seemed to recognize him and began to say something that sounded like his name. Orestes hesitated for one second before he threw another rock, splitting the man's head open.

Leander searched through the man's clothes and found two knives. Orestes walked back and picked up his shirt. Then he joined Leander and they both began to pull the body towards the house, each one holding a foot, letting the head bang against the ground as they dragged him along. Since he was heavy, they stopped several times for a rest. They brought him as far as his companion, whose body was already attracting flies. They rolled each one until it was at the edge of the cliff and then they let them fall over the edge.

"I promised myself that we would kill no one else," Leander said.

"They would have killed us. They were the two men who kidnapped me."

"They'll do nothing now. But I didn't keep my promise."

As he and Leander made their way to the house, Orestes was tempted to talk about his journey from the palace with these two men, but he realized that since neither Leander nor Mitros had ever discussed the details of how they were taken away, then Leander would not want to hear about it. It was something he would have to think about on his own.

They found Mitros and the old woman sitting at the table. The dog stood up and stretched and yawned as they came in.

"He stopped pawing the ground a while ago," Mitros said, "so we supposed whoever came went away again."

Orestes looked at Leander, who was standing in the shadows without his shirt on.

"Yes, they went away," Leander said.

"And we heard a man shout," the old woman said. "And I said to Mitros that if that man shouts again we'll go out and see what's happening. But since we didn't hear another sound we decided to stay here."

Leander nodded.

"I lost my shirt," he said.

"I have cloth left over," the old woman said. "And I can make you a new one. Maybe one for each of you. It will keep me busy."

When Orestes glanced at Leander, it seemed that he had grown older. His shoulders had widened and his face had become more narrow and thin. He appeared taller too as he stood alone in the shadows. For a second, Orestes was tempted to cross the room and touch Leander, put his hand on his face or on his torso, but he stood still.

Orestes was hungry and tired, but he felt as though he needed to do something more, that he would actually be pleased to spring into action if he were told that more men were coming.

He could not stop looking at Leander as he moved shirtless in the small room. When he caught Leander's eye, he saw that Leander too was unsettled. If the old woman had said that she needed to kill one of the sheep, or the goats, or even one of the hens, he would have been with her carrying the sharp knife. He would have been ready to help her. And so, he knew, would Leander.

They sat at the table and ate the food the woman had prepared as if it were a normal evening in their lives. The dog watched the scene from a corner of the room, observing as usual with care every morsel of food that Mitros ate, or moving closer to him every time he coughed.

Since they now knew that the dog would warn them of any intruders, neither Orestes nor Leander would have to keep guard during the night. Thus, on Leander's suggestion, Orestes shared a bed with Mitros, with the dog between them. Leander slept in the next room, the old woman at the end of the house.

During the day, they met for meals, which were cooked by the old woman and Mitros. Orestes and Leander looked after the animals and the crops, the vegetables and the trees, often working together. When all four were eating, there was never silence. They could talk about the weather, or a change in the wind; they could discuss a new sort of goat's cheese that the old woman made, or discuss an animal or something that had happened to a tree. They could make jokes about how lazy Mitros was, or how hard it was to get Orestes out of bed in the mornings, or how tall Leander had grown. They could throw bread to the dog and laugh as it ate it greedily. But the old woman did not speak of her family who had gone, and the boys did not speak of home. Orestes wondered if perhaps Mitros had told the old woman their story, or if parts of what had transpired had emerged in conversations between them.

On some days, the wind became fierce. The old woman always knew when it was about to happen. She would warn them. It could begin with a whistling sound in the night, or start during the day when it became even warmer than usual, and it could build up and last for two or three days before calming down again. When it whistled most loudly, Mitros had to stay close to the dog, which grew nervous and growled and wanted to hide. On the nights when the wind was at its most intense, when none of them could sleep and they settled in the kitchen uneasily, the old woman, having taken down a bottle of distilled fruit juice and poured a cup for herself and given the boys plenty of fruit and water, would tell them a story, promising that, if she could, she would make it last through the night.

"There was a girl," she began one night, "and she was known as the most beautiful girl that anyone had ever seen. There were different opinions about her birth. Some believed that her father was one of the old gods who had come to earth disguised as a swan. But, no matter what they thought about the father, all were agreed on the name of the girl's mother."

The old woman stopped as the wind continued around the house. As the dog moved farther into the corner, Mitros sat on the floor close by.

"What was the name of the mother?" Orestes asked. "Was she a god too?"

"No, she was mortal," the old woman said and stopped again. She seemed to be trying to think of something.

"It was the time of the gods," the old woman said. "The swan lay with her, the mother, and some say . . ."

"What do they say?" Orestes asked.

"They say that two were born from the swan as the father and the other two from a mortal father. A boy and a girl, and another boy and a girl. And the girl, the daughter of the swan, was the enchanting one. The others . . ."

She stopped again and sighed.

"The two boys are dead now," she continued, whispering. "They are dead, like all the men from that time. They died protecting their sister. That is how they died."

"Why did they have to protect her?" Leander asked.

"All the princes and kings wanted to marry her," the old

woman said. "And it was agreed that anyone who bid for her hand even if they lost the bid would have to promise to come to her husband's assistance if anything should happen to her. And that is how the war began, the war that took the boats and the men. It began because of her beauty."

The woman talked as the wind howled around the house. The three boys sat with her through the night, Orestes and Leander waking and dozing in their chairs, Mitros remaining with the dog, which was frightened by the wind.

*

Leander and Orestes learned to whistle so that even if they were apart, they could hear each other. Their main whistle was a greeting, a way of letting each other know where they were; another whistle was to say that it was time to go back to the house for food; another whistle meant that they should find each other as soon as possible; the last whistle meant intruders. They worked with Mitros, teaching him to whistle if they were late for a meal, and teaching him the loudest, sharpest whistle if the dog ever pawed the ground.

Since they could whistle if they needed each other, Orestes and Leander could work in different fields, or one could stay in the house while the other went in search of an animal. It also meant that Orestes could walk along the edge of the cliffs until he found an opening, a rocky path that led down to the ocean. He knew that the old woman worried about the waves, which could be high and rough, so he never told her that he often went there when the day was coming to an end just to be on his own and look at the water.

He found a ledge. Some days he walked down and watched the waves pushing in, crowding against each other to crash against the rocks below. Sometimes, birds flew over the sea in strange formations, some flying high and others closer to the surface of the water. It was mostly calm and still, but on the days when there was some wind, the wind seemed to toss the water far out.

Soon he convinced Leander to come with him. They sat together on the ledge as the sunlight faded. Leander seldom wore a shirt when he worked outdoors; his body was tanned. He was much taller than Orestes and bigger. He was like one of the warriors that Orestes remembered with his father, one of the men who walked purposefully in and out of his father's tent.

Orestes wanted to ask Leander if he had a plan, if he was counting the time passing, as Orestes was, by the waxing and waning of each moon, by the lambing seasons, by the way in which crops grew, and by the fruit trees with their harvest, and if he thought they would stay here for the rest of their lives, if they would remain even after the old woman died. But, as time passed, as moons grew full and thin, and no further intruders appeared, it looked as though the three of them had been forgotten, as though they had found the place where they would live safely and that any going or moving would only put them in danger.

Sometimes, Orestes gazed at the sea, searching the horizon for boats or ships. He had remembered the boats and ships all waiting in the harbor when he was with his father in the camp. But there was no sign of anything.

As they sat there together, Orestes lay back and leaned his head against Leander's chest as Leander put his arms around him and held him. Orestes knew when that happened to say nothing, and think of nothing either, merely wait until the sun dipped into the sea, when Leander would relax his arms and nudge Orestes out of the way and stand up and stretch and they would walk back together to the house.

Often at night, Mitros relayed to Orestes the stories that the old woman had told him when he was alone with her. Whispering, he recounted what she had said, trying to remember the exact words, stopping in the same way she did when he came to some of the details.

"There was a man, or maybe a king," he said, "who had four children, one girl and three boys. He loved his wife and his children and they were happy."

"When was this?" Orestes asked.

"I don't know," Mitros said.

"And then the woman died," he continued, "the mother of the four children, and they were sad until their father sent for the sister of their mother and he married her and they were happy again until she became jealous of the four children. So she ordered the children to be killed, but the servant she ordered to do the killing said that he could not do it because they were beautiful children and . . ."

He stopped for a moment as though he had forgotten the next part.

"Maybe the king would be angry," Orestes said.

"Yes, maybe. But then she came to kill them herself."

"When they were sleeping?"

"Or when they were playing. But when she came to kill them she was not able. So instead, she turned them into swans."

"And could they fly?"

"Yes. They flew away. It was part of the spell that they had to fly far away, but before they did they asked for one thing. They asked for a silver chain so that they would never be apart.

The chain was made for them and they flew away with the chain between them."

"But what happened to them?"

"They flew to one place and then to another, and then to another, and many years passed. Sometimes it was cold."

"Did they die?"

"They flew for nine hundred years. And all the years they waited and talked about going home. They talked about the day when they would fly with the silver chain still between them and they would find the place they came from. But when that time came, everyone they had known was dead. There were other people there, people they did not know, new people who were frightened when the swans landed and their wings fell off, and then their beaks and then all their feathers fell off. And they were people again. They were people but they were not children anymore. They were old. They were nine hundred years old, and all the new people ran away when they saw them."

"And what happened then?"

"They died, and then the people who ran away came back and buried them."

"And the silver chain? Did they bury that too?"

"No. The people kept the silver chain, and they sold it later, or used it for something else."

*

Slowly, the old woman weakened. Mitros made her a bed in the kitchen because she could no longer walk. She still talked to him during the day, and at mealtimes she ate some food but only if Mitros gave it to her. She did not recognize either Orestes or Leander. When they spoke to her, she did not reply.

Sometimes, she began a story about ships and men, and a woman and the waves, but she could not continue. At other times, she listed names, but they seemed to have no connection with anything. They ate in silence at the table, letting her voice come and go, barely listening since almost everything that came from her made no sense to them.

Halfway through a sentence she would often fall asleep, and then wake again and call for Mitros and he would feed her and sit close to her, bringing the dog with him, while the other two went back to work or moved to another part of the house or down to the ledge over the rocks to look out at the waves.

One evening, the woman had repeated some phrases over and over and then some names before she stopped speaking and slept. They had almost finished their food when she woke again and began to whisper. At first they could not easily hear her. It was a list of names. Orestes stood up and moved towards her.

"Can you say the names again?" he asked.

She did not pay any attention to him.

"Mitros, can you ask her to say the names again?" Orestes asked.

Mitros moved towards the woman and knelt in front of her.

"Can you hear me?" he whispered.

She stopped speaking and nodded.

"Can you say the names again?" he asked.

"The names?"

"Yes."

"This house was filled with names. Now there is only Mitros."

"And Orestes and Leander," Mitros said.

"They will go as the others went," she said.

"We will not go," Leander said in a louder voice.

The woman shook her head.

"The houses were all filled with names," she said. "All the names. This house was . . ."

She put her head down and did not say anything more. After a while, when Orestes saw that she was not breathing, they stayed close to her for some time, Mitros holding her hand.

Eventually, Orestes whispered to Leander: "What should we do?"

"She is dead. We should take her to her room, bring a light with us and stay with her until the morning," Leander said.

"Are you sure she is dead?" Mitros asked.

"Yes," Leander said. "We'll stay with her body tonight."

"And then bury her?" Orestes asked.

"Yes."

"Where?"

"Mitros will know."

As they carried her body gently down to the room at the end of the house where she slept, Mitros, who was following them with the dog, started to cough and remained huddled in a corner of the room where the woman lay, moving at intervals to touch her face and her hands and then returning to where he had been. As the night wore on, however, and he began to cough more, he had to go outside for air.

Orestes and Leander stayed with the body, now grown cold and stiff, neither of them daring to speak. This was, Orestes saw, the time they had been dreading, the time when something would have to be decided. They had been in this house, he knew, for five years. He realized that he did not know what Leander wanted to do, what he had been thinking about all the time they had been here.

He did not want to go away from here. Too much time had passed. If, when Mitros returned, Leander said that he believed that they should stay here and make no plans to leave, then Mitros would quickly assent and so would he. They would stay until they grew old as the woman had grown old.

Orestes tried to imagine which of them would die first, and who would be alone here at the end. He thought that Mitros would die first since he was the weakest. He imagined himself and Leander alone here, Leander looking after the animals and crops and he, Orestes, looking after the kitchen and the food and collecting the eggs. He imagined Leander coming in as the day ended and his having the food ready for Leander and then the conversation about the weather and the crops and the animals, and maybe they would, in time, talk about Mitros and the old woman and maybe even about home, the people they had left at home.

In the morning, Mitros took them to the place in the bushes where the old woman had said that she wanted her body to be laid. He was still coughing and holding his chest as the other two dug a hole where the woman's body could be buried. When flies gathered around her, Mitros made himself busy between gasps brushing the flies away.

The woman's eyes were still half-open, and, even though her body was inert and lifeless, there were moments when Orestes felt that she had actually moved for a second, or that she could see them and hear them as they prepared her grave. When it came to the time when they could lower her body into the hole they had dug, they hesitated. They studied the scene, immobilized.

Mitros bent down and held the woman's hand. Leander sat on the ground staring ahead. The dog crawled into the shade.

Suddenly, it struck Orestes what he might do. He stood up straight, causing both Mitros and Leander to watch him closely. As he looked at the dead body of the woman, he remembered the song that had been sung by the wife as her husband had lain poisoned by the water from the well. He cleared his throat and began to sing. He was not sure of all of the words, but he remembered the melody. He remembered also the intensity that the woman had used as she sang to the sky. Orestes looked up at the sky as the woman had. When he forgot the words, he repeated previous lines or he made them up. He forced his voice to become louder as he saw Mitros nodding to Leander. Mitros put his hands under the woman's shoulders, Leander knelt and put his arms under her legs. Slowly, they edged her to the side of the grave, lowered her gently into the ground and then filled the grave.

As all three walked back towards the house, followed by the dog, Leander asked Orestes where he had learned the song. Orestes pictured the scene—the man in agony on the ground, the guards watching implacably, the child in the woman's arms, the sky above them. It seemed like another life, or a life that had belonged to someone else.

"I don't remember where I learned it," he said.

As Mitros remained in the kitchen with the dog, Leander went into the fields and Orestes went to his ledge, hoping to be joined there by Leander so that he could find out what plans he had. But Leander did not appear.

He looked out at the sea and listened to the sound of the waves crashing below for as long as he could, and, when he grew tired waiting, he went back to the house to find Mitros on the floor coughing violently, with blood coming from his mouth. He went outside and whistled for Leander to come and then went back to the kitchen and held Mitros' head in his lap.

That night, they sat by Mitros' bed as he slept and then woke coughing and then slept again. Later, they brought him food and made sure that he was comfortable, with the dog stretched out beside him.

"We have to leave," Leander said. "We have been lucky up to now. But someday more people will come here and we won't be able to withstand them."

"I can't go," Mitros said.

"We'll wait until you're better," Leander said. "Until the coughing has gone."

"I can't go," he repeated.

"Why?" Orestes asked.

"The woman told me that as soon as I left here death would be waiting."

"For all of us?" Orestes asked.

"No, just for me."

"And us?" Orestes asked.

"She told me everything that will happen," Mitros said.

"Is it bad?" Orestes asked.

Mitros did not reply but held Orestes' gaze for some time as though he was working out what to say.

"You can tell us," Leander said.

"No, I cannot," he replied.

He closed his eyes then and remained motionless. Orestes and Leander left him sleeping and went back to the kitchen.

When they heard the loud cough again, they came to him immediately. His eyes were open; he reached out to grip Orestes' hand.

"Will you . . . ?" he began before he coughed again.

"You don't have to talk," Leander said. "Just rest."

"I want to sit up."

They helped Mitros to sit up. All the time he was holding Orestes' hand.

"Will you tell them?" he asked.

"Tell them what?" Orestes asked.

"That I was with you all these years, and tell about the old woman and the dog and the house. Will you tell them the story of us, what we did?"

"Tell who?" Orestes asked.

Leander put his hand on Orestes' shoulder, pulling him back. Mitros released his hand.

"We'll tell them that you were happy," Leander said, "and that you were looked after and that we loved you and cared for you, and that nothing bad happened to you, nothing bad at all. I will tell them and Orestes will tell them too. It's the first thing we'll do when we get home."

"Orestes . . ." Mitros began.

"Mitros, I'm here."

"Maybe what she said about what will happen isn't true," Mitros whispered.

"But what did she say?" Orestes asked.

"Will you promise to tell them?" Mitros asked in a louder voice, ignoring Orestes' question.

"Yes, I promise."

"All of them? My father and my mother, and all of them, my brothers? Maybe I have new brothers or sisters, ones I have never seen."

"We'll tell all of them."

Mitros lay back and fell asleep again. Later, Orestes went to lie down in Leander's bed, but Leander did not join him;

instead he hovered between the kitchen and where Mitros was, Orestes listening closely to his movements throughout the night.

In the morning, Orestes must have dozed off, because he was woken by Leander's hand on his shoulder.

"Mitros stopped breathing a while ago," Leander whispered.

"Have you tried to wake him?"

"He's not asleep," Leander said. "He's dead."

They waited by his body until the sun was weak in the sky and then they carried him to where they had buried the old woman, the dog following eagerly, its ears pricked up as though it could hear some distant sound. When they were ready to lower the body into the space they had made beside the old woman's body, Leander looked at Orestes, asking with his eyes if Orestes would sing the song again. Orestes moved close to the grave and sat down. He began to sing the words he knew in a low voice and then lowered it further until it was almost a whisper.

The dog seemed restless when the grave was filled. It remained there for a while with both of them, but then it slowly made its way back to the house, following them hesitantly, growling in a low voice. It sat in the kitchen in its usual place. Orestes gave it its food and water and patted it on the head and spoke to it softly.

He knew that Leander was planning to go. They had not spoken of it, but he was sure that that was the plan. He did not know what would happen then to the dog.

When he woke in the night, he moved from his own bed into Leander's, the dog following him. Leander made space for him, holding him as he settled in beside him. They were both afraid, Orestes realized, of what it would be like when they left.

He stopped going to his own bed, waiting instead until

Leander was ready for bed and then going to the room with him, the dog once more in his wake. He began to look forward to the night, to what happened between them in these hours, and to the morning when they woke.

One night, Leander seemed unable to sleep. When he had tossed and turned for a while, Orestes moved towards him in the bed. They held each other in the dark, both of them wide awake.

"I want to see my grandfather if he is still alive," Leander said. "He had two sons, but one of them died, and then my father had only one son and that is me. Maybe my grandfather is waiting for me. Ianthe, my sister, was ten when I was taken. She is a woman now, and she is waiting for me too, and my father and my mother are waiting for me and my uncles and aunts and my other grandparents, the parents of my mother."

"I don't know who is waiting for me," Orestes said. "Maybe that's what Mitros was trying to say, that there is no one waiting for me."

"Your mother is waiting for you, and Electra too," Leander said.

"But not my father?"

"Your father is dead."

"Who killed him?"

Leander did not reply for a moment and then, holding Orestes closer, he whispered: "It is enough that he is dead."

"My sister Iphigenia is dead too," Orestes said.

"I know."

"I saw her dying," Orestes said. "None of them knew that I saw her dying, and I heard her voice and I heard my mother screaming and saw her being dragged away."

"How did you see this?"

"I was on the hill in the camp. They had left me to play sword fighting with the soldiers, but the soldiers grew tired of the game after a time and then I was alone in one of the tents and I fell asleep and woke up to the sound of animals howling and I went out of the tent and lay on the ground overlooking where the heifers were being brought in and I watched as they were slaughtered. I heard the sound they made, the frightened sound that came from their bellies, and then I saw the blood spurting. And my father was there, and other men that I knew. I could smell the blood of the animals and the entrails that were everywhere, streaming everywhere. I was going to run down to my father, or maybe find my mother and Iphigenia. But then I saw them. They were in a procession, at the front of the procession, Iphigenia and my mother were both ahead of all the others, and there were men behind them. There was not a sound when they appeared. I saw them cutting my sister's hair. Then they made her kneel. Her hands and her feet were tied. And then I heard her voice and my mother's. They put something over their mouths to stop them shouting. And the men dragged my mother away and then my sister tried to reach my father, but she was dragged back. Then they put a blindfold on her. And then another man who was beside my father moved slowly towards her with a knife in his hand. And the cloth around her mouth fell away and she started to scream. The sound was like an animal. She fell over and they took her body away."

"And what happened then?"

"Then I went back into the tent and I lay down and waited. Some men came and they asked me if I wanted to play sword fighting, but I told them that I had played enough. Then my father came and he played with me and carried me on his shoulders through the camp."

"And where was your mother?"

"I was with my father's men. I must have slept in his tent for a few nights, because I remember all of them talking and then the shouting when they knew the ships could finally sail because the wind had changed. Men were rushing everywhere once the wind changed. They almost forgot about me until Achilles saw me and brought me to my father. And then my father carried me on his shoulders again through the camp to where my mother was. And then we began the journey back."

"Did you tell your mother what you saw?"

"I wondered at first if she knew that Iphigenia was dead, or if she might ask me or someone else what had happened after she was dragged away. She didn't see what happened. I saw everything. My mother didn't see and Electra wasn't there at all. I was the only one, except for the people in the crowd and my father."

"Do you want to go home to your mother and Electra?"

"Sometimes I don't, but maybe I do now."

"We have to decide."

"We'll go. And we'll take the dog?"

"We'll have to make the dog trust us so it will follow us," Leander said. "We'll get food to bring with us. We should take what food we can, and water."

Orestes put his arms around Leander to make clear that he was afraid. Leander held him.

Orestes knew as the night went on and the dawn light began that Leander was not sleeping. He could sense that Leander's eyes were open and he was thinking. He wished that they could go back to a time before, when the old woman and Mitros were still alive, or even before that, a time barely imaginable, when his mother and he and Iphigenia set out to meet his father as he prepared for battle and were welcomed by him.

He wondered, as Leander stirred, if there would ever be a future when he would remember nights like this, nights when he and Leander had been alone with each other, when they spent time whispering to each other, with the dog asleep beside them, with Mitros and the old woman in their graves not far away. He lay in bed as Leander got up. He watched him dressing, getting ready for the day. He too would have to get up and begin preparing for their departure. He would make himself busy packing food. In his mind, he began to list the things they would need for their journey.

On the morning they were to go, they found the dog lying listlessly in the kitchen, its tongue hanging out of its mouth as though it wanted water. When they offered it water, however, it did not drink.

"The dog is dying," Leander said. "He does not want to come with us."

The dog did not resist when they lifted it. They carried it down to the grave of Mitros and the old woman and they waited with it there. As the day wore on, one or the other of them got food and water, but the dog would not touch anything. All it did was whine gently, until soon even that stopped. They waited with it, whispering to it and to the old woman and Mitros, even after dark. Then they both remained silent, the silence broken only by the dog's hesitant breathing. And then there was no breath at all.

In the morning, as soon as the sun was up, they dug the grave again and added the body of the dog to the bodies of Mitros and the old woman. As soon as that was done, they went back to the house and found what they had prepared for their journey. They should start as soon as they could, Leander said, so that they would make good progress on the first day.

Electra

There is a set of winding steps some distance from the palace that leads to a sunken space that was once a garden. Some of the steps are broken, one or two have been almost completely chipped away by time or by the lizards that make their home in the gaps in the stone. Below, stunted trees do battle for space with bushes grown wild. When my sister was alive, we would go there if we needed to speak and wished to be sure that no one could hear us. As the light faded, the birdsong became intense, almost fierce. Perhaps the noise they made was a way for the birds to defy the weasels that seemed to have infested the place. We were certain then that even if someone were hiding in the shadows they would not be able to hear us.

My sister is not alive now. She will not come to this garden again.

Instead, my mother goes there. She moves out of the palace with two or three guards following her at a distance. Some days I walk with her, but we do not speak much, and often when I leave her she barely nods.

This sunken garden is where she will die. Someone will murder her here. She will lie in her own blood among the gnarled bushes.

I smile sometimes as I watch her descend the steps, her

guards alert as they lean over the stone balustrade in case she falls on the broken masonry.

It might be easy to think that in my mother's absence, and in the absence of her guards, Aegisthus is more alone and vulnerable, and that now might be a good time for someone to sneak into the room where he works, move quickly towards him and stick a knife in his chest or edge towards him as if to ask him for a favor and then, without warning, pull his head back by the hair and cut his throat as well.

It would be wrong, however, to believe that my mother's lover would be so easy to murder. He is filled with strategies and one of them, perhaps the most important, is his own survival. He is watchful. And there are men in his pay, or under his control, who are watchful too.

Aegisthus is like an animal that has come indoors for comfort and safety. He has learned to smile instead of snarl, but he is still all instinct, all nails and teeth. He can sniff out danger. He will attack first. He will arch his back and pounce at the slightest hint of a threat.

It is not a mistake to be afraid of him. I have reason to be afraid of him.

*

That day when my father returned from the war, as he greeted the elders outside, my mother ordered two of Aegisthus' friends to find me. They dragged me from the dining room, ignoring my screams and shocked protests. They pulled me struggling down the winding stairs to the floor below and they threw me into the dungeon under the kitchens and left me there for some days and nights without food or water. Then they released me. They simply opened the door of the dark room where they had kept me. They allowed me to crawl in my filth back to my room observed by everybody as though I were some abject wild animal who had been only half-tamed. They allowed me to live thereafter as though nothing untoward had occurred.

Aegisthus came to my room on the day I was released from the dungeon. He stood in the doorway and said that my mother had suffered a great deal and was in a fragile state and that it would not do to raise subjects that might upset her or remind her of what she had endured. And he said that I must not leave the palace grounds or be seen speaking to the servants or be found whispering with one of the guards.

I was not to make trouble, he said. He would see to it that I did not make trouble.

"Where is my father?" I asked him.

"He was murdered," he said.

"Who murdered him?"

"Some of his own soldiers. But they have been dealt with. We will not be hearing from them again."

"Where is my brother?"

"He has been removed from here for his own safety. He will be back soon."

"Is that where I was too? In the dungeon for my own safety?"

"You are safe now, are you not?" he asked.

"What do you want?" I asked.

"Your mother wishes to return to normal. And that is what you wish too, I am sure. We want your help in this."

He bowed to me in mock formality.

"I presume you understand," he said.

"When is my brother coming back?" I asked.

"Soon it will be safe for him. That is all your mother is waiting for. Then she will be less fretful than she is now, less worried."

*

It did not take me long to find out how my father was murdered and why my mother did not want the manner of his death mentioned. I understood then why she had sent Aegisthus to threaten me. She did not want to hear the voice of her accusing daughter. Both she and he were familiar with the web of old loyalties and allegiances that envelops this palace full of lingering echoes and whisperings. They must have known how easily I would find out what happened to my father, and also how quickly I would be told how my brother had been lured from here and on whose instructions.

My mother and her lover bought my silence with their threats, but they cannot control the night nor how word is spread.

The night belongs to me as much as it does to Aegisthus. I can move too without making a sound. I live in the shadows. I have an intimate relationship with silence and thus I am sure when it is safe for someone to whisper.

*

I am certain that Aegisthus knows where my brother is, or what his fate has been. He will, however, share this with no one. He knows what power is. His knowledge disturbs the air in this house.

He is ready to pick us up in his claws. He has us like the eagle that captures smaller birds and bites their wings off and keeps them alive so that they will nourish it when the time is right.

He is fully alert to how much he interests me. Like him,

I hear every sound, including the love noises he makes with his favored guard in one of the rooms off this corridor, or his quick, flitting movements towards the servants' quarters, where he will find a girl to satisfy him before he returns to my mother's bed and curls up there as though he has been nowhere, as though he is not impelled by some slimy and voracious appetite that has led him towards pleasure and power.

Only once have I seen Aegisthus flinch or show fear; only once have I seen the chameleon in him dart for cover.

When news came that the kidnapped boys had been released and were on their way home, with, we expected, Orestes among them, my mother and I sat with him while he remained uneasy and unsmiling.

We were waiting to welcome my brother home. As we grew impatient for more precise information about when he would arrive, my mother and I left Aegisthus' presence to ensure that the preparations for Orestes' room had been properly made. We went to the kitchens and thought of food he might like for his first meal. We spoke to each other cordially for the first time since my father's murder as we discussed the best servants to look after him. I could sense my mother's happiness at the prospect of his return.

When we went back to the room where Aegisthus was, we found that there was another man present, a stranger. It seemed to me in that moment that we were intruders, that we had interrupted this man and Aegisthus while something important, perhaps even intimate, was being spoken of. I wondered if this outsider, who was uncouth and unpleasant, had been a secret lover or supporter of Aegisthus, now come to remind him of what he was owed.

Aegisthus was facing the window when we entered; he had

his fists clenched while the visitor stood leaning against a wall near the door. When Aegisthus turned, I saw fear in his eyes. He nodded to the other man, indicating that he should leave the room. I realized that perhaps I should go too, that this would be a moment when, whatever had happened, Aegisthus and my mother would need to be together. Instead of leaving, however, I sat down. I made it plain that it would take more than a polite request to dislodge me. I would wait with my mother to hear from Aegisthus what it was that had caused that look of fear.

My mother, in the presence of Aegisthus, would often at that time become girlish and silly, and then at intervals petulant and oddly demanding. Nothing she said was of any interest. She had learned to sound stupid. The heat, some flowers, how tired she was, the food, the slowness of some of the female servants, the insolence of one particular guard—these were her subjects. I often wondered what would happen to her chirping voice, the jokey inconsequentiality of her tone, or her way of suggesting something and then stopping herself, if it were to be openly stated that the guard in question felt that he had a right to be insolent to her because he was sometimes to be found panting in the arms of Aegisthus, and that two or three of the female servants, as she must know, were slow because they were either pregnant with Aegisthus' child or had already had a baby by him. One of them, I understood, had even had twins.

The rooms beneath us were thus filled with fecundity as the corridors were filled with rough desire. While it was convenient for my mother to pretend that none of this was happening, that she was somehow too foolish or distracted to notice, it was clear that she, like me, allowed nothing to escape her. She was not foolish. She was not distracted. Beneath all her simpering and insinuation, there was fury, there was steel.

"Who is that man who was here?" she asked.

"What man?" Aegisthus asked.

"That unpleasant man."

"Just a messenger."

"Normally messengers don't come in here. And that is a good thing, because that man has left a smell behind him in this room. Perhaps that is because he has not bathed for some time."

Aegisthus shrugged.

"Oh, why is there no wind?" my mother asked the air around her. "I am exhausted."

Aegisthus clenched his fists even harder.

"I have a feeling there is news," my mother said, raising her voice so that it would be apparent to Aegisthus that she was addressing him.

When she caught my eye, she pointed to Aegisthus, as if I could somehow make him respond.

I looked at her coldly.

"What message did the messenger bring?" she asked more loudly.

There was silence now, which none of us, it seemed, wanted to break. My mother was wearing a vague smile; she was like someone who had eaten something sour and was doing everything to disguise her discomfort.

It had never struck me before, but it came to me forcefully at this moment, that she and Aegisthus had come to dislike each other. I had previously imagined them in some warm arrangement, circling each other happily by day and locked in each other's arms in the parts of the night when Aegisthus was not wandering freely in the palace. Now I noted a hard detachment. They had each taken the measure of the other and learned the outlines of some foul truth.

It amused me how natural they made this appear; it was not something that seemed ready to break. I understood their dilemma. It would be difficult, I thought, for my mother and Aegisthus to separate. Too much had happened.

As I sat in silence with them, I imagined what must fill their dreams in the hard hours, how the sound of muffled cries must press down darkly on their hours of slumber as much as when they are awake.

I watched them for some time. I contemplated my mother opening and closing her eyes, Aegisthus not moving once. What I witnessed was almost as private as the most intimate act. I saw them together as though naked.

*

I gravitate from their world, the world of speech and real time and mere human urges, towards a world that has always been here. Each day, I appeal to the gods to help me prevail, I appeal to them to oversee my brother's days and help him return, I appeal to them to give my own spirit strength when the time comes. I am with the gods in their watchfulness as I watch too.

My room is an outpost of the underworld. I live each day with my father and my sister. They are my companions. When I go to my father's grave, I breathe in the stillness in the place where his body lies. I hold my breath so that this new air fills my body and I release my breath slowly. My father comes towards me then from his place of darkness. I walk to the palace with his shadow close, hovering near me.

He approaches the palace with care. He knows that there are people of whom he should, even in death, be wary. I do not make a sound while he finds a space in this room to settle.

And then as soon as I whisper her name, my sister Iphigenia appears, first as a faint disturbance in the air. They edge
towards each other.

At the beginning, I feared for them. I believed that my sister
had come into our presence to remind my father of how she
died, to speak to him of how he watched coldly as she was sacrificed. I believed that she had come as accuser to cast him into
a darkness beyond the one where he lived.

Instead, my sister Iphigenia, dressed in wedding clothes,
more pale and beautiful as she became substantial, inched
soundlessly towards my father, ready to embrace him or hold
him or seek comfort from his ghost.

I wanted to ask her then if she did not remember. I wanted
to ask if the manner of her death had been erased from her
memory, if she lived now as if those things had not occurred.

Perhaps the days before her death, and the way death was
given to her, are nothing in the place where she is. Perhaps the
gods keep the memory of death locked up in their store, jeal-
ously guarded. Instead, the gods release feelings that were once
pure or sweet. Feelings that mattered once. They allow love to
matter since love can do no harm to the dead.

They approach each other, my father and my sister, their
movements hesitant. I am not sure that, once they have seen
each other, they still see me. I am not sure that the living interest them. They have too many needs that belong to themselves
only; they have too much to share.

Thus I do not speak to my father and my sister as their
spirits hover gracefully in this room. It is enough for me that I
have them here.

But there was a question I wished to ask them. I wanted to
know where my brother was. I divined some days that they

were alert to this; they were waiting for my question, but they drifted away before I could mention his name.

On one of those afternoons, soon after that encounter between Aegisthus and the man, there was sudden shouting from the corridor and then the sound of men running. And then I heard my mother's voice shrieking.

Once I realized that neither of my visiting spirits was aware of these noises, I did not move but waited with them. I heard more shouts coming from outside the palace; then one of the guards came to the door to let me know that my mother wished me to be with her now as the boys, the kidnapped boys, were finally about to arrive and we must be there to welcome Orestes.

As soon as my brother's name was spoken, I sensed my father and my sister become more densely present, more fiercely active. I felt my father tugging at my sleeve, my sister holding my hand. And then there was stillness as the sound of the guard's footsteps faded.

I decided to speak my brother's name myself. When I whispered it, and then said it again more loudly, I heard a voice, a quickened sound in response, but I could make out no words. My sister put her arms around me as though to hold me in place. I struggled for a moment to free myself as my father tugged at my sleeve again trying to get my attention.

"My brother is coming back finally," I whispered. "Orestes is coming."

"No," Iphigenia said. Her voice, or a voice that was like her voice, was almost loud.

"No," my father repeated, his voice fainter.

"I have to go and see my brother, to welcome him," I said.

And then I was no longer being held. I smiled in relief at

the thought that my father and my sister might have moved to the front of the palace so that they could be there when my brother appeared. I ran as fast as I could along the corridor and towards the door. Men's voices were rising in unison from outside the palace.

When I heard cheering and whistling, I wanted to be with my mother so that in those first moments Orestes would see us standing together to welcome him home.

When the first boy to arrive was lifted up and shown to the crowd, the cheering continued, but I could see how unsettled people quickly became. Some looked around as though searching to see if there was another person who had witnessed what they had witnessed—the pale, frightened face of the boy, his darting eyes like the eyes of an animal that had been held in a cage and was now even more frightened by the noise of freedom.

My mother caught my hand in hers. She watched and then gasped and let out small cries and began to shout at those around her, telling them that Orestes must be brought directly to her, that he was not to be lifted into the air by others, that he was the son of Agamemnon and he was not to be handled as the others were being handled.

It was then that I noticed Aegisthus standing in the crowd. His face was tense with worry, his brow furrowed, his eyes cast down. When he looked up, he caught my eye. I knew then that Orestes was not among those who had been released. I knew as other boys were lifted high with shouts of welcome and cries of relief that my brother was not among these boys and, as I looked around at some men who were glancing nervously at my mother, I became aware that they knew that too. Maybe everyone knew. The only one who did not know was my mother, who was all heat and breath and voice and blind expectation.

I watched Aegisthus as the boys were taken home by their joyous relatives. When the crowd began to disperse, he was left with two of the families whose sons had not returned either. They had crowded around him, and when he managed to assuage their fears with promises and assurances he was left with my mother. I stood beside her as she gazed at him imperiously.

"Where is Orestes?" she asked him.

"I do not know," he replied.

"Could you find out?" she asked.

"I understood that he was with the rest of the boys," he said.

"Did you?" she asked.

Her tone was cold, direct, controlled, but there was also rage in her voice.

"So who was that messenger, the one who left the smell behind him?" she asked.

"He came to tell me that the boys were on their way."

"And that Orestes was not among them?"

Aegisthus bowed his head.

"He will be found," he said.

"Have the men who accompanied the boys brought before me," my mother said.

"They did not come all the way," Aegisthus said. "They left the boys in the care of others once they had come part of the way."

"Have them followed and brought back," my mother said. "Do that now. When they are here, have them presented to me. This has gone on for long enough. I will not tolerate it any further. I will not be treated like this by you."

I kept away from my mother, but from the sounds of groups of men in the corridor and the pitch of my mother's voice as she issued instructions and the silence that ensued, I deduced that vicious antagonisms were at play around me. I slipped out quietly to my father's grave, but even there I felt that the air was unyielding and that no set of whispers, however imploring, would cause the dead to venture beyond their own realm.

That night when I went to the door of my mother's room, I heard her weeping and I heard Aegisthus' voice trying to soothe her and then her dismissing him, telling him to get away from her.

The following morning, I was woken by further shouts from outside the palace. Once more, I heard the sound of men in the corridor. I dressed carefully. I thought I would find my mother and Aegisthus and sit with them, if only to confirm what I had been told by one of the guards—that Aegisthus had, up to recently, known Orestes' whereabouts, had been responsible for him and had believed that he would return with the others, but that somehow Orestes and two other boys had got away from his henchmen.

Theodotus, the grandfather of Leander, one of the boys who was still missing, and the father of the third boy, Mitros, who was also not among the group that came home, appeared with some of their followers, demanding an urgent meeting with my mother and with Aegisthus.

Of the men who had stayed when my father went to battle, Theodotus was the most respected and revered. He had come often to the palace to talk about the whereabouts of the kidnapped boys, explaining each time that Leander was his only grandson.

I greeted these men waiting in the corridor. I followed them into my mother's room and I stood in the corner watching them as, without even looking at Aegisthus, Theodotus told my mother that they had ascertained from the boys who had come home that Orestes had escaped with two friends, one of them Theodotus' grandson, Leander, and the other Mitros' son, also called Mitros. The three boys had fled just days before the others were released, he said, having killed one of the guards. No one had any idea where they had gone.

"They will be found," my mother said, as though none of this were a surprise to her. "I have arranged that they will be found."

"All of the boys were beaten and badly treated," Theodotus said, as the other man stood humbly beside him. "Some of them were almost starved."

"This has nothing to do with us," my mother said.

Theodotus smiled at her faintly. As he bowed his head, he politely indicated that he understood why she might speak like this but that he did not believe her. Then he bowed towards me. But neither he nor the other man looked at Aegisthus. In the way they held themselves, they suggested that he was somehow beneath their contempt.

Some days later, the two men who had accompanied the boys most of the way were brought to the palace and escorted towards my mother's room like prisoners. They were told to wait in the corridor while men whose sons had come back gathered inside the room with Theodotus and Mitros. As I passed the two men, I turned and looked at them closely; they seemed to be terrified. I went into my mother's room once more and stood in the corner.

When the two men were brought before her, my mother immediately put up her hand to stop them speaking.

"We know he escaped with the two others. We don't need

to be told that. We simply need you to find them, all three of them. You must have some idea where they went when they escaped. What I am saying is: follow them, find them, bring them here. Nothing more, nothing less. No excuses. And start now. I am in anguish about this."

One of them made as though to speak.

"I don't want to hear anything from you," my mother said. "If you wish to ask a question, then ask Aegisthus on your way out. I want to see my son; that is what I want. I do not want to listen to anything else. And I do not want him or his companions ill-treated in any way. If I hear the slightest complaint from them, I shall personally cut your ears off, both of you."

They humbly left, with Aegisthus following. As the others went out of the room too, I waited behind, noticing how filled with pride my mother was. She was touching her own face tenderly, softly, and then gently putting her hands on her hair. She glanced self-consciously around her, like an ungainly peacock. She sat as if she had a large audience and might dismiss everyone at any moment or give some order that would impress everyone with its aura of pure willfulness and sharp menace. When she spotted me, she stood up and smiled.

"It will be so wonderful to have Orestes back," she said, looking around still at some imaginary crowd. "And perhaps it is for the best that he did not come with the others and have that mob to greet him. I will make sure that he arrives alone, with the other two boys perhaps coming a day or two later."

She smiled sweetly. I could not wait to get back to my room. I had a feeling that she would spend the rest of the day trying on dresses and checking her hair and her face, thus to be ready to perform when the time came to receive Orestes and be seen by the crowd as the adoring mother welcoming her son on his return.

*

Over the months that followed, Theodotus often came to the palace with the other man, Mitros. Both were always received formally, with others sometimes invited to witness the encounter, my mother talking with great authority about how they would have to be patient. Even though Aegisthus watched from the side, ushering the visitors out when it was time to go, they never once addressed him or looked at him.

My mother and I often spoke of Orestes and where he might be. I knew that relations between her and Aegisthus were difficult so I took my meals alone and went each day to the grave and returned with my father's spirit close to me. I whispered also to my sister. But Iphigenia's presence and that of my father were faint; at times they were hardly there.

I was aware of tensions all around me; there were days when no one moved in the corridors of the palace, days and nights when my mother did not leave her room and Aegisthus seemed more soundless than usual. For some time, they received no one, no one at all. When I ventured into the corridor, the guards stood immobile like figures that had been turned to stone.

*

One morning, I was woken by the sound of men's voices. Theodotus and Mitros had gathered ten other men, who stood in a row behind them, and they, in turn, had brought relatives and retainers to support them. I went past the guards to the front of the palace and approached Theodotus. I discovered that for some time my mother had been refusing to meet either him or Mitros, and that Aegisthus had told them that they were not to come to the palace again unless summoned.

"Tell your mother that we demand to be allowed into her presence," Theodotus said, as Mitros and the others stood beside him nodding.

I pointed inwards, emphasizing that all of them could enter the palace freely if they wanted. I spoke to the guards and told them that my mother had said that she wished to see these visitors. I ran ahead as the men, led by Theodotus and Mitros, walked through the corridors towards my mother's room, but they were soon stopped by other guards, who came running from all directions.

"Let me through," I told the guards.

Inside her room, my mother was standing at the window and Aegisthus was seated. They were looking at each other harshly as if difficult words had just been said, or might be uttered soon. They both turned to look at me with a mixture of malice and grim familiarity.

"Tell the men to wait," my mother said. "I will see them soon, but only two of them."

"I am not your messenger," I said.

Aegisthus stood and stared at me. It frightened me and made me edge towards the door. But then I grew brave and walked across the room and stood close to my mother. Once Aegisthus went outside, I heard the voices of the men becoming louder. Soon the men pushed their way into the room, led by Mitros, with Theodotus following. They stood facing my mother.

As Aegisthus moved quietly towards the corner, my mother found a seat, having crossed the room like someone with many

other important things on her mind. When she had made herself comfortable, she focused on Theodotus.

"How dare you crowd into my room? Is this what it has
come to? After all I have done?"

Theodotus smiled courteously. He was about to speak when
he was interrupted by Mitros.

"After all you have done! What have you done?" Mitros
asked. His face was red with anger.

"I have been working tirelessly to ensure the return of the
three boys," my mother said. "When the first two guards we
sent did not return, we dispatched others among our most
trustworthy—"

"You kidnapped the boys in the first place," Mitros interrupted. "It was done on your orders. And your own son!"

Aegisthus went angrily towards Mitros but was pushed
away by one of the other men. My mother put her hand to
her mouth and stared straight ahead. When Theodotus tried
to speak, Mitros interrupted again.

"And you, and you alone, murdered your husband," Mitros
said directly to my mother. "It was done by your hand. Your
hand alone."

My mother stood up. A few of the group crept towards the
door and quickly left the room.

"You made us sit and eat while his body lay there, and then
pretend that we had not witnessed your pleasure. You made us live
as though nothing had happened. You frightened us into silence."

"That's enough!" Theodotus shouted at Mitros.

"We came to say that we wish to send a small army to search
for the boys," Theodotus went on. "We have been trying to
meet you for some time to discuss this."

"You kidnapped the boys," Mitros said, pointing at my

mother. "It was done on your orders to frighten us. And it was your hand and no one else's that wielded the knife that murdered Agamemnon. It was not done on your orders. It was done by you! By you only."

"My friend is stricken with grief for his son," Theodotus said. "His wife is very delicate and may not have long to live."

"I am stricken with the truth," Mitros said. "I have spoken the truth. Will anyone deny that what I have said is true? Will you, yes, you?"

He looked to Aegisthus, who shrugged.

When he directed his attention to me, I almost smiled. What the maids in the kitchens and the guards in the corridors knew, but what had been only whispered, had been stated clearly for the first time. Now that the truth had been spoken, I felt free to go towards my mother and hold her hard by the wrists and shake her.

When I turned towards the men who were still there, I noticed that some of them appeared uneasy now, but others wore a determined, fearless look, seeming to have been emboldened by Mitros' words and by what I had done.

And then I glanced towards Aegisthus. He had begun staring at me again. I moved to the side, suddenly terrified. When I looked over again, I saw that his gaze had hardened and intensified. He was staring at no one else except me, as if I were the one who had openly accused my mother in public of kidnapping my brother and murdering my father, as if I were the one who would need to be dealt with when these men had left.

"You are hysterical. I have no interest in anything you have to say," my mother said to Mitros, before turning to Theodotus. "And no army, large or small, will be sent from here without my orders."

"We need to search for them," Theodotus said.

"We have sent men who know the terrain and we await their return," my mother said. "Let us meet again in some days, perhaps when tempers are less frayed. And perhaps you might ask your friend to withdraw the words he has spoken? I see that he has disturbed my daughter's fragile peace of mind with his lies. My daughter is not strong."

All of the men stood their ground.

My mother stood up and raised her voice.

"I insist that you leave at once, and if you"—she pointed her finger at Mitros—"approach the palace again, then I will have you detained immediately for spreading vile and malicious lies."

"You murdered your own husband with a knife," Mitros said. "You tricked him. And you had your own son kidnapped. And my son, and all the others. That man in the corner is just your puppet."

He pointed again at Aegisthus.

"I will call the guards and they will have you removed," my mother said.

"And your daughter!" Mitros said.

"My daughter?"

"You led her to be murdered."

My mother lunged towards him and tried to hit him across the face but he moved back.

"You led her to be murdered!" Mitros said again. "And you had that one"—he pointed at me—"locked up in a dungeon like a dog while you did your evil work murdering your husband."

He spat on the ground as two men dragged him out of the room. The last one to go was Theodotus, who turned to my mother and whispered: "In a few days, perhaps I could come alone? This has been a disgrace. None of us imagined that he would speak like this."

My mother offered him a crooked, exaggerated smile.

"I think you should take your friend home."

When they had all gone, I noticed that Aegisthus' gaze was still on me. As my mother turned as if to say something, I fled from the room.

*

Later, I was almost asleep when I felt a presence in the doorway. I knew who it was. I was expecting him.

"Do not come into my room," I said.

Aegisthus smiled as he stood there.

"You know why I am here," he said.

"Do not come into my room," I repeated.

"Your mother—" he began.

"I don't want to hear about my mother," I interrupted.

"It's difficult for her, this waiting, and these men do not help. You must not repeat to her what you heard today. She has asked me to convey that to you."

"I should not repeat what everyone heard? What was said in broad daylight?"

"And also, if your brother should come back, then it is essential that you do not discuss any of this with him."

"When is he coming back?"

"No one knows where he is. But he could return at any time. And it will be your mother's task to inform him what has happened."

"To misinform him, you mean?"

"Have I made myself clear? You must not discuss any of what was said today with him."

"He will find out. Someone will tell him."

"By which time he will have become accustomed to his mother's role and to mine. He will know that we look after everyone's interests. Everything else is in the past."

"You want him to trust you? After all that has happened?"

"Why would he not trust us?" He almost laughed. "He will trust you, I'm sure, as much as we all do."

"If I find that you have defied your mother, then you'll see a side of me that perhaps you have not seen yet. There is another floor below the dungeon."

He pointed his finger downwards as though I did not know where the dungeon was.

"And your mother, as I said, has asked me to emphasize that she does not want any of this discussed at all at any time, even if you and she are alone. She has heard enough about it."

He did not bother denying what Mitros had said. Instead, his demanding that I not repeat it even to my mother moved it merely into the realm of uncomfortable, awkward fact, something that might disrupt the ease my mother pretended to feel.

She had murdered my father and left his body to rot under the sun. She had sent me and my brother into darkness. She had arranged the kidnapping of the children. But she wanted all that set aside, as you might a plate of uneaten, unappetizing food.

I wanted to go to her room and insist that she hear me as I told her clearly once more what she had done to my brother and to me so that we would not be witnesses to the fact that she, with no permission from the gods, having consulted no one among the elders, decided that my father would die. I wanted to make sure that she heard me when I repeated what Mitros had said so that it would be heard by the gods themselves: that she alone had wielded the knife that killed my father.

I pictured her when she came back from my sister's sacrifice. I remembered her silences and her rages, her darting, shifting moods, her willfulness, her haughtiness.

Now it had been said in the open who she was. She was a woman filled with a scheming hunger for murder.

When she stood waiting to welcome my father, with Aegisthus inside the palace, it was the beginning of a long performance, a performance that started with smiles and ended with shrieks.

Did she not understand that the servants knew what she had done, that the servants had seen her leave my father's bloodied body, her eyes filled with satisfaction, and that the news of what she did had spread like fire in a dry and windy season?

Yet all day she and Aegisthus enacted their fiction. If they could keep us from reminding them of what they did, then they could live in a world of their own invention. They wanted silence so they could continue with their roles as the innocent ones since there were no other parts they could perform without feeling an urge to turn on each other and turn on us all. The role of murderess and kidnapper was, I saw, somehow beyond my mother's reach. For her, it was something that merely happened once. It was in the past and was not to be mentioned. And the role of puppet and assistant to a murderess was not a role that Aegisthus could easily play either without becoming hungry for more drama, more blood, more savagery.

As Aegisthus still stood and watched me, with all his malevolence on display, I saw that I was in danger unless I agreed to be the frail daughter, the sweet simpleton, who visits her father's grave and speaks to his ghost, the witness who barely remembered all of the evidence.

I would join them in the game of innocence for as long as

I needed to. I would assist my mother in her role as someone who had known grief and was now almost foolish, distracted, harmless. We would play the parts together even if my brother came back.

"We will be watching you," Aegisthus said. "And if your brother should appear, then we will be watching you more closely still. At any time if you want to visit the floor below the dungeon, you merely have to let me know. It is there for you. And it would be best, if you value your safety, still not to venture beyond the palace grounds. We would like to know where you are."

Once he had left, I told myself that I would, when the time was right, have my mother murdered. And I would, as soon as the first chance came, have Aegisthus murdered too. I would ask the gods to be on my side as I planned how this would be achieved.

*

Some days after the encounter between my mother and Mitros and Theodotus, I was stopped by one of the guards in the corridor when I had accompanied my father back to his grave and stayed there until his spirit returned to rest.

"I have a message for you," he said. "It is from Cobon, Theodotus' son. He wants you to go to their house. He says you must go there urgently. He cannot come here. He is afraid. They are all afraid. You must not mention that I have spoken to you."

"I am forbidden from leaving the palace and its grounds," I said.

"He would not ask if it were not important."

I felt at first that I could not go, and I wondered if this was a trap that had been set by Aegisthus for me. I wavered between deciding to go out by the side door I used to go to my father's grave and imagining bravely walking to the front and down the steps, aware that I would be watched by the guards and that Aegisthus would be quickly alerted to my departure. I wavered between moments of reckless courage when I was ready to defy him, and then the shivering knowledge that I could not face the dungeon again. I decided I would use the side door.

At my father's grave, I checked that there was no one watching. Furtively, I slipped between the gravestones, and found the old path that was overgrown, the path by the dried-up stream along which people used to carry the bodies to be buried. Few come this way anymore. No one wanted to be in these ghostly spaces.

What I noticed, even as I passed houses where I knew entire families lived, was shuttered silence. I realized quickly, as I flitted from shadow to shadow, that I should not have come out at all. I was sure that I had already been seen. As I made my way to the house of Theodotus, I was sure that some man would already have gone to the palace and, as a way of ingratiating himself, informed Aegisthus of my movements.

Even Theodotus' house was shuttered. I went around by the side and tapped on the window. Eventually, I heard someone whispering. As I waited, I could hear further movements from within the house, a lock being pulled back and footsteps. And then a woman's voice. After a while, Raisa, Cobon's wife, and her mother appeared at a door and beckoned me to enter. They whispered to me to follow them to an inner room that was almost fully dark.

As my eyes got used to the darkness, I saw that the whole family was there in the room—Theodotus' wife, Dacia, Raisa's parents and her sister and her sister's husband and their children, five or six of them gathered around their father and mother, and then also Raisa and Cobon's daughter, Ianthe. She gazed at me from a corner of the room, her two hands clenched into fists and held against her mouth. I had not seen her since she was a child; she was almost a young woman now.

"What has happened?" I asked.

None of them spoke as one of the children started to cry.

"Where is Theodotus?" I asked.

"That is why we asked to see you," Cobon said. "We thought that you might know."

"I know nothing."

"The men who took Leander, the same men, they came and took my father-in-law in the night," Raisa said.

"They didn't speak this time," Ianthe said, as she began to cry, "but the last time when they came for my brother, they said that they were here on the orders of your mother."

"I am not my mother," I said, and then immediately saw how accusing their looks were. I tried to think of something more to say that would make clear to them that I could not help them. In thinking, however, I had left silence for too long. I had allowed the accusing stares to mark me in some way.

"Can you ask her?" Cobon said gently. "Can you ask your mother?"

I understood that it would sound untrue if I explained to them how I lived and how distant I was from my mother and Aegisthus. These people sought help for themselves; they had no interest in hearing how afraid I was.

"I have no power," I said. "I am only—"

"And there is more," Raisa said, interrupting.

I wondered if they had taken someone else from the family. I looked from face to face in the semidarkness, unsure if someone else was missing.

"What?" I asked. "Tell me."

"Mitros," Cobon said.

"They took him too?"

"We don't know."

"He's not in his house?"

"There is no house," Raisa said quietly. "I'll take you out and show you where his house was."

"It's not safe to go out," her father said.

"They have taken my son and they have taken my husband's father," Raisa replied. "If they want me too, they can have me."

It did not occur to them that going out might not be safe for me either, as Raisa motioned me to come with her. I noticed how proud and defiant she was once she was outside the house. She was like a woman asking to be taken into custody, a woman ready to sacrifice herself. I walked slowly and carefully beside her.

When we came to the place where Mitros' house had been, there was nothing. Some trees and scrub, that was all. There was no sign that there had been a large house and a garden and olive trees all around it.

"Two days ago, there was a house here," Raisa said in a loud voice. "There was a family living in the house. Everyone who passed knew it was the house of Mitros. Now there is nothing. Those trees there were planted in the night. They were not there yesterday. They were taken from elsewhere. The house was reduced to rubble and then the rubble was carted away. The foundations were covered over. Where are the people? Where are Mitros' family? Where are Mitros' servants? Someone has tried to pretend that they never lived here. But they did. I remember them. I will remember them as long as I have breath."

By this time, people had gathered and were listening. Raisa then turned towards me. She wished me to witness this. I knew then that I would have to get away from her, but I did not want her to believe that I was in league with my mother and Aegisthus. I stood as though alone. I let my eyes linger on the space where the house had been. I did not lower my head. As I faced Raisa, I felt strengthened by her, enough to want to suggest that I was with her. But I was determined that no one among this crowd would be able to convey to Aegisthus or to my mother any words that I spoke.

What I wanted was Raisa to return home, and I wanted to return home too.

"Where is my son?" Raisa shouted to the crowd. "Where is my husband's father? Where are Mitros and his family?"

Then she looked at me.

"Will you ask your mother where they are?"

She was challenging me, waiting for a response. If I turned away without speaking, I knew, I would appear as an accomplice to my mother and her lover. If I stood my ground, on the other hand, I would be forced to reply.

I called to my father's ghost and to my sister's dead body. I called to the gods on high. I asked them to silence this woman, to make her move away from me.

As I stared at Raisa, it was my uncertainty that seemed to unsettle her. I tried to suggest that if the men could come in the night and make a house disappear, if they could take the two most powerful elders, then asking me to help was almost foolish.

But I also wished to emphasize that I was in possession of a power that came from the grave and from the gods, a power that could not easily be named or eliminated. I wanted her to know that, despite my weakness, I would, at some time in the future, prevail.

"I have no power now," I said. "But there will come a time. There will come a time."

Raisa turned and walked proudly back towards her own house and her own family. It was only when she was some distance away that I saw her body buckle and I heard her broken cries.

I filled my lungs with breath and did not move, forcing those who had been watching me to drift away. I would go back, I decided, through the open spaces. As I walked, I looked at nobody I met, but when I approached the palace, I saw the figure of Aegisthus waiting for me. He was smiling. He was the same figure of pure charm who had beguiled my mother those years before. He made as though to help me as I came near the steps. I allowed him to guide me as my mother's errant daughter, into the palace and through the corridors to my room.

*

In the years that followed, as I began to abandon hope that I would ever see my brother again, I realized that, as a woman with no husband, I was powerless and would remain so. All I had were my ghosts and my memories. Even my resolute will would mean nothing, would come to nothing.

I watched the men who came to my mother's table, the ones she had singled out from my father's soldiers to protect the places that my father had conquered. Sometimes they came to consult with her and remained for weeks.

On those nights when there were feasts for them in the dining room, I noticed a giddy watchfulness as every guest was aware that outside here the naked body of my father had once lain beside the body of a beautiful woman dressed in red whom he had brought back from the wars.

The guests were in the presence now of the woman who had murdered him, who had done so, it was known, without any permission from the gods. This gave my mother a strange, malignant power. It made her presence glow as the evening wore on. She dominated the room, yet no one seemed nervous; instead, they were excited, fired up, loquacious. Death and all its drama filled them with a satisfaction that lasted until the very end of the evening.

I believed at first that time and circumstances would cause any one of these men to realize how much power could come into his hands were I, with my sister dead and my brother missing, to become his wife.

I ordered the seamstresses to go through the wardrobe of my sister Iphigenia, always more elaborate than mine, since she was the favored one, to see what was left there after all the years. We selected some robes and dresses that might be adapted for a sister who was less beautiful.

At first, I did not wear what they made for me to any of the dinners, but I often tried them on in the afternoon and wore them when I was alone.

As I attended the dinners, I imagined myself in my sister's robes, my hair carefully coiled and my face whitened with black lines around my eyes. I imagined what it would be like to be noticed and to make an impression.

I would remain silent, I told myself, once I was dressed in these new clothes. I would smile, but not too much, and I would seem content, as though I possessed some inner light.

I watched the visitors and dreamed of how easy it might be for one of them to stay here with us, and how we would secretly arrange our alliance. I imagined how unsettled my mother and Aegisthus would become as I took a husband.

We would have guards fully loyal to us, and sources of treasure that were ours alone. And we would bide our time, or move fast, as we judged right. We would do what I could not do on my own.

I would choose my evening. I would decide between one of the smaller dinners that my mother held, or a larger occasion, perhaps a celebration of some fresh victory, some new set of spoils.

When news came that there had been a revolt in one of the more distant places and that the rebels had held out for weeks, creating murder and mayhem, killing the wife of an old ally of my father's and putting his children to the sword, we soon learned that the warrior himself, Dinos, and a small band of his soldiers had survived the initial massacre and finally defeated the marauding forces, so that peace had been restored. Many executions had taken place.

The idea that Dinos, who had lost so much, had been fully loyal caused my mother great joy. She sent him well-equipped forces to assist him and also many personal gifts. She granted land to his father, who lived near the palace. And she also sent one of Aegisthus' closest allies to replace Dinos, should he wish to return to see his father and be received in glory. She spoke often of his bravery, of how handsome he was and how much he was admired.

It struck me then that such a husband would set me free. He would be strong and cunning enough to withstand my mother and Aegisthus and, since news of his exploits had spread, his name would be known by all. Should he wish to marry again, he would not be opposed. And should he wish to marry the daughter of Agamemnon, with whom he had often served, then that would seem natural, almost part of what was due to him.

We would be careful at first, I thought. He could advise my mother and Aegisthus. And slowly he would begin to see how poisonous they both were, how they stank of blood, and how necessary it was for both my mother and her lover to be sent to a place where they could cause no further damage.

Preparations began for Dinos' arrival. It was agreed that a large spectacle in the streets would be put on to honor him and this would be followed by a feast.

For that, I decided to have the seamstress create for me a sumptuous robe that was close in its shape and texture to one that my sister had once worn. Each day, a maid came to refashion my hair and another servant came with unguents and sweet water to soften my skin. After a few weeks, when the dress was ready, the seamstress and her helpers and the other servants came to my room and watched me as I prepared myself.

When I was alone with the spirits of my father and my sister, I put on the dress and pulled my hair back so my face would be clearly seen. As I proudly moved around the room I felt that I was under their care. Before the feast for Dinos, I wanted their approval.

For several days before the spectacle and the feast, Dinos was in the palace. He was received by my mother and Aegisthus, who held, I was told, formal meetings with him about supplies of troops and other support that he needed to ensure no further rebellions took place. There was also a private dinner for him and his father at which, I was informed by one of the servants, he expressed himself inconsolable at the loss of his wife and his children. But he did not weep. At all times, he maintained a distance, like a commander. He was handsome, one of my maids told me, one of the most handsome men she had ever seen.

Since I did not see my mother during these days, she sent word by one of her servants that she would be less than pleased if I did not attend the feast, although it would, for safety reasons, be best not to go into the streets beforehand for the spectacle.

I imagined entering the great dining room at the moment when everyone was already there. I saw the door opening and I heard the silence, the few seconds when no one seemed to be speaking, when attention could easily be drawn towards the door. I saw Dinos' father move towards me, making space for me as I went with him towards the main table. And then I imagined Dinos himself turning.

All afternoon, the maids worked on my hair and my skin. The dress was taken for one further alteration and then returned. An hour before the guests assembled, I was ready. Once the lines had been put around my eyes, I asked the seamstress and the servants to leave me so that I could compose myself. One servant, however, I asked to remain close to my room so she could tell me when the guests were all there.

Slowly, I summoned up my sister's spirit. I touched my face as though it were her face. I whispered to my father. When the servant beckoned, I was ready. I walked alone down the corridor to the dining room. I stood back as the servant opened the doors and then I walked alone into the room, looking at no one directly, but ready to catch the eye of anyone who looked at me.

What I heard first was my mother's voice. She was telling a story about how, when she had heard the news of the insurrection, she had appealed immediately to the gods and then how, on the advice of the gods, she had sent her most trusted soldiers to go to Dinos' aid and put down the revolt with speed and efficiency. She spoke of the gods in a way that was perfunctory, almost dismissive, and that, I thought, might have been noticed by everyone in the room.

And then she saw me. I was still standing at the door. In one second, when I raised my eyes, I caught her gaze. She stopped speaking.

"Oh, no," she said in a louder voice than before. "I have heard all week that there was something afoot with Electra, but I never foresaw this."

She brushed guests aside as she stepped towards me, but there was still a wide space between me and her, enough for her to have to shout for me to hear her.

"And who is responsible for this?" she asked.

I glanced at some of the others, who were staring at me. There was no one close to me. The doors behind me had been shut.

"Oh, go and sit down," she said, "before too many people see you. Aegisthus, can you take Electra to the table and keep her company? Or find someone who will."

Aegisthus whispered to one of his associates, who accompanied me to the table. I sat between him and one of his friends and looked away or stared straight ahead as they made idle comments to each other. A few times, I directed my gaze at Dinos, but he did not once acknowledge my presence. There were many dishes served and then fine speeches. The wine flowed. For most of the guests, it seemed, the memory of my father's murder had faded. But it had not faded for me. As I watched my mother and Dinos speaking, as I saw my mother's eyes flash as she told him some story, as I watched her exude all her charm as she listened to him, I thought of my father until he was more real, more vehemently present in this room than any of these people who were in thrall to my mother and her lover and their power.

At the end of the evening, I managed to leave as others were departing. And thus no one noticed me as I made my way back to my room.

All I wanted then was a sign from my father and my sister that my brother was still alive and that he would return. But I waited to ask, I waited until I was sure, until I knew that the saying of his name would not merely cause disruption in the air.

One day, I whispered it. I said the name. At first, there was silence. In another whisper, I asked them to send me a signal if he was still alive. I stood against the door to make sure we would not be disturbed.

But there was nothing, no sign.

Later, I went again to my father's grave. I was sure my sister's spirit was still with me. The air was thundery, the light purple. As I waited at the grave, I tried to move nearer my father's spirit than I had ever been before. And it was then, as the rain came in heavy drops, that I understood what would happen.

Orestes was alive. I knew that then. But he was somewhere else, in a house where he was safe, where he was protected. It would be some time before he would return. But it was here, at this grave, that I would see him.

He would come, I was told, he would come in time. All I had to do was wait.

Orestes

The stones, carefully chosen to defend them from the dogs in the farm below, were heavy and slowed them down as they set out. It was the early morning. Leander, speaking about strategy and tactics, was so filled with purpose as they walked on that Orestes understood it was a way of distracting them both from thinking about Mitros and the old woman and the house that, no matter what happened, he imagined they would not see again.

Once they neared the place where they had been surrounded by dogs, they moved even more cautiously. Soon, after every few steps, Leander put his finger to his lips and indicated that they should stop and listen. But there was only intermittent birdsong and the distant roar of waves crashing against rocks.

When they reached the house, they saw that it was uninhabited, almost derelict. They stood still, looking behind them and then to the side. As they walked warily along the overgrown path to the door, Orestes listened for the sound of dogs or goats, but there was nothing. The door was half-rotted and it swung unsteadily on its hinges when he pushed it in.

Orestes pictured the scene he remembered—the man and his wife, the dogs, the goats, the aura of husbandry and harmony that he and his two companions seemed to have threatened. He wondered how it had ended, if the man and his wife had been frightened by something, or if they had made a slow, rational decision to leave.

Since they had presumed that they would be attacked, that the farmer would set dogs on them at the first sign of their approach, and since they came tense and fully alert, the emptiness they found, the silence, was almost disappointing. For a second, as he caught Leander's eye, Orestes felt that his companion was also let down by finding nothing here.

Leander motioned to Orestes, suggesting that they move on. He said that they should drop one of their sacks of stones but still carry the other in case they were attacked by dogs along the way.

They walked towards the morning sun. What was strange was that there was no sign of life at all, other than foxes in the undergrowth, some rabbits and hares running away in fright, and the sound of crickets and birdsong. The houses they passed had either been burned down or had fallen into ruin.

Orestes would not have demurred had Leander suggested that they return to the old woman's house, that their journey so far had been just a useful way to check the terrain. But Leander appeared determined to proceed.

*

"The only safe way now is to climb," Leander said. "Soon, if we keep on these paths, we will meet someone. There will have to be streams in the mountains. If we ration what food we have, there is enough for two or three days more."

"How far are we from the palace?" Orestes asked.

"It's hard to say. But I'm sure that this is the best way to go. I can tell the direction by the sun."

Orestes nodded. He could sense that their time in the house

of the old woman already meant little to Leander. It was merely where they had been. He was fully focused now on their journey, and on making it safe for them.

They had been climbing, and then, having found quail's eggs and wild fruit, they rested for some hours before setting out again. Leander looked regularly at the sky, but he often seemed unsure which way they should take. Since none of the mountain paths was straight, it was hard to press forward in a single direction.

The palace was on a plain. Thus no matter how much they climbed or descended, they would have to walk two days or maybe even three through flat and inhabited countryside before they reached it. If they could find a habitation, Orestes thought, they could identify themselves and offer some reward to anyone who would accompany them on the rest of their journey, but then they could also be kidnapped again.

As the rocky landscape gave way to soft hills, Leander, having set a trap, managed to catch and kill a rabbit. He had carried with him materials to light a fire, which he did with some difficulty. Although they were hungry, it was hard to eat the meat, which was burned on the outside and almost raw on the inside.

When they started walking again, they came across a flock of sheep and stood for a moment listening.

"We might be much closer than we think," Leander said. "Or we might have spent a day going in the wrong direction. We had to follow the valley."

Since they had found the sheep, Orestes presumed that they would soon come across a village and a cluster of houses, but the landscape appeared more and more bare and desolate and there was a whistling wind that blew sand into their eyes.

"Are we coming near the sea?" Orestes asked.

"I don't know, but at least we are safe. The main thing is to be alert. Someone could be watching us even now."

Orestes looked around, aware of how exposed they were, how the dull colors and the scarce light would make it easy for someone, even a group, to watch and wait without being seen.

All they could do was walk. Orestes did not need Leander to tell him that once the walk was downhill, they would have to reach somewhere sheltered with less wind.

When the wind stopped whistling, it was replaced by mist, which came first in swirls and eddies. Sometimes the sun burned through it and they could see into the distance, but at other times the mist thickened and enveloped them in a dense fog and they had to keep close to each other.

As they made their way forward, Orestes ceased to care about hunger or thirst, he ceased even to feel tiredness. He felt the warmth of Leander's shoulder when he rested his hand on him and the strength of his will and this gave him comfort.

Later, as the fog lifted, they could see a thin ridge that was cut through by a fast-flowing stream. They sat down by the stream, cupping the water in their hands to drink.

"I know where we are," Leander said. "There is a village half a day away. I came here once with my uncles and cousins. We were hunting. My mother's family comes from the village. If we can reach it, then we are safe. The house where her brothers live is there. But we have to be careful—there are some houses on the way and I don't know who lives in them."

Orestes could feel Leander's increasing eagerness. Moving quickly now, he seemed even more locked into his own world. It was as though he had already arrived at his destination. All the houses they passed were empty, and when they searched for food they found nothing. The houses were not in ruins but they looked as if they had been abandoned for some time.

"Leander," he said.

"What?"

"Is it wise for me to come with you?"

"Why?"

"Because of my father or my mother."

"I think it's best for us not to say who you are. We'll tell them that you are just one of the other boys who was kidnapped."

This was, Orestes saw, something that Leander had already worked out.

Once they came to the house of his mother's family, Leander shouted out his own name. As people slowly appeared, they ran towards him and embraced him, repeating his name, with one woman insisting as she began to weep that he had his grandfather's voice and she would have recognized it anywhere.

Orestes stood apart until one of them noticed him. He was not introduced by name, but was welcomed into the house almost as warmly as Leander. He saw how dignified Leander remained as more and more of his relatives came to greet him.

During the day and night they spent in the house, the family barely spoke to Orestes. It became apparent to him that Leander had told them not to speak freely in the presence of his companion.

When he went to the room they had given him, he expected that he would be joined by Leander. But Leander did not join him. Instead, he came into the room in the morning to wake him and let him know that they would wait until nightfall to leave, as the moon was full enough and it would be safer to move through the countryside by its light.

When they set out, they were accompanied first by two of

Leander's uncles, who left them at a crossroads. Once they were alone, Orestes ventured to ask Leander if he had learned what had happened while they had been away.

"Things are bad," Leander said.

"Where?"

"In my house," Leander said.

He did not explain further.

"We must go to my house first, both of us," Leander said eventually.

"Why?"

"That's the advice I have been given. This time, I will tell them who you are."

"Is my mother still alive?" Orestes asked.

"Yes."

"Electra?"

"Yes."

"In the palace?"

"Yes."

They did not speak again for some time. Leander walked alongside him, linking arms with him, catching his hand at times and holding it or putting his arm around him and slowing down as they made their way through the night. While Orestes was comforted by this, he also understood that it was perhaps a way for Leander to tell him that they were together now but would soon be apart, that what had happened between them in the old woman's house would not happen again.

As the dawn came up, Orestes observed a lightness in Leander as he gazed around him in animated wonder, stopping to examine even the smallest thing. Orestes did not want to break the spell by asking Leander how long he should stay at his house. They had also not discussed what to do about Mitros' family, who would surely come looking for their son when they discovered that Leander had returned.

They walked by houses they recognized. Dogs barked as they passed, but Orestes felt no sense of danger. Soon Orestes found that he had passed the place where he might have turned in the direction of the palace; he was quietly following Leander towards his own house.

Near the house itself, Leander clicked his fingers and whistled and then one of the dogs from the house came close to him. Leander whispered to the dog and rubbed its head as the dog snuggled against him, wagging its tail. Leander knelt down and put his face against the dog's face. With all the dogs following them, they walked around to the back.

It was obvious that everyone inside was still sleeping. Orestes wondered at what point Leander was going to shout his father's name or his mother's name or that of his grandfather or his sister. Instead, Leander tried the doors but they were all locked. They sat on a step in silence, listening, until a servant going to get water opened a door and saw them. She instantly dropped the receptacle in fright and ran inside, pursued by Leander. Catching her, he put his hand over her mouth and held her by the wrist as he explained in a low voice who he was. With Orestes standing near him, Leander told the frightened servant that he did not want the family to be woken with the news of his arrival. He wanted food and drink placed on the table for himself and Orestes as though it were a normal morning and he had never been away.

The servant seemed nervous and unsure as she prepared the table and brought eggs and cured meat and bread and cheese and olives. Even as she found the pitcher and went outside again to fetch water, she glanced back warily at the two visitors and stood well away from them once she had returned.

Leander's mother was the first to come into the room. As soon as she saw them, she screamed and ran along the corridor to the bedrooms. When Leander followed her, Orestes could hear Leander's mother calling all the family, urging them to get up quickly and gather in the room that could be locked.

"They have come back," she shouted. "The men have come back."

Leander walked quickly down the corridor, shouting his own name, shouting that he had returned. But nothing he said calmed the crying that came from the rooms. After a while, he returned to the kitchen and spoke to the servant.

"Can you tell them that I am Leander and I have come back?"

"They won't believe me," she said.

"Can you cut a lock of my hair and show it to my mother?" he asked.

"Your hair has changed," she said. "You have changed. I didn't recognize you."

"Can you not convince them?"

"They are afraid since the old man was taken."

Leander looked darkly at Orestes. Since he did not express surprise, this, clearly, was what he had learned in the house of his mother's family.

Leander stood at the kitchen door.

"It's Leander," he shouted. "I was kidnapped and I escaped and now I am home. Please come out. I am at the table. I am Leander."

He returned and sat down.

"Let's just eat," he said to Orestes. "One of them will have to come out."

Orestes wondered if he could slip away. He was aware that Leander barely noticed him now. Their arrival, which Orestes could see he had carefully planned, had not worked out the way he had foreseen. As they ate, still watched over nervously by the servant, no one appeared. Eventually, Leander stood up again and went outside and began calling in through the windows, shouting out his own name, telling them once more that he had come back.

The first to emerge was a young woman. She stood at the entrance to the kitchen staring at both visitors, not speaking. She was in her nightclothes. Orestes saw how tall she was and how black her hair and how dark her eyes. When Leander moved from his chair to embrace her, she stepped backwards, recoiling.

"We want you to leave," she said. "There has been enough suffering. Who else do you want to take?"

"Ianthe," Leander said softly. "You are my sister. Is there anything I can do to make you believe that I am Leander?"

She let out a deep cry before running down the corridor.

Soon they came in ones and twos and stood in the kitchen doorway, Cobon and Raisa and Raisa's parents and Cobon's mother, Dacia, and another couple with some children whom Orestes presumed must be part of Raisa's wider family.

Raisa was the first to cross the kitchen floor and touch Leander.

"Who is that?" she asked, pointing to Orestes.

"Orestes," Leander said.

"What is he doing here?" she asked.

"He escaped with me."

"And Mitros?"

"We must go and tell his family that he died," Leander said.

Raisa let out a sound, almost like a laugh.

"There is nowhere to go. All of them were killed or taken."

"All of who?"

"All of Mitros' family."

"When?"

"When your grandfather was killed or taken."

"I didn't know that," Leander said, as they all watched him. "They didn't tell me that in the village."

Slowly, Ianthe approached him again. She began to touch Leander's face and his shoulders and his back and chest. But still the others hovered at the entrance to the kitchen.

"We thought that you were dead," Ianthe said. "It will take us some time to believe that you are alive."

"Did anyone follow you here?" Cobon asked as he crossed the room.

"No one," Leander said.

"Are you sure?"

"Yes."

"Why has he come here with you?" his father asked, pointing to Orestes.

"I was told in the village that it would be safer," Leander said.

"Perhaps that was wise," Cobon said. "He should stay here for now so that they don't know you've arrived."

"Who should not know?" Orestes asked.

"Your mother and Aegisthus," Cobon said. The hatred in his voice was palpable.

*

Leander and Orestes possessed a set of references that were like a private language; in the old woman's house, the discussion of weather or food or farm animals had evolved into a sort of mild banter with many comments exchanged on each other's failings and incapacities. Now they had to restrain themselves when the family was there, they had to try not to talk too much, since the talk between them disturbed the others.

Orestes noticed how guarded everyone in the household was. Cobon went out every day to oversee supplies of food, or to go to the market, but he came back sullen and downcast. It became clear that the only news worth imparting would be news of his father's whereabouts, but since Cobon did not speak, it was presumed that he had found out nothing in the lanes or in the marketplace.

Ianthe alone seemed to understand or appreciate how Orestes and Leander spoke and she showed this only when she was on her own with them. The rest of the time she joined the family in their silent disapproval of the two newcomers' way of talking and joking with each other.

A few times in the first days, they had tried to discuss their escape and talk about the house of the old woman but they had been met by puzzlement and vacant expressions. All of the family spent their time embracing Leander and telling him about the morning when he was kidnapped. But no one wanted to know in any detail precisely where he had been, or what had happened to him. He had been away from them; that was enough.

In the house, Orestes soon observed that there were whisperings between the men in which Leander was included and from which he was left out.

Since Leander's mother's father could not keep his voice down, Orestes heard them talk of the need for Leander to go back to the village of his mother's family and join them in seeking out one of his mother's brothers, who had fought with

Agamemnon in the war and returned with him victorious, only
to be led away with the captured slaves.

They were ready now for a revolt, Orestes heard the old
man saying, as their captors had grown lazy and less alert, and
were not as well armed as they used to be. The captors would
not be easy to overthrow, the old man said, but there might
never be a better time. Leander should leave soon.

*

Slowly and, it seemed, deliberately, the family found a way of
bringing Leander into their conversations and disrupting the
private way he and Orestes had of communicating. In doing
this, they managed to ignore Orestes. When Leander witnessed this, it made him uncomfortable, but all his efforts to
have Orestes included in the life of the house failed.

When Orestes told him finally that he wanted to go home,
he did not express surprise.

"Your sister goes to the graveyard each afternoon," Leander
said.

"Have you seen her?"

"My mother and my sister have."

"If we go there, will we see her?"

"Once you leave this house, you'll be noticed. They'll want
you back in the palace."

"Is there something I shouldn't tell them?"

"Don't tell them that we stayed with my mother's family
on the way. And you mustn't repeat anything you heard in this
house."

"Can I tell them that I came back with you?"

Leander hesitated before he replied.

"My father was concerned about drawing attention to my

return. That's why he wanted you to stay here, so they would not know. But he agrees that it might be better now for you to go. Someone will find out you're here. Maybe say as little as possible."

"Is there anything—?"

"If you discover anything about my grandfather, you must send word. Even the smallest thing."

"Who captured him?"

"Orestes, don't ask."

"Did Aegisthus kidnap him?"

"Someone close to Aegisthus. Perhaps it was someone close to Aegisthus."

"I will do what I can."

After a few days, guided by Raisa and Ianthe, they went to the graveyard in the afternoon, using the narrow lanes and paths. As they hid behind a gravestone, Orestes watched Electra, standing at a grave, whispering prayers and raising her arms towards the sky.

"That is your father's grave," Raisa whispered.

It was hard for Orestes to imagine that the man he remembered, his large, imposing father, was lying inert below the ground, his body reduced to its bones.

Slowly, they approached the grave, Raisa and Ianthe remaining in the distance. When Electra looked up, Orestes felt an urgent need to go towards her and embrace her, but he felt a need just as pressing to keep her at bay, as though her presence represented the real world in all its hardness and he preferred to remain in the soft, temporary cocoon that had been made for him.

At first she did not look at him but directed her attention to Leander. Then she fixed her eyes sharply, completely, on Orestes.

"My prayers have been answered. The gods have smiled on me."

"I have brought him home," Leander said gently to Electra. "I have delivered him safely to you."

A number of palace guards moved quickly in their direction before Leander stepped away from them and turned towards his mother and his sister. As Orestes' eyes followed him, Leander did not look back.

*

The guards ran ahead to let his mother know that her son had finally returned. As he and Electra walked towards the palace on the path that led from the graveyard, his mother was standing alone waiting for him, fully unprotected and utterly vulnerable. When he was very close to her, she raised her arms towards the sky.

"This is all I have wanted," she said. "And I must give thanks."

His mother embraced him and made him follow her into the palace, shouting out instructions about his room and what food they would have and calling for Aegisthus to come from wherever he was. She embraced him further and kissed him and directed servants to find her a tailor who could make new and suitable attire for her son.

Once Aegisthus came, Orestes followed the example of Leander when they were with his mother's family in the village. He attempted to be dignified. He edged away as though he had larger matters to consider when he saw that his mother's lover wished to embrace him. And all of the time, he noticed how keenly Electra observed him.

The next day, when he was being fitted for new clothes, his mother came into the room and circled him, giving elaborate advice to the tailor. She was all warmth and bustling comment.

"You have become so tall," she said. "You are taller than your father was."

A shadow crossed her face as she spoke and there was a sort of nervousness in her voice.

"I have something to ask you," he said.

"There must be many things you want to find out."

"Yes, there are, but just now I want to ask if you know anything about Leander's grandfather."

"Nothing," his mother said. "Nothing at all."

Her face reddened as she held his gaze.

"It has been a very difficult time," she continued, "and there are many rumors. Have they asked you to inquire about him?"

"No, but they said that he has been kidnapped. They're worried."

"It is most unfortunate. But it's best not to become involved in what I imagine is a dispute between families. I hope you understand that."

Orestes nodded.

"And the most important thing for us is that you are home. Maybe we should not think about anything else for the moment."

*

Even though his mother and his sister treated him as a boy, asking if he had enough to eat and if his bed was comfortable enough, everywhere he went in the palace he was greeted with respect, sometimes with a sort of awe. For the guards and the servants, he was his father's son, come back to take his rightful place.

This meant that when he walked through the corridors, or even when he was alone sometimes, he became aware of his role and his importance. Sometimes, however, it was as though he were still in the house of Leander's family. His mother had a way of cutting off all conversation by constantly thanking the gods for his return and punctuating this with many mentions of how much he had been missed and how much she and Aegisthus had done to effect his release.

Like his mother, Electra was happier offering him accounts of what his absence had meant to her and how relieved she was now that he had returned. He found that both his mother and his sister became nervous if they thought that he was even going to speak; if he seemed ready to say something, they rushed to ask him further questions about the state of his comfort, as if to make clear that, as far as they were concerned, he was still the boy, the son, the younger brother, who had been kidnapped and had now come home.

Like the family of Leander, they had no interest, as far as he could make out, in what had happened to him and where he had been. Aegisthus always smiled when he saw Orestes, but at meals he allowed Clytemnestra to dominate, leaving the room at intervals when one of his minions came with a message for him, a frown often darkening his face.

From the beginning, Orestes was warned about his safety; usually several guards followed him wherever he went. Once, however, when he diverted their attention, he made his way to Leander's house, only to be coldly told by Raisa that Leander was no longer there and she did not know his whereabouts.

One day, as he was sitting at the table in his mother's room with his mother and Aegisthus and Electra, he saw that they had run out of easy topics and had exhausted the subject of him and his comfort. He felt a tension in the room and looked from one to the other to see who would attempt to break it. He could almost hear his mother trying to think of something soft and pacifying to say.

"You know," she finally began, "there is a line of people each morning to see me, to ask me about land and water rights, or some come to consult me about inheritance and old disputes. Aegisthus says that it is too much, that we must send those people away. Some of the visitors could even be dangerous. But I know them. I knew those people when your father was alive. They come because they trust me as they trusted your father. In the mornings sometimes I have them brought into the palace. And often that is enough for them, and perhaps even for those left waiting. We have allowed them to come into the palace. I use that room where your father's guards used to be. I sit and I listen. Someday soon, Orestes, you must come with me and help me. You must listen too. Will you come with me?"

He found himself nodding coldly, as he thought Leander might have done, while his mother continued talking about all the tasks she had, going into more and more excited detail as the others remained silent.

"Can you tell me what happened after my father came back from the wars?" Orestes interrupted.

His mother put her hands to her mouth, looking nervously at Aegisthus and making as though to stand up before settling back in her chair. Then she cleared her throat and looked at him sharply.

"We are the most fortunate people," she said. "We are so very lucky to be alive. And for that we have to thank Aegisthus. He was the one who found out about the conspiracy against all of us and it was his supporters who came in time to quash the revolt that would have meant the end of us all."

Electra stared at the floor and then at the window.

"Who killed my father?" Orestes asked.

"That is what I was coming to," his mother replied. "Some of your father's own men were plotting against him. Oh, they looked like his friends! Oh, they gave the impression that they were happy to obey him! I must admit that I saw nothing strange when he arrived. Perhaps it was because I was so relieved to have him home that I suspected nothing. I was so relieved to have all the burdens of office lifted from me."

She stopped and put her hands to her mouth again and looked towards the window.

"But what happened?" Orestes asked.

"I can hardly say it," his mother replied. "We found out in time to rescue you and your sister, and in time for me to be hidden away too. But for your father, it was too late, it was too late. I cannot bear to think of it."

Her voice was shaking.

"Rescue me?" Orestes asked. "Did you say 'rescue' me?"

"We tried to make sure you were safe," his mother said.

"Why was I taken so far away by those men," he asked, "if they just wanted to rescue me and make sure I was safe?"

"To make sure that your life would be spared," his mother replied. "And to make sure that no one among our enemies would find you. They would have come for you if we had not done that."

"Who gave the order to take me to that place and not to some other place?"

"It was a mistake," she said. "We soon realized it was a mistake. When I thought about it later, I knew it was a mistake."

Her voice began to quaver.

"You see, Orestes, I had no control over those men. That was Aegisthus' doing, but he had no control either. I thought it was the safest thing to do. And then we sent those two men looking for you and they did not come back. And then we sent others, but they could not find you. And I thought I had failed and we had lost you. I believed that your father was lost and that you were lost too. And your sister Iphigenia too. I thought that I had only Electra. They told us when they came back from looking for you that you could not be found. We did everything, but we had no control. Aegisthus, did we have control?"

Aegisthus knocked over his drink. Quickly, as he retrieved it, he gave Orestes' mother the fiercest, most threatening look. And then he calmly refilled his glass.

"It was a time filled with panic," his mother went on. "And we tried to do our best. And all I can do is thank the gods that we at least are safe."

"I was not safe where you sent me."

"Orestes," his mother said, "it was not my doing."

Orestes pushed his chair back and stood up and moved across the room.

"Why is Aegisthus here?" he asked.

"He is here to guard us."

"Why is he here in the room with us? At the table with us?"

Orestes noticed Electra's mouth open in surprise.

"There has been a revolt," his mother said.

"Is that why he needs to sit with us?" Orestes asked, looking directly at Aegisthus. "Surely we can have our meals without him at the table?"

"Orestes," his mother said, "he is all I have. We are all in danger."

As Orestes returned to the table, passing Aegisthus, he lingered behind him and reached down and tossed Aegisthus' hair, as if fondly and familiarly, just as the old woman used to do with Mitros.

Aegisthus stood up as if he had been threatened or attacked.

"Orestes, do not do that!" his mother shouted.

"I am sure he is very welcome here," Orestes said and took his seat again.

*

Later, when he went over what his mother had said, it was her voice he remembered, and the sad, perplexed expression on her face when she mentioned his father and Iphigenia. He had not intended to challenge Aegisthus as openly as he did. He had said what he did almost as a joke, but somehow in the saying it had turned, gone out of his control, in a way that such a conversation between himself and Leander would never have, but would have led instead to laughter. And then he had tossed Aegisthus' hair to make clear that he meant him no harm. The response from Aegisthus and his mother showed him how much on edge they were.

When Electra came to his room that evening, he was about to explain this to her when she said that she could not stay for long, but needed him to know that he had to be careful, that he was being watched and that every word he said was being noted.

"Watched by whom?" he asked.

"They need to know whose side you are on."

"Do you mean my mother and Aegisthus?"

"Watch everything you say. Ask no more questions."

She looked towards the door as though there might be someone listening.

"I must go," she whispered.

The following day, when Orestes was going from his own room to his mother's quarters, he saw Aegisthus coming in his direction. Orestes stopped, ready to greet Aegisthus, pleased to have a moment with him uninterrupted, a moment when he might, if he were allowed to speak, refer in some way to what had happened the previous day. Aegisthus, however, as soon as he saw Orestes, turned as if he had forgotten something and walked away.

Each day, Orestes formed the habit of spending time with both his mother and Electra. He sat with his mother in a room at the front of the palace in the late morning. Often they saw supplicants, but usually they were alone. One day, when a visitor had spoken about a revolt, she waited until she was on her own with her son before referring to the subject again.

"You heard us talking about a revolt," she said. "There have always been revolts. There are always factions and there is always unrest. We are always at war. We get daily reports. And what I learned from your father and what you must learn is that a trusted friend is the one you can least trust. For each ally, I have a shadow ally, and even then I have other shadows, all of them watching, all of them reporting. That is how we keep power, by never trusting. I will take you through who they are. You can also talk to Aegisthus, who is always vigilant. Orestes, our enemies have to be lucky just once but we must be vigilant every second of every day. Now that you have returned, you can become my eyes and ears. But you must trust no one."

What struck him was how different his mother could be when they were eating together, or receiving a guest, or when he was walking with her in the garden. She could be worried one minute and then all chatter and easy, friendly talk.

Electra let it be known that she was not to be disturbed for much of the afternoon. She went each day to her father's grave and then returned to her room. By the time the sun was going down, she would receive him. When he referred to her warnings about what he should say and do, she brushed him off, and when he asked her if she knew the names of the men who had killed his father, or anything about Leander's grandfather, she went silent and pointed to the door.

Instead, in this time they had alone, his sister became interested in where he had been. She was less anxious in his company. When he told her what had happened when he was taken away and how he had escaped, she paid close attention.

Although he went into great detail, he did not tell her about the killing of the guard or of the two men. And he tried not to say too much about Leander. But it was the house of the old woman that interested Electra most. He found that telling her about the old woman and Mitros gave him a sort of comfort and he looked forward each day to seeing his sister.

Sometimes, Electra spoke of the gods and her belief in them, invoking their names and speaking of the power they had.

"We live in a strange time," Electra said. "A time when the gods are fading. Some of us still see them but there are times when we don't. Their power is waning. Soon it will be a different world. It will be ruled by the light of day. Soon it will be a world barely worth inhabiting. You should feel lucky that you were touched by the old world, that in that house it brushed you with its wings."

He did not know how to reply to this. Once Electra had spoken of the gods, she would look desolate, and then, when she had checked that no one was listening at the door, she would begin to speak of what was happening in the world outside the palace. When she told him about the revolt, he knew not to repeat what his mother had said, that there were always revolts. Instead, he listened carefully.

He was surprised at how much she seemed to know of the plains beyond the mountains, and surprised also to be told that the rebels hiding in the mountains were not in retreat but gathering their strength, making alliances and growing in number.

He wondered about the accuracy of what she said, however, when she told him that she did not know the names of anyone involved. Orestes presumed that Leander was among them now, as well as members of his family. But he did not mention this.

*

He began to observe that his mother was more preoccupied and had less time for him. Once, as they were sitting together, Aegisthus came into the room and made a gesture to her that he did not expect Orestes to notice. As his mother tried to return to the topic under discussion, he could see that she was no longer concentrating on him. Soon she made an excuse, saying that she would have to go and deal with the servants. But Orestes did not believe her; he knew it was something more serious.

*

The palace was silent at night. Sometimes Orestes slept deeply and woke in the morning wishing it were the night before and he was facing dreams and oblivion rather than the pervading unease of daylight, as more and more men came to consult his mother and Aegisthus, and his mother tried to disguise her worry by growing more ebullient during meals. Electra, in turn, became more withdrawn.

But as he grew accustomed to the silence, he realized that it was not entirely real. He started to hear sounds—someone moving quietly in the corridor, for example, or faint whispers, and then nothing for a while. Soon, as he stationed himself outside his room in the darkest hours, he saw that Aegisthus came and went, moving quickly, and that his mother often walked the corridor too. He even noticed Electra crossing the corridor from her room to a room on the opposite side.

The guards merely stood watch. It was not their job, it seemed, to stop any of the incumbents from straying in the palace, but rather to protect them from outsiders. At the beginning, he supposed that they never shifted from their appointed stations, almost like pieces of furniture. One night, however, he stood watching while Aegisthus left the room where he normally slept with Orestes' mother. Orestes saw him walking slowly towards one of the guards, beckoning to him and indicating that he should follow him. None of the other guards appeared to register their presence as they made their way into one of the seldom-used rooms at the front of the palace. Orestes waited for a while to see if they would return, and when they did not, he went stealthily down the corridor himself, passing guards whom he pretended not to see. He stood outside the door of the room where Aegisthus and the guard had gone.

The sounds he heard were familiar to him, and unmistakable. He wondered if his mother ever followed Aegisthus in the night like this herself and heard this panting and hot breathing.

It made him wonder also when he thought of Electra. Did she too cross the corridor in the shadows for a secret assignation? Immediately, he thought of what Leander would say when he was told about this, how many questions he would have and comments he would make. But then it struck him that he would not be able to share this with Leander. He would have to keep this to himself until Leander returned.

One night when he woke, he saw Electra in the corridor, with one of the guards following her into a room. He saw another guard approach and enter the room as well. All he heard as he listened outside were whispers, the voices so low that he could not even tell who was whispering. The tone was serious, whatever the subject.

Gradually, he was able to distinguish the guards from one another. Only two of them would go with Aegisthus, but several more would cross the corridor to whisper with Electra. One night he stood and watched his mother as she walked up and down the corridor; he wondered if she too would slip into one of the rooms and be followed by a guard. But her way of moving was too self-absorbed for that; she was like someone sleepwalking or trying to work out a difficult problem. Even though she passed near him, he knew that she would not notice him. There was something on her mind that she was going over in a great, undisturbable solitude.

Some of the guards who were there by day often became night guards. One of the day guards, he had known from before the time he was kidnapped. This guard's father, a guard too, had always been ready to amuse Orestes when he wanted to have a sword fight. Orestes remembered that he had often brought his son with him; the boy was easygoing and willing to play with him, even though he was a few years older.

Now this boy grown into a man stood guard close to Orestes' door during the day. At the beginning, his demeanor was formal; he barely nodded at Orestes as he passed. When

Orestes spoke to him, reminding him of the sword fighting and asking about his father, the guard remained curt
and stern. When he changed to night duty, he still hardly
acknowledged Orestes.

Slowly, however, the guard began to change. As soon as he
came on duty, he would alert Orestes to his presence, let him
know that the other guard had gone and that he had replaced
him. It was as if he believed that Orestes would be pleased,
would feel more at ease with someone he knew.

One night, Orestes woke and, while still lying in bed,
cleared his throat. It was just a single sound, something that he
thought no one in the corridor would be able to hear. But the
guard heard it and came into the room and sat on the side of
the bed and asked him if he needed anything. When Orestes
replied that he had merely woken and believed that he would
soon return to sleep, the guard touched him for a second and
then took his hand away.

"I am with Leander," he whispered. "My father is a friend of
his grandfather. Leander has asked me to be here. It has taken
time because no one must realize."

"Where is Leander?" Orestes asked.

"In the mountains with the rebels."

They listened out in case there was a sound from the corridor.

"Leander says that you are with him," the guard whispered.

"I am his friend."

"He says that you will support him."

"Tell him—" Orestes began.

"I must go," the guard said. "I will come again when I can."

The next time the guard came, he made clear that they
could not speak at all, that there was too much movement in

the corridors. On a further visit, however, he stayed for longer, telling Orestes that he had no more information about what was happening, or where Leander was, but as soon as he had news he would convey it.

His presence in the room some nights became part of the slow ritual for Orestes of being back in the palace, with times each day marked out for Electra, with times marked out for his mother, who needed his company more since Aegisthus had gone to raise an army to deal once and for all, she said, with this latest revolt.

At the beginning, he tried to ask the guard questions, but the guard would put his hand over his mouth, signaling that someone could be listening at the door. Even when they were together, the guard managed not to make a sound and tried to encourage Orestes, no matter what happened between them in the darkness of the room, not to disrupt the stillness. That, too, became part of the ritual.

One night, as he had been in the room and was preparing to make his way back to his station, the guard motioned Orestes to follow him. They both then stood in the corridor, the guard listening out. When there was pure silence, he took Orestes by the hand and accompanied him back into his room, stood close to him in the corner that was farthest away from the door and began to whisper.

"Theodotus and Mitros are alive," he said.

"No," Orestes whispered. "Mitros is dead. I was with him when he died."

"His father, Mitros, is alive, and Theodotus too. Leander has asked that you go to where they are held. That is the message I have. The place where they are being held is not far from here."

"Are they being guarded?"

"Yes, but at night there is no one."

"Can we get help to have them released? Can we ask Leander's father?"

"It must be done from the palace, Leander insists. Cobon cannot approach the palace. The men are being held underground in the gardens," the guard said. "And we have to move quickly, as Mitros will not live much longer."

"Can you do it alone, or with some others?" Orestes asked.

"We need someone to lead us."

"Who's holding them?" Orestes asked.

"I don't know," the guard said. "I only know that Theodotus is the grandfather of Leander. And Leander wants him free. That's the message I've been told to give you."

The next night, the guard said that he had been in touch with Cobon, who had arranged a hiding place for the two men. Once they had reached a spot beyond the graveyard, Cobon could meet them there. He would have help, or he would ensure that there was no one in the lanes to stop them. Some of the guards were loyal to Leander, and they would make sure of this.

Orestes did not want to send an open message of support to Leander, since he was with the rebels. That would look like disloyalty or defiance to his mother. Nor did he want to deny Leander what he had asked. Nor did he wish to share the news the guard had given him with his sister. He was alone with this, he saw. He could do nothing, or he could, as requested, accompany the guard to the place where he claimed that the men were being held.

If he did this and found them, he could then make a further decision there. As he pondered on what the likely outcome would be, he told himself that he was his father's son, who could, if he wished, exert power in the palace, but he was also the son of his mother, who had warned him to trust no one.

His father, it struck him, would never have done nothing. He remembered his father's strong voice and tone of command. If his father were here, he might move warily, but he would never stay in his room out of fear. He would take action.

The guard and he worked out a plan, the guard having secured a key to one of the rooms beyond the kitchens that had a side entrance, from which they both could leave when there was no moon.

*

Two nights later, Orestes was awake and ready when the guard came into his room.

Outside, they stood still for some time so that their eyes would become accustomed to the dark. They walked away from the palace, veering to the side of the sunken garden towards the empty spaces beyond. Without speaking, they crossed the dried-up stream.

When they came to the place beneath which the guard said that the men were held, they scrambled with their hands to find the hard surface of a trapdoor under the layer of earth. When they found the trapdoor, they pulled it up to find a rank smell coming from below not just of soil and rotting undergrowth, but of human waste.

Orestes made his way down steps into the dark. When he reached a clay floor, he called the names of the two kidnapped men. But he heard nothing at first, no voice.

When he finally heard a groan, he said his own name and Leander's name, adding that he had come to release them. He heard someone whisper the name Mitros. Trying to locate the sound, he explored the underground space while not losing his bearings. Even though there was no light, he began to sense where the two men were. When he stretched out his hands, he was caught by another pair of hands that felt strong and bony, intent on holding on to him.

"You'll have to help me lift him up," a voice said, a voice that sounded almost in control.

He and the guard lifted the man Orestes guessed was Mitros to his feet and then guided him across the floor to the steps. They had to push Mitros up step by step and hold him in case he fell back. He was breathless and had no strength. As they neared the surface, Orestes edged by him and Mitros winced with pain; he was being crushed against the side of the opening. Orestes pulled him up by the wrists and helped him to stand as the other man, whom he knew as Theodotus, emerged.

They made their way slowly out of the palace grounds and through the graveyard, with Mitros, held between Orestes and the guard, muttering to himself and moaning.

Compared to the darkness of the underground prison, the night itself seemed almost bright. When they had passed the first house at a turning of the lane, the guard motioned to Orestes to stop. Cobon was standing against a wall, waiting. The guard said he would go back to the palace, leaving Orestes and Cobon to take the two men to their hiding place.

Moving forward, they met no one. Orestes did not know if guards were usually placed in these lanes throughout the night, but he imagined that the lanes were closely watched. In the fastness of the palace, he had presumed that the immediate hinterland, where so much potential danger lay, was vigilantly controlled, especially at night. But there was no one now. The guard had been right, and this meant, Orestes realized, that Leander and his associates must have considerable secret support among the guards and that security had become lax in the absence of Aegisthus.

Thus they were able to aim towards their destination without anyone stopping them. As far as Orestes could discern, no one even saw them passing. The house was small and nondescript. The door was opened by a woman who ushered them inside. Soon she brought them food and drinks and accompanied Mitros to an inner room so that he could lie down.

Orestes was aware that he would have to leave soon to make his way back to the palace before the dawn. If he could help it, he did not want to have to explain to his mother or Electra what he had done.

"Where is Leander?" Theodotus asked.

"He's not here," Cobon said.

"Where is he?"

"He has gone to free his uncles. There is a revolt," Cobon said.

"Where is Mitros, the boy?" Theodotus asked, looking at Orestes.

"He is dead," Orestes whispered. "He died before we returned."

Theodotus sighed.

"Do not tell his father," he said. "His father has been living only so that he could see his son."

"I must tell him," Orestes said. "I must tell him that Mitros was happy as he died."

"No one is happy as they die," Theodotus said. "His father will not live long. You must tell him that his son returned with you and with Leander and then left with Leander again, but will soon come back. You must make him believe that it is true."

Orestes did not move. He wished that he could leave now.

"You must go to him immediately. He is waiting and that is what he is waiting for, and when his family come you must tell them what you have done so that they will say the same."

"His family?" Orestes asked, looking at Cobon.

"Someone must go and tell Mitros' family that he has been freed," Theodotus said.

"There is no family," Cobon said quickly. "His house was razed to the ground. They say that his family were all killed and they are buried there. We thought he was buried with them. He must have been taken before they were killed."

Theodotus gasped and bowed his head.

"He will not live long. He should be told that his son was released and has gone with Leander and he should be told also that his wife and his other sons and his daughters fled when he was captured and are some distance from here."

"He'll ask to see them," Cobon said.

"Tell him that when it is safe they will come."

"But what if he lives?" Cobon asked.

"I do not know what we will do if he lives," Theodotus replied.

They heard low groans coming from the room where Mitros was.

"Go to him now," Theodotus said.

Mitros, when Orestes came into the room, was breathing with great difficulty. He reached out, trying to find Orestes' hand.

"Is he safe, my son?" Mitros asked.

"Yes," Orestes replied. "We escaped from where they held us."

"And what happened then?"

"We found a house by the edge of the sea. There was an old woman who looked after us. She loved your son the most."

Mitros shivered and appeared to smile for a moment. He tried to sit up.

"Where is your mother?" he asked.

"She is in the palace," Orestes said.

"Sleeping," Mitros said, "as only the wicked sleep."

Orestes thought for a moment that he was making a joke.

"All of the trouble starts with her," Mitros went on, still trying to sit up, pushing Orestes away when he tried to help.

"She ordered the kidnappings," he continued, "so she could frighten us. And then she killed Agamemnon, your father, killed him with her own hand, and left his body to rot in front of the palace. She made us pass his body as he lay unburied."

"My mother did not kill my father, she—" Orestes began.

"It was done by your mother with her own hand," Mitros interrupted.

His tone was flat and factual and almost weary. It was clear that he believed that he was speaking the truth.

"Was Aegisthus with her?"

"Aegisthus is no one," Mitros said. "She did the killing. All the killing. All of it."

He was sitting up fully now and had gripped one of Orestes' wrists.

"But she did not kill Iphigenia—" Orestes began again.

"The gods demanded that Iphigenia be sacrificed," Mitros said. "It was the hardest choice. The gods can be hard."

"But it was not my mother," Orestes said. "It was done by my father."

"That is right. It was not your mother," Mitros said.

For a moment, there was silence. Orestes listened to make sure that Mitros was still breathing.

"And my son is safe?" Mitros eventually asked.

"Yes," Orestes said. "He is with Leander. He will return soon."

He could feel Mitros' gaze on him in the half-light offered by the small lamp in the room.

"Are you sure that it was my mother that killed my father?" he asked Mitros.

"Yes. It was her knife."

"Does anyone else know?"

"Everyone knows."

Mitros released his grip on his wrist and instead reached out for Orestes' hand and held it. And then he began to sob.

"My family, the boys and girls . . ." he began.

"They are all fine," Orestes said, "and they'll come here when it's safe."

"Your mother killed them," Mitros said. "My wife, the boys, the girls. They were killed by her men as I watched. She gave the orders for that."

Orestes was ready to contradict him, to tell him again that he would see them soon, but Mitros was not listening. He was speaking as though to himself.

"I heard their cries as they died," Mitros said. "And then they took me away."

In all their time buried under the ground together, Orestes realized, Mitros must not have told Theodotus that he had witnessed his family being killed. They must not have spoken about this.

"But your son is alive," Orestes said softly.

"Yes, yes," the old man replied in a tone of sadness and resignation.

Orestes was not sure that Mitros believed him.

"Wait," Mitros said, "and move close."

Orestes knelt down by the bed.

"Your mother murdered your father," Mitros whispered. "She lured him into the palace. She had the knife ready once they were close. It was her plan. She wanted his power. I swear on my children that this is the truth. And there is only one, one alone, who can revenge what she did, who can revenge that killing and the other killings, and that is you. You are the one. That is why the gods have spared you and sent you back. That is why you are here, so I can tell you this. Now it is your duty as the son of Agamemnon to revenge his murder."

He put his hand gently on Orestes' head and left it there as his breathing became stronger and more even.

When Cobon came to say that he wanted Orestes to leave now, he said that he would walk with him through the lanes.

"No, I will go alone," Orestes said.

He returned as the first rays of the dawn appeared. Slipping in by the door beyond the kitchens, he moved stealthily through the lower corridors and then up the smaller set of stairs to the main corridor.

In his room, he thought about his mother and how she had tried to entice him to follow her and Aegisthus and learn about power and authority under their guidance. He could have become one of them.

He felt a surge of rage against her and also against Aegisthus, who had taken the place of his father and strutted in the palace as though he had a right to rule. As he went over what had happened, however, it was the figure of his mother alone that stayed with him. Thinking about her gave him a sort of strength. She was the one in control. As morning noises began, he saw her as the one who had taken power. The revenge could be against Aegisthus too, but it would first have to be against her.

He almost smiled when he thought that he would not need to consult Leander or Electra or anyone. But then he saw that he would need Electra's support. He would need to move his sister close to him. He could not work on his own.

As the morning went on, however, he wondered about what Mitros had told him. The man had seemed so certain when he spoke. It had sounded so true. Yet Mitros had suffered so much. It might have been something that he had imagined and then begun to believe.

Surely Electra, Orestes thought, would have told him as soon as he returned if it were his mother who had killed his father. Electra was in the room when his mother had given her account of his father's murder. Surely she would have given some indication if his mother were not telling the truth.

As he puzzled over what he should believe, he decided that he would tell Electra what Mitros had said and then watch her response. He wished that Leander were with him so that he could ask him what to do.

*

In the afternoon, as he and his mother were talking, his mother leaned towards him affectionately.

"Orestes," she said, "I need to take you into my confidence. As you know, there has been a revolt and Aegisthus has been involved in quelling it. But these rebels are more determined than the others who came before. They do not stay in the same place. They disappear and then reappear even stronger. Aegisthus has many loyal supporters. He is a brave warrior, but he is not a military leader as your father was. And his supporters are rough. They know how to attack fiercely. But they are bandits before they are anything."

She stood up and walked around the room.

"Orestes, Aegisthus has brought me great trouble. I need you to know that. I can tell that to you as to no one else."

Orestes watched her as she was about to say something more and then stopped. Suddenly, she came towards him and held him by the shoulders.

"This revolt is more determined and serious than anything we have known. All I have now is you. I trust you and I trust Dinos, who is a warrior as cunning as your father was. I trust no one else. I have had Dinos watched and shadowed and am as sure of his loyalty as I am of anyone's. I want to send you to him. I cannot afford to lose you. For those who are leading the revolt, you are the prize. No one cares about me or about Electra. It is you they will come to capture. Therefore you cannot be here. We are vulnerable here."

Orestes looked at her as she finished. For one second, he was sure that he was being sent away because his mother had discovered what he had done the previous night. But then, as she spoke to him in greater detail of how much protection he would have as he moved across the countryside, he was less certain. By the end of the conversation, when it was agreed that he and his mother would meet the next day to discuss safety with the men who would be his bodyguards on the journey, he merely knew that he was being sent away, but could not decide whether it was because he had displeased his mother or whether she genuinely wished to protect him.

When he went to Electra's room, she expressed astonishment.

"Dinos' wife and his children were all killed in a revolt," she said. "He put it down with immense ferocity. But it remains a most dangerous place. And my mother wants to send you there?"

Orestes nodded.

"She says she trusts Dinos," he said.

"I'm sure she admires him enormously," Electra said.

"She says that the revolt is serious."

"It's also spreading. Aegisthus is putting down only one of the revolts. He won't be able to put all of them down. They will be waiting for him. She has sent him to his death."

"Who decided that he should go?" Orestes asked.

"She made him feel that since he is a warrior, then he would have to go. She left him no choice. She schemed so that he would go. Nothing happens without her. It is she who decides."

"On the day when my father came back from the war," Orestes asked, "did my mother also decide—?"

"She is all charm and sweetness since you returned, isn't she?" Electra interrupted.

"Why don't you answer me? When my father came back, did my mother decide what happened?"

"Why don't you ask her? You spend plenty of time with her."

"If I ask her if it was she who killed my father, will she answer me?"

"Who do you think killed your father?" Electra asked.

"Is that a question?" he replied.

Electra moved some flowers around in a vase.

"If it is, I myself would like to hear my mother's answer," she said.

"I would like to hear yours," Orestes said.

"Did Theodotus and Mitros not tell you?" she asked.

"What do you mean?"

"When you rescued them?"

"How do you know I rescued them?"

She carried the vase to a table nearer the door.

"This is a house of whispers," she said.

"Does my mother know that I rescued them?"

"Why don't you ask her that too? But not just now, as she and I are due a walk in the garden."

"Who told you about the rescue?"

"It doesn't matter who told me. What matters is that you must not meddle in things that are beyond you."

"Leander is my friend. Theodotus is his grandfather."

"Leander is leading one of the revolts," Electra said. "He is, unless he is victorious, not your friend. He is your enemy."

"He has gone to free his uncles, his mother's brothers. They were kidnapped when I was kidnapped. You must have seen me being taken away."

"I was being held in the dungeon at that time," Electra said. She was standing now with her back to the door.

"Who held you?"

"Why don't you ask your mother that too?"

"I am asking you."

"You must learn to listen. I notice you are sometimes listening outside the room where I am at night. But you don't hear anything, do you?"

"You were in the palace when my father was killed?"

"Yes, I was. Indeed, I was. I have told you that I was in the dungeon."

"So you saw nothing?"

"There was a small window in my cell. I saw a chink of light."

"So you don't know—?"

"Of course I know," Electra interrupted. "I know every-thing!"

"And you won't tell me?"

"I'll tell you when I can. Now I must go and walk in the garden with my mother and you must return to your room."

*

That night, when the guard appeared, he whispered: "You must go to Leander's house. As soon as the palace is busy in the morning, you must go there."

"Who has requested this?" Orestes asked.

"It is urgent," the guard said.

"My sister knows that I helped rescue Theodotus and Mitros."

"You were seen," the guard said. "And you'll be seen going to Leander's too. But this is more important than anything."

"Has Cobon asked to see me?"

"I don't know. My message is simply that when the sun is in the sky you must go there."

The guard stayed with him for a while, but did not speak again. Later, as Orestes lay in bed alone, the figure of Lean-der came sharply into his mind. He pictured him as decisive, watchful. He would make no mistakes. He put Leander's level-headedness, his clear-eyed sense of purpose against an image of his mother and Aegisthus. And it struck him forcibly that in any battle between them, Leander would prevail. He did not know what would happen then, but he made the decision as first light came that he would do as he was asked. He would go to the house. He could always claim, if his mother remonstrated with him, that, since she had not told him, he had no idea Leander was part of the revolt. He would warn Electra not to tell his mother that he knew. He could say that he merely went to see his friend to inform him of his own imminent departure.

He woke late, and quietly left the palace by the side door, walking by the graveyard and the dried-up stream. He veered between feeling brave and feeling nervous. He kept his head down as he passed people on the lanes and crossed a small, busy marketplace.

When he arrived, he thought it odd that the front door was wide open and that, even in the hallway, there was no sign of any servants or any of the family. Everything was deserted, silent. He started calling out names, Cobon and Raisa, Ianthe and Dacia, and then calling his own name, as Leander had done, so they would know he was not a stranger.

But then as he moved farther into the interior of the house, there was a smell that was familiar to him from his time with the old woman, when the occasional goat or lamb fell off the cliff and started to rot.

That smell came to him now more powerfully than ever before. When he called out the names again, his own breath was fouled by the sharpness of the stench coming from the main room of the house.

There was, he saw, a mound of bodies with the buzz of glistening black flies all around them. The mound had been neatly made, dead body placed on top of dead body, each balanced against another, creating what was close to a single mass. He had to turn away to vomit. When he returned and noticed something moving on a piece of white flesh, he saw that the skin was alive with wriggling maggots.

Worried why he had been sent here and whether anyone might be waiting in one of the other rooms, he found a piece of cloth and, putting it over his nose and mouth, he looked

around the house, gasping with shock when he found the bodies of Theodotus and Mitros lying on a blood-soaked bed with
flies all around them.

He went back to the main room, and in disgust and fear he
dragged one of the bodies from the top of the mound by the
ankles, letting it land with a hard, lifeless thud on the ground
before turning it over to see the face of Raisa, her throat cut
from ear to ear, her eyes wide open.

As far as he could make out, all of Leander's family were
dead, and all of the servants. And as the buzzing flies landed
on his own face and hands, and as the fetid and rotting smell
seemed to intensify now that he had dislodged one of the bodies, he decided that he should go back to the palace and find
Electra, that he should, before he did anything else, tell her
what he had seen. She would return with him and then he
would not be alone when other people arrived to find the mass
of bodies.

As that thought came to him, he heard a low whimpering
and he wondered if some animal, a weasel or a rat, had bur-
rowed its way into the mound of bodies. But then he heard a
girl's voice. It was deep within the pile of inert bodies so that
all he could do was begin to separate them to locate its source.
When a hand reached towards him, with the flies fierce all
around it, he recoiled, darted to the corner of the room. And
when he turned, he saw Ianthe tunneling out of the mound and
getting to her feet. She screamed when she saw him, screamed
in fear, trying to bury herself once more in the pile of corpses
as though they would offer her a place of safety.

"Ianthe, it's Orestes," he said. "I won't hurt you."

He went back to the pile of bodies and pulled some more
away, finding among them the body of Cobon and the body

of the woman who had given refuge to Theodotus and Mitros when they had escaped, and the bodies of two children huddled together. Ianthe, when he attempted to reach her, was like a wild animal whose lair had been desecrated. She curled and struggled to shelter under one of the bodies so he could not get to her. He called her name and said his own name again, but his efforts to pacify her made her scream more, call out in dread, call the names of her mother and her father, call for Leander.

"I'll help you," he said as he took her by the wrists. He lifted her and held her body, which was covered in a slime of blood, against him. From the strength of her resistance, he presumed that she did not have a serious injury. When he managed to get her outside, away from the stench and the flies, he saw that the blood on her clothes and on her skin was not her own blood.

"You must come with me," he said. "Away from here."

When she finally spoke, he could not at first make out what she said because of her sobbing. He had to ask her over and over what she was trying to say, imploring her to speak more slowly. And then he heard the words.

"You did this!" she said.

"No, I did not!" he replied.

"The men who did this were your mother's men."

"My mother's men are not mine."

"We were getting ready to flee. Theodotus and Mitros had just arrived," she said in between sobs. "Mitros was so weak. He wanted us to leave him behind but we would not. You had someone watching us, you must have known we were going to escape."

"I had no one watching. I did not know. I didn't know anything."

He forced her to walk with him, having to pull her forward

several times as she tried to go back to the house. They went together through the lanes and then into the market space and then into the open area in front of the palace; people who saw them edged out of sight, frightened by Ianthe's unkempt appearance and by the dried blood on her clothes and on her hair.

In the palace, Orestes found Electra, who took Ianthe into her room.

"Electra," Orestes said. "They have killed all of Ianthe's family. I found them. They are all dead."

Electra went towards the door as if to guard the room from any intruders.

"She told me who ordered the killings," Orestes said.

As Ianthe cried out further in fear and pain, both Electra and Orestes moved to help her.

"Why did you bring her here?" Electra asked.

"Where else could we have gone?" Orestes asked.

Electra looked at him darkly, impatiently.

With Orestes waiting outside, Electra bathed Ianthe and dressed her in fresh clothes. When she finally called him back and they both were holding Ianthe as she whimpered and shivered, they were suddenly confronted by their mother, who had arrived in the room with two guards.

"What is this girl doing here?" his mother asked.

She spoke with a mixture of pure fury and command that Orestes had never heard before.

"She will stay here for the moment," Electra said.

"Who gave orders that she come here?" his mother asked.

"I did," Electra said.

"Under whose authority?"

"Under my own," Electra replied, "as my father's daughter

and my mother's daughter and the sister of Orestes and the sister of Iphigenia."

"I know whose daughter you are, and whose sister. Do you realize that there has been a revolt? She cannot stay here."

"In a day or two she will go," Electra said calmly. "I have given her my word that she can stay."

"I do not want her near me," his mother said.

"She will not leave this room," Electra replied.

"I can assure you that she will not!"

Orestes looked from his mother to his sister, noting that neither of them even glanced at him. In their rage, he had become invisible to them. As they stood glaring at each other, he was determined not to give in to the temptation to say that he was the one who had found Ianthe. He would not insist that she was here on his orders. He knew that it was best now to keep silent. For the moment, he would need to keep his mother's gaze on his sister and away from him.

Not long before, he might have wondered why his mother did not ask what had actually happened to Ianthe, or asked himself why his mother did not demand to be told why Ianthe's clothes, soaked in blood, were on the floor, or why Ianthe remained immobile and impassive in the room, like some captive, helpless creature.

Now he did not wonder. Now it was clear to him. His mother had ordered the killings, just as she had ordered the kidnappings, just as she had wielded the knife that killed his father.

He watched her with cold anger.

*

Later, as he dined alone with his mother, he noticed that she was subdued and complained of a pain in her head.

"Your sister," she said, "has become a great thorn. One would imagine that now of all times she would come and sup with us and keep us company. When I pray at night, I thank the gods for what they have given me. I thank them for you. At least, my son has returned and is with me. I thank them, despite everything, despite all the disappointments, despite all the treachery."

Her smile was warm and kind, with a hint of forbearance and resignation. But there was something in her posture and her voice that let him know in ominous undercurrents that she was fully aware of what he had done, of his part in the release of Mitros and Theodotus and his going alone, without consulting her, to the house of Leander, where he had found the dead bodies. In her tone he also detected a warning, a suggestion of the steel and the hardness she had displayed in Electra's room, and he could not wait to be away from her.

"Come kiss me before you leave me," she said as he stood up. "It is a time when all of us must take care. We must watch everything and listen out for even a smallest whisper."

*

Orestes' guard was missing and there was no replacement standing near his door. He slept fitfully, waking after a while to the sound of someone in his room. As he sat up in fright, Electra whispered to him to be quiet, not to stir.

"Your mother is asleep and the guards who are loyal to her did not see me as I came here," she said. "I have one of my own guards at the door. If you hear a sound, it will be a warning for us to be silent, completely silent."

"What do you want?" Orestes asked.

"Now that Aegisthus is not here, we can act. She has lost her protector. She will not want to be alone with me now, or even close to me. When she walked in the garden with me today before you came back, she kept her distance, but she will not walk in the garden with me again. She will take no more risks. She is afraid."

"Of what?"

"Of what I will do to her."

Orestes felt for a second as though he had stopped breathing.

"There are loose steps on the way down to the sunken garden," Electra continued. "She goes there every day. It is part of her walk once I have left her. In the afternoon tomorrow you will go with her. You will behave normally. Three guards will follow you, but as you approach the steps, two will overcome the third and then they will withdraw. It will be done quietly. Do not look too closely. Do not draw attention to it. The knife you will use will be under the loose stone on the third step as you walk down. There will be only one chance. If you miss the chance, she will have both of us killed."

"You want me to stab her?" Orestes asked.

"Yes. She killed your father with her own hands, she ordered your kidnapping and the taking of Theodotus and Mitros. She ordered the killing of all their families."

"I saw them killing Iphigenia," Orestes said, almost as a way of changing the subject, distracting her. "I saw that."

"It does not matter what you saw," Electra said.

"It was my father," Orestes said. "I saw my father watching—"

"Are you afraid?" Electra asked.

"Of what?"

"Of killing?"

"No."

"Once it is done, the guards who are loyal to us will open the palace gates and others will come to dispatch the guards who have remained loyal to her. They will kill the men whom she sent to destroy the family of Theodotus. The palace will then be ours."

"How do you know that two of the guards tomorrow are with you?" Orestes asked.

"I have worked and prepared for tomorrow. She will not suspect you. No one knows how brave you are."

"How do you know?"

Electra thought for a second and smiled.

"That is what I have prayed for," she said. "That you would turn out to be brave. I know that you are brave."

"I have killed before," Orestes said.

"We will have all our enemies dealt with once we have the power," Electra continued, ignoring what he had said.

Orestes was silent.

"The plan is in place," Electra continued. "You are the only one who can do it."

"Can we not capture her? Send her away?"

"Send her where? Listen, one of the other guards will come into the corridor soon. I cannot stay here with you. I will not be free to see you until this is done. I will remain in my room with Ianthe until the word has come that my mother is dead. I will pray to the gods for it to succeed."

"The knife will be there?"

"It is there now. The third step, the stone that is loose."

She left him alone then.

As the night wore on, he knew that he would do as his sister had asked. He would revenge his father's death. The next day he would do everything to make his mother trust him. He would be kind to her and appear meek and willing to do as she said and then he would be brave.

In the full light of morning, he found himself almost envy-
ing his mother that she could be decisive enough to kill a
whole family and then calm enough to walk in her garden or
sit at meals talking casually. She must have been the same, he
thought, on the day she killed his father. He remembered her
smiling at the palace doors, all warmth.

She knew how to kill, he thought. She knew what killing
was like. But then it struck him that he did too, that he had
not waited for Leander's instructions before he had killed the
guard and the men who came to the old woman's house. He
had taken advantage of the moment. The only thing he could
do now was ask for help from his father's spirit, ask for strength,
but ask also for the gift of not making his strength apparent
until the moment it was needed.

He would not have to ask for courage, he thought. He had
courage already.

*

When they met in her room, his mother told him that she
would have to expedite his departure.

"Soon," she said, "some of the roads will not be safe. It is a
dangerous time. Dinos has sent a message saying that he can
ensure your safety now. He will meet you halfway, but he will
send some of his men ahead so they will find you earlier. It is
best if you leave at first light. I have chosen the most trusted
and able guards to protect you for the early stage of the journey.
We don't know what will happen here. For the rebels, as I have
told you, you would be the golden prize, your father's only son."

If his mother could pretend with such breathless ease, he
thought, then he could also pretend. He concentrated on every
inflection of his own voice, every gesture. He made himself

seem willing to acquiesce, but also fully involved with all the details as though he had power and needed to weigh them up. He made it seem as though the only thing on his mind was how he might best begin his journey.

As they ate together, he listened attentively to his mother while trying not to watch her too closely. When he told her that he was tired and had not slept well, adding that he would go to bed early this evening, she said that she would go to bed early too so she could be up before dawn to see him on his way.

He stayed with her as she prepared to go for a walk in the garden. He avoided looking at the guards waiting outside her door to accompany her as he said, as casually as he could, that maybe he would walk with her too, that the walk would help him sleep once night came.

As he had invoked his father's help, he also envisioned what was coming as something that the gods had ordained and that was fully under their control.

His mother picked some flowers and then looked at the sky and the sun, talking about the heat, expressing the view that Orestes' room was best in winter, retaining the heat, but it was also the worst in summer. As she made towards the steps to the sunken garden, she wondered if perhaps he should change to another room when he returned, a cooler room.

When they had descended three or four steps, Orestes heard a gasp from one of the guards. He looked behind and saw him being overpowered by the other two.

His mother heard it as well and turned. She was almost facing him as he bent over to find the knife. Instantly, when she saw him picking it up, she let out a cry and tried to get past him and force him down into the shrubbery below. But he moved in towards the wall and managed to pull her to him and stab her in the back and then withdraw the knife. With all his strength, he pushed her so that she fell into the overgrowth.

When he found her, she was lying on her back. He could see her eyes clearly, the panic in them, as he tried to stab her in the neck. She defended herself with her arms, holding him until her strength gave out. All she could do now was cry for help. He stabbed her in the chest and neck and then held her down until all the life went out of her.

Clytemnestra

There will come a time when the shadows fold in on me. I know that. But I am awake now or almost awake. I remember some things—outlines come to me, and the faint sound of voices. What linger most are traces, traces of people, presences, sounds. Mostly I walk among the shades, but sometimes a hint of someone comes close, someone whose name I once knew, or whose voice and face were real to me, someone I once loved perhaps. I am not sure.

There is one remnant that comes and persists, however. It is my mother at some moment in the distant past; she is helpless, being held down. I can hear cries, her cries, and the shriller cries of a figure above her, or lying on her, and then louder cries as the figure flits away, a figure with a beak and wings, with the shape of wings, the wings beating in the air, and my mother lying breathless, whimpering. But I do not know what this means or why it comes to me.

I feel that if I remain still, something more will come. It is hard not to wander in these spaces when there is silence. There are presences I wish to encounter, presences that are close but not close enough to touch or be seen. I cannot think of the names, their names. And I cannot see faces clearly although there are moments when I have been quiet, when I have made no effort for some time to remember or focus, moments when a face approaches, the face of someone I have known, but it fades before it becomes anyone I can recognize.

I know that there was feeling, and that is the difference between where I am now and the place I was once. There was a time, I know, when I felt rage and I felt sorrow. But now I have lost what leads to rage and sorrow. Maybe the only reason I wander in these spaces has to do with some other feeling, or what is left of it. Maybe that feeling is love. There is someone whom I love still, or have loved and protected, but I cannot be sure of that. No name will come. Some words come, but not the words I want, which are the names. If I can say the names, I will know then whom I loved and I will find them, or know how to see them. I will lure them into the shadows when the time is right.

No one in their world knows how little there is here. It is all blankness, strangeness, silence. Hardly anything moves. There are echoes like distant water flowing under rock, and then sometimes that sound comes nearer but it is still faint. If I listen too eagerly, it disappears.

Maybe there are things that did not come to an end when I was there, and they linger now like words that need to be said, or words that have escaped me and will come or might come or must come as I wait here. It will take time. I do not know how much time I have, or how much time there is. But I know that I must fade, that I cannot persist in this state. The fading will be gradual. By the end I will not know anything. What I am hoping for is one more surge, some hours or even moments when I will go back into the world and settle into it briefly as though I were alive.

In the meantime, there is memory, which connects and attaches and withdraws. It is almost something. A vague thought hovers but is never stable. Like a figure with wings, it edges towards what has been, or was. I live on the inside of what has substance. I can feel some large set of pressing desires brushing past.

All I am left with though are the grey traces, the clues.

This must be what shadow is like, or aftermath. Some lines or shapes that must have made sense at one time, or may still make sense, but seem random now. If only I could follow what their intention was, or whisper to whoever made them. That desire is the closest I have come to pure feeling, and it is not close at all. I will be left here for the hours or days or years I have been allotted. No longer than that.

Being perplexed and bewildered replaces truth and knowledge, replaces what is real and tangible. The space I inhabit is like a sad gift that was offered but will soon be withdrawn.

And then a word occurred to me, a word of which I was sure. It was the word "dream." Once the word came, I knew what "dream" was or had been, and I was certain then that I was not dreaming in this nullness, that none of what is happening is dream; it is real, it is actual.

And then other words appeared like stars in the darkening sky. I became desperate to take possession of each one, but I could not hold on to them. They were falling or glittering or moving farther away. It was enough, however, to have seen them to get some idea of their power and know that some of them would return and, like the light from a full moon on a dark night, become part of a shadowy stability that was guiding me.

I walked in the corridors of that palace where I had once lived. I could almost remember some things that had happened. There was an image of someone in a garden, or on steps that led to a garden, staring hard, breathing hard, but then nothing, just stillness in the garden and then there was not even a garden, there was merely a space.

But I was still awake. I was waiting, knowing that there would be change, that it would not always be like this. I was aware how easy it would be, once I was in those corridors again, for one of the guards to notice me if I made a sound or if I moved quickly so that there would be some disturbance in the air. And then, slowly, I began to understand why I was here and who I was looking for. His name did not come to me, and I was not able to picture his face, but I felt that he was close.

I could imagine the guard who had seen me, or who had noticed my presence, consulting one of the other guards, and then both of them approaching him, the one I am searching for, or his friend who looks after him.

My husband is dead and my daughter. They have become pure shade. My other daughter is here, but the one I am searching for is my son.

I am awake; the words I knew are sleeping. Sometimes they turn in the night, or make some sound in their vast dreaming, and then they wake too. Often, if only for a second, they open their eyes and watch me. I hold their gaze so that they might remember me as they fall back into sleep. I study them then in their inert state. I am alert to any movement they make. I can hear their dark groanings in the night, intermittent against their breathing. I can see them reach their arms towards me to be lifted.

I can tell the difference between night and day now. I know the silence that descends on the gardens and corridors at night, a silence broken only by the soft movements of the guards or of cats. This is my realm, where I am free to wander. As I come from the garden, I am aware that the guards can feel a movement in the air. It would just take one more thing to let them know that I am with them. A sound. A darting gesture.

When the time came, I knew that I would hear his name, my son's name, enough to whisper it, like someone imploring. It would come to me when I needed it.

"Orestes," I whispered on one of those nights, and then I withdrew into the shadows.

"Orestes," I repeated, letting my voice echo down the corridor.

I saw two of the guards running back and forth and then summoning the other one, my son's friend, who strutted up and down, checking doorways and corners.

I waited until he had gone and then I whispered to one of the guards.

"Tell Orestes that I am his mother. He must come alone into the corridor. He must be alone."

The guard made as though to run, but then stopped himself.

"Speak again," he said quietly, his head bowed.

"Tell Orestes to come alone," I said.

"Now?" he asked.

"Soon. Orestes must come soon."

"Do you mean to cause him harm?"

"No, I do not mean to cause him harm."

Orestes

By the time news came that Dinos had been killed and Aegisthus captured and their troops had been routed and that Leander, with an army, was coming back towards the palace, Electra had taken up residence in her mother's room, having placed a bed in the corner for Ianthe. Some days as he ate with them, it struck Orestes that his sister was dealing with the servants precisely as his mother had. Electra's very voice, like her mother's, had a way of emphasizing that she controlled things even when it was clear that she was deeply preoccupied by something else. At times, it hardly mattered what she said.

Orestes found this almost comforting since he himself had little to say. Ianthe did not speak at all; she looked into the middle distance as if the idea of speech were foreign to her, an unnecessary distraction.

Electra had not come to Orestes' room after the murder of their mother. Once he returned to his room that day, he had heard her shouting in the corridor. He presumed at some stage that his sister would come to talk to him, sit by his bed, comfort him, praise him, ask him to share with her every detail of what occurred. But she had been too busy making sure that her mother's guards were surprised and strangled or hacked to death, and then that the guards whose loyalty was in doubt were put into the dungeon.

That evening, Orestes ate alone in his room. After supper, he slept for a while. When he woke and went into the corridor, he saw that his own guard was absent. As he walked up and down, noting the guards who stood at intervals, he felt an overwhelming desire to be visited in his room by one of them. He puzzled over what signals Aegisthus had given so that a guard might follow him to a room at night. By flickering light from braziers in the walls, Orestes looked carefully at each one as he passed, but they behaved as they usually did, they pretended that they did not see him.

In bed, he thought about how Leander would soon return. He thought about Leander's losing all his family except his sister. Although news of what had happened to Dinos and Aegisthus and their army had reached the palace, he did not think that any messages had gone in the other direction. He wondered then if Leander knew he had no family anymore except Ianthe, just as he, Orestes, had no one except Electra.

He would tell Leander when they were alone how he had found the bodies and how he had killed his mother, who had ordered these killings. What he had done, he thought, would make them closer to each other, as Electra and Ianthe were close. The two women had, indeed, become inseparable, just as he and Leander in their last months after the death of Mitros had never left each other's side. He pictured his mother's room at night and imagined Ianthe in all her strange beauty moving to be with his sister as Leander used to move in the darkness to be with him. Once he thought about this, his longing to see Leander again and to be with him in the night became intense and lasted into the morning and began to fill his days as he waited for his friend to return.

*

One morning as he arrived in his sister's room, he found her in a state of agitation. As Ianthe watched calmly, Electra said that a message from Leander had come to their mother in the form of a military command. Leander had said that he wanted space created where he could keep prisoners and he wanted twelve of the elders to be gathered and nothing to be done without their agreement until he and his army arrived. He also said that he wanted his family to be notified that he would soon be coming home.

"It's hard to know what to say," Electra declared. "I cannot send a message to him to let him know what has happened to his family, because he forbade the messenger who came to disclose his whereabouts. And of course I cannot convey the news of my mother's death to him. His message suggests that he has some authority, but here in the palace the authority is ours."

Orestes wanted to say to her that neither she nor anyone else in the palace had authority. They were protected by some guards, but he was not even sure, since news of the army's defeat had spread, that these guards were fully loyal anymore.

"Can I take it," Electra said impatiently, "that you agree with me?"

"What size is Leander's army?" Orestes asked.

"I don't know," she replied.

"What size is our army?"

"We have no army. The last of the army went with Dinos. But we have the palace guarded and guarded well by men who are loyal to me."

"Loyal to you?"

"To us. To both of us."

"Are you sure that Leander is actually leading an army?"

"It's what I have been told. He led the army that was victorious, or he is the survivor among those who led that army. I have also been told that he holds Aegisthus prisoner. And I will ensure that if Aegisthus comes here, he will be dealt with instantly."

Orestes glanced at Ianthe, who pushed back her hair from her brow and looked at both him and his sister, suggesting that she had concerns more pressing than those of her two companions. He realized that she would have to tell her brother what had happened to the rest of the family.

*

The army came in the night. Leander's first act was to have the palace surrounded. He then demanded a meeting with Clytemnestra and the elders. Once Electra received the request, she summoned Orestes to her room.

"I have not replied to his message," she said.

Ianthe, in a corner of the room, covered her body with a blanket.

"I suggest we admit Leander to the palace immediately," Orestes said.

"On what terms?" Electra asked.

"He is my friend and Ianthe's brother."

"He is the leader of an army," Electra said.

"Electra," he said, "he will come in whether we agree to his arrival or not. Resisting him makes no sense."

"Are you deserting me?" she asked.

Orestes did not reply.

"His messenger is waiting at the door," Electra said. Her voice was quiet with suppressed rage. "It is on your head if we invite him in here."

Orestes and his sister went to the palace doors and ordered

them to be opened. Leander, outside, was surrounded by his followers. Since there was shouting and cheering all around, no one heard Orestes when he said that he was inviting Leander into the palace.

"You must come alone," he said.

As Leander stopped and touched him gently on the shoulder, Orestes saw a freshly healed wound down one whole side of Leander's face. The flesh had been sliced open with a sword.

"You must come alone," he repeated in a louder voice.

"I will come with my guards," Leander said. "No one who comes alone to this house is safe."

He brushed past Orestes, accompanied by five guards. As Leander marched through the corridor, Orestes tried to keep pace with him, with Electra following. A number of times Orestes made an effort to catch Leander's attention but, in his determination to go to Clytemnestra's room without being detained, Leander did not heed him.

When Leander and his guards broke into the room, Ianthe was standing in the shadows so that at first he did not see her.

"Where is your mother?" Leander asked Electra, as she and Orestes arrived behind him.

When she did not reply, he turned to Orestes.

"I demand to see your mother."

"She is dead," Electra said.

"No one told me of this," Leander said.

"No one could find you," Electra replied.

At that moment, it seemed to Orestes that the light in the room changed, as if the burning lamps on the wall had developed the power of sheer sunlight. Ianthe moved towards her brother. Her feet were bare, her hair hung loose; she appeared to be immensely frail, almost ghostly.

"Why is my sister here?" Leander asked.

He looked at Electra, who did not answer him. Then he turned to Orestes, lowered his voice and appealed directly to him.

"Why is my sister here?"

"The house was attacked," Orestes said.

"My house?" he asked. "Our house?"

"Yes," Orestes said quietly, holding Leander's gaze. "Your father . . ."

"Where is my father?" he asked.

"He is dead," Orestes said and sighed. "All of them are dead."

"My mother?"

"Yes. All of them."

"Your sister—" Electra began.

"My sister what?" Leander interrupted. "What is my sister to you?"

"We found her," Electra said. "She has been in our care."

"Who found her?" Leander asked. The scar on his face was livid with purples and reds.

"I did," Orestes said.

Leander's hands moved to his face, and then his arms began reaching outwards away from him, as though beyond his control.

"The house was attacked?" he asked.

"Yes," Orestes said.

"All of them were killed, you said?" he asked softly. "All of them are dead now?"

He went towards Orestes and faced him, and then faced Electra, before walking to the window.

"Allow me one minute when I do not have to believe this," he said. "And then tell me again if it is true."

The silence lasted only for a few seconds before he spoke again.

"Is it true?" he asked.

When no one answered him, he repeated what he had asked, a cold fury in his voice.

"Is it true?"

"It is true," Electra whispered.

"And your mother?" he asked. "How did she die?"

"I killed her," Orestes said.

"You killed your mother?"

"Yes."

"Who said that you could?" Leander asked. He did not wait for a reply but began to shout the question, repeating it several times until Electra defiantly replied: "I said that he could. The gods said that he could."

"The gods have nothing to do with us," Leander shouted. "Nothing! We will get nothing more from them. Their time is over."

"My mother ordered the killings," Orestes said. "She—"

"I do not want to hear what she did," Leander said. "She is dead now. Is that not enough?"

Leander walked over to Ianthe and held his sister close to him and did not speak. Orestes was aware of Electra, sure that she understood, as he did, that she had one moment when she could try to assert her authority, but that if she did so, then Leander would have her and him taken away. Leander was breathing heavily, his eyes darting from one object in the room to another as Electra seemed to be intoning a prayer.

"I need the kitchens opened," Leander said finally. "The troops have not eaten for days. I need the twelve elders I asked for to assemble here. I need space in the dungeon now. Are the cells in the dungeon empty?"

He looked from Electra to Orestes.

"Will one of you answer me?"

"No, they are not empty," Electra said calmly. "The guards who were loyal to my mother are there."

"Make sure that they are unarmed and put them in one of the rooms," Leander said. "And I need the kitchens opened now, and the elders sent for. I need to see them now."

Orestes watched as Electra, scowling and imperious in her movements, crossed the room and spoke to one of the guards.

*

As the morning progressed, the palace became like a marketplace, with food being brought to the kitchens, the front rooms filled with soldiers eating or sleeping or sitting in groups talking, and the corridors noisy with messengers and prisoners and women looking for their husbands or their brothers or their sons.

When the elders came together in a building close to the palace that had not been used for many years, Leander explained that he needed guidance on what should be done with Aegisthus, who was now under heavy guard in the dungeon. When Electra expressed the opinion that it was obvious what to do with him, some of the elders agreed with her.

"It is not obvious," Leander said. "Aegisthus knows every detail of what has been happening here. He is the only one alive who knows. There may even be kidnapped people such as my grandfather and Mitros and his family imprisoned in isolated places. Only he knows where these places are. He is the only person we can use to free them."

While he was speaking, Ianthe made her way towards him, waiting until he had finished, and then whispered into his ear. He listened attentively, nodding his head, as if she had imparted some fact that was interesting but not of any great consequence. And then he turned away and doubled up in pain. Orestes thought for a moment that he should go to him and comfort him, but Leander was kneeling, unapproachable, heaving as he sobbed. All they could do was watch him in silence. When Ianthe reached towards him, Leander found her hand and held it.

*

Later, it was decided by Leander with a majority of the elders that Aegisthus' life would be spared but that he would have his legs broken, thus preventing him from wandering in the palace and fomenting conspiracies. Once he recovered, Leander decreed, he could be brought into the assembly room and included in the deliberations, but he would have to be watched carefully.

When Electra protested, demanding that he be put to death, she was overruled.

"There has been enough killing, there are enough dead bodies," Leander said.

Since Orestes found Ianthe a more congenial companion than Leander or his sister, who had begun to ignore him, and often pretended that he was not there during these meetings about the fate of their enemies, he made sure that he was sitting near her.

When Ianthe started to come to Orestes' room at night, he did not ask her if she had been sent by Electra or how she explained her absence to his sister, or indeed if her brother was aware of what she was doing.

As they lay together, Orestes was surprised at how much he wanted her and how the prospect of being with her at night made his days easier. Ianthe was hesitant with him at first, almost afraid to be touched. But soon she put her arms around him and let herself be held and they slept close to each other.

Orestes observed a change in Electra now that Leander had returned. She no longer went to her father's grave. She had become brisk, almost sharp. Since she spent her day issuing instructions, consulting Leander and the elders, exercising control, her movements were now decisive and direct and her voice deeper, her tone more exact and precise. She did not mention the gods or the spirits of the dead, but spoke rather of distant regions that would have to be brought under control. She was like someone who had been woken from a dream.

He wondered how much of this was an act and under what pressure it might fall apart, as her earlier pose as the daughter who lived by the light of the gods had fallen apart.

In the largest room in the palace, Electra spent her day with Leander. When they needed the elders, they called for them. It occurred to Orestes sometimes how much his mother would have loved this new dispensation, the urgent messages, the orders being formulated, the times being allotted for meetings with those in line outside the palace.

He noticed how much his sister and Leander deferred to Aegisthus, whose knowledge of old family feuds or ancient disputes over boundaries or what land was the most fertile or which individuals could not be trusted was detailed and accurate. Aegisthus sat in a chair as if nothing had happened. When it came time to move, the loss of power in his legs seemed like merely a minor irritant, or an extra quality that made him endearing.

Indeed, since he had taken up residence in Electra's old room, where Leander insisted, in response to Electra's protests, that he could be watched most vigilantly, Aegisthus had many visitors at night, beginning with the servants, who came with food for him and with warm greetings from the kitchen. Since Electra objected to his presence at meals, banishing him to his own quarters once the day's business had been completed, Aegisthus took advantage of this. News spread that the best cuts of meat and the freshest pastries made their way to his solitary table. Once the food had been eaten, other visitors came, some of whom did not leave until dawn.

Since his emergence from the dungeon, Aegisthus paid Orestes close attention. He had obviously been told that it was Orestes who had killed Clytemnestra, and Orestes could see that the idea both puzzled his mother's former lover and deepened his interest in her son.

Once, when they were discussing a plan for irrigation with some of the elders and Aegisthus began to speak, Orestes caught Electra's eye. As she smiled darkly at him, he nodded to her. It was plain to him then that his sister had no intention of tolerating Aegisthus' presence for much longer. No matter what Leander or the elders thought, he saw, Aegisthus would be quietly murdered when everything else had become calm. Orestes still had the knife he had used to kill his mother. It was hidden in his room. Once Electra gave him the sign, he would be ready to use it again.

*

Since they had returned, he and Leander had never once spoken about the place where they had been held, or their escape, or the old woman's house, or Mitros. What happened in that time came to Orestes now as moments, single images, flashes of memory, things made all the brighter because they did not easily connect. He felt that Leander, having found out how near they were to being released when they escaped, did not want those years to be discussed. They would be consigned to oblivion, Orestes thought. Even though he could not revisit them with Leander, he did so in his imagination when he was alone. But it was not enough; they would shrink, shrivel, fade away until a time would come when what happened might not have been. He was the only one who would remember.

And a few times when he met some of the boys, now grown men, who had been in the place of detention with him, he saw that they had been avoiding him since his return. Indeed, he thought, it was only now that he began to hear again their names. As they came with their fathers to the palace, they nodded to him in polite recognition, but nothing more.

Leander had made a room for himself at the front of the palace where he oversaw the arrival of troops. It was he who decided which guards were on duty, and since the guards reported directly to him, Orestes presumed that he knew precisely when Ianthe moved each night from Electra's room to Orestes' room, returning in the hour before the first glimmer of dawn. On a number of occasions when he saw Ianthe to the door, he was tempted to go down the corridor to see if her brother was awake, but he was afraid of what he might find if he were to surprise Leander in his quarters.

He felt sometimes that both his sister and Leander had willfully abandoned him, that he reminded them of events they wanted to gloss over, forget. They were reluctant to be alone with him. He was no longer of any interest to them, just as the gods and the spirits no longer appeared to interest Electra or events that had happened in the past no longer interested Leander.

Orestes was still living somewhere that was shadowy, haunted;

it was a region that both Electra and Leander had lived in too but
had left for a place that shone with a promise that his very presence seemed to dilute. It was strange to him that, while he had
remained in the palace, Leander had gone out into the world,
and that while he had remained within the orbit of his mother
and Electra and Ianthe, Leander had become a warrior like
Orestes' own father. More and more, his killing of his mother
seemed almost unreal to him, something that no one mentioned,
as though it had not happened.

*

One day, when he came into Electra's room, she was at the
window in deep discussion with a lone figure. Orestes watched
them quietly for a time. When the man turned, he saw that it
was the guard, the one with whom he had rescued Theodotus and Mitros. It was clear from the guard's relaxed posture
and willingness to interrupt his sister that they were talking as
equals or as two people who were well acquainted with each
other.

Immediately, they stopped talking, the guard moving away,
pretending to be occupied with something else, Electra strid-
ing across the room busily. It was as if they had been found out.

As Orestes observed them, his concentration was broken by
Ianthe, who asked him to come and sit with her. He pretended
that he was listening to her as he went over in his mind the
scene he had witnessed, the obvious familiarity between his sister and the guard and the feeling that they had not wanted him
to see them together.

Increasingly, as Electra appeared sometimes not even to see
him, and as Leander continued to ignore him, and as they and
the elders left him out of all their schemes, he felt as though

he had been singled out for solitude. All of them, maybe even Ianthe, were at ease in a complex web of plans and alliances whose intricacies only they understood. It made him wish that he were small again, living in a time when these things did not matter to him, when he was the little boy who wanted to engage adults in mock sword fights.

*

Ianthe spent her day in the room where there was most activity. She knew each messenger by name and noted what time each one left and was expected to return. She also remembered what had been decided or on what matters the various elders had asked to be consulted. Usually she said little. She had a way, Orestes noticed, of listening and then seeming to be about to speak and then thinking better of it. She gave the impression that she was wrapped up in her own thoughts while also paying close attention to everything.

When she told Orestes that she was pregnant, he asked her to wait for some time before telling Electra and Leander. He wanted something in the palace to be his alone, some secret to be known by no one except him.

"I have already told them," Ianthe said.

"Before you told me?"

"I am telling you now."

"Why did you tell them first?"

She did not reply.

The following day, Orestes watched Leander pretend to be involved in deep conversations with some of the elders. Eventually, Orestes pushed past the men around him.

"I need to talk to you," he said.

"We are sending messengers out today, so it is busy."

"This is my father's palace," Orestes said. "No one speaks to me in that tone."

"What do you want?"

Leander was clearly irritated. A number of the elders began to move nearer so they could hear the conversation.

"I need time with you in private."

"Perhaps once the day's work is done."

"Leander," Orestes whispered, "I will go to my room now, and I will expect you to follow me there."

In the room, Orestes had prepared what he would say. Once Leander appeared, however, he began to shift about as he spoke, as though he were thinking aloud and talking to someone who was in the habit of obeying orders.

"A great deal happened here in your absence," he said. "I studied the systems we use. For example, how we raise taxes, or how we deal with the outlying regions. Other than Aegisthus, I am the one who knows most. Some of the elders know some things, but it is best not to trust them. They need to be watched."

Leander leaned against the wall and listened to him.

"When I am included, I am paying real attention to the deliberations," Orestes went on, "and I feel that it would be better if things were confined to a smaller group. And some of the information that is being offered is wrong, some of the decisions misguided. I know the information to be wrong. I am sure the decisions are misguided."

"With whom did you study our systems so that you are so sure?" Leander asked.

"With my mother."

"And you want us to believe that what she told you was true?"

"We studied the systems of administration."

"And then you murdered her?"

"She gave the orders for your family to be killed. It was done on her orders. She is the one who killed my father."

"I know all of that," Leander said.

"Leander, I am with you. When you were away, I did what you asked me to do."

"I asked for nothing."

"You sent me a message telling me to help release your grandfather and Mitros."

"I sent you no message. I was in battle. I did not know where my grandfather was. If you had not released my grandfather, he might be with us now."

"Who sent the message then if you did not?"

"I have other things to think about," Leander said.

As they stared at each other, the atmosphere becoming more hostile, Leander beckoned to Orestes. When Orestes came towards him, he reached out and touched his face and his hair.

"The elders do not want you to be involved in anything," Leander said. "They do not even want you in the room listening to us. You are there only because Electra and I have insisted. The elders want you sent away."

"Why?"

"Can you name another man who has ever done what you have done?"

"If I had not killed my mother, you would not be here now."

"Yes, I would."

Leander pulled Orestes closer to him.

"My sister is fragile," he said. "When you found her, she was seeking death. I want you to be with her, stay with her. I do not want you to leave her side."

"There are grave matters . . ." Orestes began.

"They are for me to deal with, and for your sister and the elders."

"I am my father's son," Orestes said.

"Perhaps you should pray to have that burden lifted from you. Maybe that is the last wish the gods may grant."

Orestes was shaking. He started to sob.

"You must live with what you did," Leander said. "What you did is all you have. But now that my sister is pregnant, you will marry her and look after her. But nothing else. It has been decided that you will be involved in nothing else."

*

When it was announced that Orestes and Ianthe would be married, both Ianthe and her brother were firm in their view that the wedding ceremony should be brief and private. It took place in a small room off the larger assembly hall in the palace gardens. Once the vows had been exchanged, no one spoke. Orestes could almost sense his sister and his wife and Leander looking around them in the silence, alert to the names of the dead, alert to the ones who had been murdered, whose absence filled the air.

*

Over meals, when the elders had left for the day and no more messengers were arriving, Leander and Ianthe both spoke openly about their parents and grandparents and their cousins. Their tone was filled with simple sorrow as well as pride. Once or twice, Orestes found himself looking at Electra, wondering if they too could begin mentioning their sister or their parents, even just saying their names or recalling something that one of them had done or said, but he realized from Electra's bowed head that it was something that would not happen.

Once, when he saw the guard with whom he had rescued Theodotus and Mitros leading a group of prisoners from the dungeon, which had become vastly overcrowded, to another place of detention, he wanted to stop him and ask who had told him where the two men were being held and how Electra managed to know so quickly what had happened. He was almost ready to accuse the guard of collaborating with his sister until it struck him that the guard would suggest that he confront Electra herself. He knew that he could not do that. For a second, as they locked eyes, he noted a look of guilt, almost shame, on the guard's face before he passed on with the prisoners.

Each night, Ianthe prepared for bed in his room, but repaired at some point to Electra's quarters for a short time, coming back with news or some fresh opinion that Electra had shared with her. Orestes enjoyed touching her stomach, asking her to imagine what part of the child was where, or whether it was a boy or a girl.

When, one night, Ianthe told him how soon she thought the child would come, he expressed surprise. She moved towards him and whispered: "Electra is the only one who knows this. Leander does not know and your sister advised me not to tell him and she has advised me not to tell you either."

Orestes felt tense, presuming that the midwife who had come to the palace had told Ianthe and Electra that the child was in danger or might not live.

"You must not tell Electra that I have told you," Ianthe said. "She made me agree that I would only tell you that the baby might come before its time."

"What do you mean?"

"When you found me, I was already with child," Ianthe whispered.

"Are you sure?"

"Yes, I am. I felt I was, even then. My mother and my grandmother had told me what I would feel. When I came to the palace first I was not certain, but soon I was, soon I was sure."

"Who were you with?"

"They forced me, the men, they forced me while all of the others, including my grandfather, watched, and then, while I looked on, they killed the others and stacked them neatly as you saw. I presumed that I would be the last to be killed and so I waited. But they left me and they didn't come back and so I found a place under the bodies. I wanted to be with those who had died, buried between them."

"I am not the father of the child?" Orestes asked.

"I don't think that what we do in the dark can make me pregnant. For that to happen, it must be different."

Orestes held her to him, but did not speak.

"But I have not told Electra that," Ianthe said. "And I will not tell her."

She sighed and put her arms around him.

"When I knew first that I was to have a child," she continued, "I was ready to dash my head against the stone outside, or find a knife. I was ready to do that until your sister began to wash me at night and touch me, and then you too began to hold me, and then my brother came back. But I'll leave you now. The marriage has been a mistake. I'll ask my mother's family in the village to take me in. I'll clean for them, do what I can for them. I will have the child there. The child is already moving. I will walk to their village."

"I don't want you to go," Orestes said.

"You won't want me when there is a child."

"Did you see the man who caused this?" he asked as he touched her stomach. "Did you see his face? Do you know his name?"

"There were five of them," Ianthe said. "I was attacked by all of them. There was not just one."

"But the child is in you, not in them," Orestes said. "They are all dead. They were all killed."

"Yes, the child is in me."

"And the child grew here in our house and will be born in our house."

"No, it won't be born here. I'll go."

"Does my sister want you to go?"

"I haven't told her that I'll go."

"But I am your husband. I don't want you to go."

"You won't want the baby."

"It is the baby that grew in you. It's your baby."

"But it's not yours."

"It grew in you as I held you. It grew in the night when you were here with me."

"I can't tell my brother," Ianthe said. "I can't tell him anything of this. There has been too much."

"You must tell Electra that you said nothing to me either."

"When the baby is born," she said, "you will think of the men. That is what you will think of."

"Does my sister want you to have the baby and stay?" Orestes asked.

"Yes, but she also wanted me not to tell you what happened."

"But she wants you to stay?"

"Yes."

"Then that's what you will do. There cannot be anyone else . . ."

He felt that he was choking as he tried to stop himself from crying.

"Orestes, what? I can't hear you."

"We cannot lose anyone else. I lost my sister, I lost my father and . . ."

He hesitated and then held her nearer to him.

"My mother moves in the corridor at night."

Ianthe sat up and looked around her.

"Have you seen your mother?" she asked. "You have seen her?"

"No, but she is there. Not every night and not for long but some nights some part of her is here and then moves away. Sometimes she is close. She is close now."

"What does she want?"

"I do not know. But I cannot lose, we cannot lose, anyone else. There has been enough death."

"Yes," she said, "there has been enough death."

*

In the weeks that followed, as he moved between his own room and the room where the others gathered, where Ianthe also spent her days and which was filled with visitors and messengers and the voice of Leander, shouting out orders, the scar on his face often growing red, Orestes began to feel the hostility from the elders. He was not wanted here, he saw, the same as he had not been needed anywhere, except when Electra needed him to do something that she would not do herself or when Leander needed him to escape with him so they could protect Mitros.

When he came into a room, he saw that no one looked up or people brushed by him. He could stay here if he wanted or go back to his own room and listen to the sounds of the day outside in the corridor in the full realization that they had nothing to do with him. He could imagine that, compared to what had happened, these sounds did not matter, or perhaps he was the one who did not matter. Like the messengers who came and went with urgent missives, he himself, he saw, had his uses. He had proved to them that he was someone who would do anything.

But now he was living in the shadows, spending each day in a pale aftermath.

When he lay with Ianthe at night he felt that she too was distant from him, as the child in her was distant, the child that he had believed was his, the child to whom he would be the ghostly father since the real father, whoever he was, had been consigned to dust.

Ianthe noticed his listlessness and encouraged him to stay longer when he came to the meeting room for the discussions among Electra, Leander, Aegisthus and the elders. A few times as he made to stand up and leave, she signaled to him to stay with her and listen.

They were discussing what to do with the slaves whom his father had captured all those years before. The slaves had been made to work clearing rocks from fields and building irrigation canals, but now, since Leander's victory, they were roaming the countryside in groups, marauding settlements and attacking houses.

As Orestes listened, he was surprised that no one suggested sending troops to round the slaves up, kill their leaders and put them back to work. Not long before, he was sure, this would have been Aegisthus' view and his mother's, and perhaps it was even what his father would have done and with the agreement of the elders. But now Aegisthus spoke of a territory where there was spring water in abundance but no irrigation and where the land was in much need of work.

When Aegisthus described it, Leander suggested that this land be given not only to the slaves but to the men who had been sent away with them and who had no families. It should be divided into small parcels so that each one would own something. Electra spoke then about the seeds and the implements that could be distributed and what crops might grow. One of the elders reminded them that some of the slaves were actually in captivity close by and perhaps could be released, before Aegisthus interjected to say that some of these slaves were dangerous and they should be released only in twos and threes, having been carefully vetted. He believed also, he said, that the slaves who were roaming would have to be forcibly removed to this new territory as they would not go willingly.

Some of them, he said, even had hopes that they would be sent back to their country of origin, which could not happen since their land had been resettled by soldiers who had fought in the wars against them.

At the end, when Leander asked Orestes in a desultory tone if he had anything to contribute, he shook his head. But before he did so, he saw the elders looking away and Electra and Aegisthus becoming involved in something else. He wondered if Leander had drawn attention to him just to mock him.

But once he stayed in the room with them, he found that since he listened intensely and was never preoccupied by what he himself should say next, he could remember with accuracy a previous argument or a solution of which they had lost sight. When there had been a complex discussion, or detailed evidence that contradicted other evidence, Orestes could remember what the others had forgotten or remembered hazily. On a few occasions, he was ready to correct them, tell them precisely what had been said or agreed. But since he saw that they had no interest in what he might say, he did not intervene.

He did not merely notice them and the words they used, but as he looked from one to the other, he felt other presences in the room, people who had dealt in a different way with these same matters in the past. He felt his father's spirit hovering and the spirits of Theodotus and Mitros and other spirits whose names he did not know.

But more than anything, he saw his mother in the room and saw her in Electra. He saw his mother's face and heard her voice when he looked at his sister or listened to her speak. And then he would notice a faint presence or a change in the light and he would realize that it was his mother. He would hold Ianthe's hand and keep her close so that the disturbance would fade and the atmosphere become calm again.

*

Orestes was not surprised when Leander came alone to his room one evening, while Ianthe was still with Electra. He had almost been waiting for this. In the half-light, he observed that Leander's scar was white at the edges and seemed almost open like a lip.

"The guards have heard a voice in the corridor at night," Leander said. "At first, they say, it was only a disturbance in the air. Last night, however, they ran to my room because a woman's voice spoke."

"What did she say?"

"She said your name. The guard heard her say your name and then he ran in fright to my room. When I came out, I noticed a coldness in the corridor. Nothing else."

"And so there was nothing?"

"Orestes, the guard saw your mother. It was your mother. He knew her and recognized her fully. He heard her voice and he asked her if she meant you harm."

"What did she say?"

"She said that she does not mean you harm, but that you must come into the corridor alone. I have arranged for the guards not to be at their stations tonight. For some hours in the fastness of the night there will be no one in the corridor."

"Does my sister know?"

"Only the guards who heard her voice know, and I know."

"Will you be close by?"

"I will be in my room."

"What will I tell Ianthe?"

"Ask her to stay with your sister. It is near her time so perhaps she needs to be with your sister. I will tell Electra that the midwife has sent a message that it is best for Ianthe to stay in Electra's room. You will be alone."

"Are you sure I should do this?" Orestes asked. "Are you sure this is not a trap that has been set by Aegisthus or by one of our enemies?"

"I swear to you, by the memory of my grandfather whom I loved, that I believe that your mother has walked in the corridor."

*

They ate together with Electra and Ianthe as though there were nothing strange. Once supper was finished, Orestes and Leander withdrew. As he passed the guards in the corridor, Orestes saw how nervous they seemed. Leander held him in a warm, familiar, comforting embrace and then released him and walked down the corridor to his own room. Orestes waited alone, checking at intervals if the guards were still at their stations.

When he saw that they were gone, he waited in the corridor, unsure whether he should stand still and wait or walk up and down to see if she would appear.

As he returned and lingered at the doorway to his room, there was nothing. No sound, no change in the air. He shifted his position a few steps and then back. What came to him now, as it sometimes did when he was alone at night, was the distant sound of animals bellowing in fright, and then the more piercing cries of agony from the heifers, and then the smell of blood and fear and raw animal intestines that rose from the place of sacrifice. And then his sister dressed in white and cries from her and from his mother.

As these sounds came to him now, he looked around him. He had moved into the middle of the corridor, and she was there, his mother. She was saying words that he could not make out. He whispered to her that he was Orestes and he was waiting for her. Suddenly, two hands gripped him firmly by the waist and he was swung around. Then the hands released him. He knew that he must only whisper, he could not call out in case he alerted Electra or Ianthe.

"I am here," he whispered.

When his mother appeared again, she was wearing white as though dressed for a wedding or a feast. She was younger than he remembered her. As she moved away from him, he followed her, then stopped as she stopped.

"I am Orestes," he whispered.

"Orestes," she whispered.

He could see her clearly now. Her face was even younger.

"There is no one," she whispered.

"There is," he said. "I am here. It is me."

"No one," she repeated.

She said the words "no one" twice more, and then, as her image began to fade, as the shadows grew around her, it seemed to him that she had some fierce and sudden intimation of what had happened, how she had died. She gazed at him in surprise and then in pain, and then she gasped in anguish before she disappeared.

When he felt a cold wind in the corridor, he knew that she would not come back.

*

He waited alone in the silence for some time, and when he was sure that there was no trace of her he went to Leander's room. He found it empty. He then ran the length of the corridor to find his sister and Ianthe, but he could not locate them. In the corridor again, he went to Aegisthus' room, to discover that he was in bed with the guard, the one who had come with messages he claimed were from Leander. When Orestes asked where Leander was, Aegisthus said that Leander had been shouting Orestes' name in the corridor some time earlier, and he should ask the guards in the corridor where Leander had gone.

"There are no guards in the corridor," Orestes said.

Aegisthus appeared ready to spring to the door in alarm, but instead he motioned the guard to go and look.

"They are in their usual places," the guard said, having peered into the corridor.

As Orestes passed the guard, he took him in from head to toe until he was sure that he let him understand that he would be dealt with in some way or other in due course.

When he himself stood in the corridor, he was instantly approached by two of the guards.

"Leander has been looking for you," one of them said. "He has sent guards out to search for you."

"He is not in his room," Orestes said.

"He is with his sister. She is in labor," the guard said.

"Where is she?"

"In the new room."

The guards accompanied him to the room that had been decorated for Ianthe and her child. Ianthe was lying on the bed. She was being held and comforted by Electra. Leander was standing close to them.

"We couldn't find you," Leander said.

"I was in the corridor," Orestes replied.

"We were all in the corridor," Leander said. "No one could find you. It was a peaceful night until her pains came. You were not in your room or anywhere else so we sent some guards searching for you and we sent others to get the midwife."

Ianthe cried out. She was unable to control her breathing. Electra pulled her hair back from her brow and sponged her face with cold water, soothing her as she spoke.

"It will not be long now," Electra said. "The midwife will not be long."

Leander made a sign to Orestes that they should leave. Orestes thought it was strange that just a few minutes earlier he had been desperate to find Leander to tell him what he had seen but now, as they moved towards the steps of the palace to wait for the guards and the midwife, and as the light of dawn appeared, making the stone red and golden, what had happened seemed already to have faded as the darkness itself had faded.

He moved beside Leander, putting his hand on his back and saying nothing. Even as they saw the guards coming, hurrying, the midwife between them, they did not speak. Once she was at the top step, however, Leander told the guards that they could wait at the palace doors while he and Orestes went with the woman to where Ianthe and Electra were waiting.

"She is in time," Leander whispered to Orestes. "She is here in time."

When they led the midwife into the room, they stood in the doorway looking at each other nervously as Ianthe cried out again in pain. The midwife examined her and then sternly told the men to go outside.

All they could do now was wait as they heard the noise of people getting ready for the day, and then the voices inside of Electra and the midwife calming Ianthe, whose moans they could hear clearly as they walked the corridor together.

They made their way outside and stood on the steps, taking in the dawn light, fuller now, more complete, as it always would be once the day began, no matter who came and went, or who was born, or what was forgotten or remembered. In time, what had happened would haunt no one and belong to no one, once they themselves had passed on into the darkness and into the abiding shadows.

Orestes suggested to Leander that they return to wait outside the room. Leander nodded and touched Orestes' shoulder. Almost afraid to look at each other, the two went back into the corridor and stood together without saying a word, listening to every sound.

AUTHOR'S NOTE

Much of this novel is based on imagination and does not have a source in any text. Indeed, some characters and many events in *House of Names* do not appear at all in earlier versions of this story. But the main protagonists— Clytemnestra, Agamemnon, Iphigenia, Electra and Orestes— and the shape of the narrative are taken from Aeschylus' *The Oresteia*, Sophocles' *Electra* and Euripides' *Electra, Orestes* and *Iphigenia at Aulis*.

I am grateful to the many translators of these plays, most notably David Grene, Richmond Lattimore, Robert Fagles, W. B. Stanford, Anne Carson, W. S. Merwin, Janet Lembke, David Kovacs, Philip Vellacott, George Thomson and Robert W. Corrigan.

I am grateful also to my agent Peter Straus; to Catriona Crowe, Robinson Murphy and Ed Mulhall, who read the book as I worked on it; to Natalie Haynes and Edith Hall; to Mary Mount at Penguin in the UK; to Angela Rohan, as always; to Nan Graham and Daniel Loedel at Scribner in New York.